CEYLON SAPPHIRES

CEYLON
SAPPHIRES

MAILAN DOQUANG

THE MYSTERIOUS PRESS
NEW YORK

CEYLON SAPPHIRES

Mysterious Press
An Imprint of Penzler Publishers
58 Warren Street
New York, N.Y. 10007

Copyright © 2025 by Mailan Doquang

First Mysterious Press edition

Interior design by Maria Fernandez

Library of Congress Control Number: 2024949905

Cloth ISBN: 978-1-61316-647-5
ebook ISBN: 978-1-61316-648-2

10 9 8 7 6 5 4 3 2 1

Printed in the United States of America
Distributed by W. W. Norton & Company

Dedication TK

PART I

1

THE LOUVRE MUSEUM, PARIS

T he gallery was empty save for the lone artist on the far end of the room, a student judging from her high ponytail and the awkward way she held her paintbrush. She stood before a splattered easel, back straight, bespectacled eyes trained on the painting she was in the early stages of copying: a three-quarter length portrait of Count Alcide de la Rivallière in his art studio. It was an odd choice given the Louvre's plethora of treasures. The sitter's dark breeches and cropped jacket were decidedly plain. His expression fell squarely on the side of boredom. Centuries-old varnish darkened the simple background.

Noah Ballard barely gave the painting a passing glance before zeroing in on the artist. "No, no, no," he muttered when she wiped her dirty hands on her coveralls. The Louvre's director had assured him that the galleries would be empty. In turn, Noah had promised his client privacy as she paid homage to her illustrious forebears. Preparation was everything in the security business. His had been perfect, until now.

Noah turned to apologize to his client, only to be silenced by a flick of her wrist. He didn't press the issue. Working for the one percent required a light touch under the best of circumstances, and this job was more demanding than most. Fifty-nine-year-old Margot Steiner—née Bonaparte—wasn't just the rich wife of a pharmaceutical executive; she was royalty, a distinguished member of the House of Bonaparte. As in, Napoleon Bonaparte, the ruthless French general who ruled Europe with an iron fist. Mrs. Steiner was Napoleon's great-great-grand-niece through the emperor's youngest brother, a woman whose pedigree was as impeccable as her appearance was refined.

Mrs. Steiner sashayed past Noah, Givenchy boots clacking, cashmere coat swooshing as if of its own accord. She stopped in front of the largest painting in the room: Jacques-Louis David's famed *Coronation of Napoleon* of 1807. The painting depicted, in glorious detail, Napoleon crowning Josephine empress of France before an assembly of elites at Notre-Dame Cathedral. Mrs. Steiner gazed at the painting in silent reverence, unconsciously mimicking the actions of the fictive spectators in David's work. Her hand found the bejeweled necklace at her throat, a museum-quality piece ostensibly commissioned by the emperor himself. Her eyelids fluttered shut.

Noah suppressed a yawn as the minutes ticked away. He and Mrs. Steiner had been touring galleries for the better part of an hour, far too long after the night he'd had. It wasn't like him to drink to excess, but the strawberry shortcake at the hotel bar had insisted on doing Jägermeister shots, and that was after they'd shared a bottle of champagne.

Cham-pleasure, the woman had purred as she'd refilled his empty glass for the third time. Or was it the fourth? A twinge in Noah's right temple reminded him of his folly. He rubbed the pain away with the tips of his fingers and glanced at his watch. *Five more minutes,* he thought with relief. Mrs. Steiner had a plane to catch.

Crack!

Noah's head swiveled. The budding artist had lowered the mast of her easel and was tossing tubes of oil paint into the built-in storage drawer, haphazardly, by the looks of it. She slammed the lid shut and secured the brass latch. Noah watched with mild amusement as she fought with the easel's retractable legs, her long ponytail bobbing and swaying in time with her efforts. A smirk spread across his face when she bent over to retrieve an errant butterfly nut. For a split second, he thought of offering to help, but the view was just right from where he was standing.

"Ahem."

Noah jumped to attention. Mrs. Steiner had finished communing with Napoleon and was eyeing him with obvious annoyance.

"Am I interrupting something?" she asked. Her accent was haughty and French, which was two ways of saying nearly the same thing.

"N-no, of course not," he stammered, embarrassed to have been caught off guard. "This way, please."

Noah led his client out of the cordoned gallery toward the staircase displaying the winged Nike of Samothrace, a monumental statue of the goddess of Victory alighting on the prow of a marble warship. He hadn't the foggiest idea who Nike was, nor did he care. His only concern was getting his client away from the masses milling around the sculpture.

"Oh!" Mrs. Steiner exclaimed when they neared the crowd. Her reaction was understandable. Women of her rank were not accustomed to moving among plebs.

"Stay close, ma'am," Noah said, shielding her as if they were escaping a war zone.

As it turned out, Mrs. Steiner was right to be nervous. The mood in the staircase was animated, some might even say rowdy. Gone was the quiet, almost meditative atmosphere of the galleries. In its place was a jumble of sights and sounds. To the left, a group of middle school boys tore up the steps ahead of a teacher who looked like he deeply regretted his life choices. To the right, a woman chastised her wayward twins in a language Noah didn't recognize. The cacophony of voices bounced off the stone walls and the lofty vaulted ceiling. Noah caught a glimpse of the artist from the neoclassical gallery amid the mayhem. She'd barely made it past them when she clipped a bearded man with such force her easel slipped from her grasp. It hit the ground with a loud clunk. The drawer popped open. Paint tubes tumbled out. The crowd trampled them instantly, turning the stairs into a veritable Jackson Pollock.

Noah experienced the disaster that followed as though it happened in slow motion. Mrs. Steiner stepped in a pool of cadmium yellow paint. Her foot slid out from under her. Noah reached for her arm, only to lose his balance in the process. Even as he was airborne, he couldn't help but wonder if the previous night's bacchanalia was to blame. A consummate professional, he twisted his body and broke his fall with the padded flesh of his thigh.

Mrs. Steiner was not so lucky. A high-pitched cry rose from her lips as she fell onto her backside. Her cry turned into a pained groan when her head smacked the stone steps. She rolled onto her side, her hair askew, her cashmere coat streaked with paint. Strangers rushed to the rescue. Their hands were everywhere as they hoisted her into sitting position and did what they could to clean her up.

"Back away," Noah sputtered as he crawled through the ring of Good Samaritans.

They continued to fuss and fret.

"I said back away!"

Murmurs of indignation arose. The pack dispersed. A security guard wearing a concerned expression approached. Noah shooed him away with both hands.

"Are you alright?" he asked, searching his client's eyes for telltale signs of a concussion.

She whimpered softly and nodded.

"Come with me."

Noah rose to his feet and offered Mrs. Steiner his hand. She clung to him as if her life depended on it. They were a pitiful sight as they hobbled down the staircase toward the museum's exit, their paint-smeared bodies garnering curious looks along the way.

The great volume of I.M. Pei's glass pyramid eventually came into view. The minutes it took to reach it were the longest of Noah's life. His heart leapt at the sight of the escalator. He ushered Mrs. Steiner onto it, then through the vestibule. Out the door they went, a gust of heated air lingering in their wake.

Noah's breath came in short, audible spurts as he dragged Mrs. Steiner across the courtyard and through the Passage Richelieu, an entrance reserved for groups and VIPs. Relief coursed through him when they finally stepped onto the sidewalk. Behind them lay the Louvre's iconic facade. In front of them was the impossibly chic Rue de Rivoli. Noah silently thanked the heavens as he shoved his client into the backseat of a waiting Bentley and hurried to the passenger side. "Go!" he yelled before he'd even closed the door. The tires squealed as the driver sped to Le Bourget, the airport of choice for moneyed Europeans.

It took many minutes for Noah's breathing to return to normal. It took several more for his brain to process what had happened. He was about to go into damage control when he heard a piercing shriek from behind. His head snapped back. His insides lurched. One look at Mrs. Steiner's stricken face told him everything he needed to know. Napoleon's necklace was gone.

⚬━━⚬

Down the stairs . . . left at the Mars Rotunda . . . toward the Classical and Hellenistic galleries . . .

Rune Sarasin had rehearsed her escape countless times in the last week, but no amount of preparation—mental or otherwise—could make her feel good about this job. It was too public. Too reckless. Way outside her comfort zone. None of that mattered. She had a debt to pay, and Charles Lemaire was collecting. He was a trafficker. A purveyor of illicit gemstones with an insatiable clientele. He smuggled pigeon blood rubies from Myanmar into Thailand, but having Rune under his thumb for the last four months had opened a slew of opportunities for him. His latest instructions: Produce the Bonaparte necklace or suffer the consequences. Rune knew from experience that it was no choice at all.

The clip-clopping of soles hitting the stone floor caught her attention. Her ponytail swung pendulum-like as she stole a glance over her shoulder. No one appeared to be following her, but she quickened her gait, nonetheless.

Past the Venus de Milo . . . through the Southern Italian galleries . . . up a short flight of stairs . . .

The crowd thinned. A quiet darkness descended, mirroring Rune's mood. Her name meant "happy" in Thai, but "grumpy" was more appropriate of late. "Sleepy" would be her second pick if she had to choose another dwarf. Deep elevens formed between her eyebrows, the kind people paid top dollar to erase. She took a hard left, anxious to put as much distance between herself and the incident with Margot Steiner as possible.

The Department of Egyptian Antiquities beckoned. A gilded mummy glowed under the gallery's diffuse light. Rune averted her gaze. Seeing a woman trapped inside a glass case hit too close to home. The fact that she'd been dead for over two thousand years hardly made a difference.

Another left transported Rune to Dura Europos, an ancient caravan city in the train wreck that was now Syria. She strode past fanciful sculptures of deities and curious zoomorphic vessels, remnants of the region's more prosperous past. A sign for the restrooms appeared up ahead. She hurried to close the distance, ignoring the stink as she slipped into the last available stall.

Fan-freaking-tastic, she thought when the lock failed to latch. She wanted to bash the door until it came off its hinges. Instead, she pressed her back against it and gazed at the ceiling.

Five . . . four . . . three . . . two . . . one . . .

Rune's measured countdown did not have its usual calming effect. She took a deep breath, then another to steady her frayed nerves. When that didn't work, she closed her eyes and tried to picture herself somewhere else—at a spa, on a beach, in a goddamned grocery store—anywhere but this smelly bathroom.

Whirr!

The sound of the hand dryer jolted Rune out of her inertia.

Move! her inner voice yelled.

She shed her eyeglasses and shapeless coveralls and stuffed them into the plastic bag she brought along for exactly this purpose. Her wig came off next, revealing a short, shaggy mullet that was in dire need of some TLC. She lowered her hand to the pocket of her jeans to make sure the necklace was still inside. It wasn't paranoia. She had a history of losing Lemaire's gems. Only after she was sure she had what she came for did she zip up her plain black jacket and flush the toilet. In her line of work, no detail was too minor.

All the sinks were occupied when Rune emerged from her stall. She tossed her bag into the trash with a casualness she was far from feeling, then queued behind two teens who looked like they'd slept in their clothes.

"I heard she blocked him on everything," said a girl suffering from acute bedhead.

"That's what happens to cheaters," replied her racoon-eyed friend.

Indeed. Rune's mouth tugged up at the corners. The low stakes drama was just the distraction she needed. By the time the sink freed up, she felt more like herself than she had all day. She had every reason to feel good. The hard part was over. Security wasn't on to her, and even if they were, she no longer fit the profile. A quick glance at her reflection confirmed her assessment. Gone was the youthful art student with the jaunty ponytail who wreaked havoc in the grand staircase not long ago. The woman staring back at her seemed older, more guarded. She leaned closer to the mirror. Her unusual features, an arresting synthesis of her Thai father and whey-haired American mother, looked ashen in the bathroom's unforgiving light. Her uncommonly large eyes, a tempestuous swirl of greens, golds, and browns, were tired and bloodshot. She pulled her lipstick from her pocket. Cherry red, her favorite. Her gold rings came out next, one for every finger. Seeing them was almost enough to lift her spirits.

Rune's glimmer of optimism vaporized the moment she stepped out of the bathroom. An extra-large security guard stood in the middle of the gallery, telescoping above the crowd. His tense face and alert posture told her everything she needed to know. She was busted. She swore under her breath and scanned the room until she located a tour group heading away from the guard. No one noticed when she quietly joined their ranks. She kept her head low and shadowed them until they reached a gallery displaying archaeological finds from Susa, the capital of the ancient Persian Empire.

"The Frieze of Griffins once adorned the palace of Darius the Great, the third king of Persia," said a bow-tied docent in smooth BBC English.

A few members of the group nodded, but most were too busy taking selfies with said griffins to pay him any mind. Rune searched for an escape route.

"French archaeologists uncovered tens of thousands of artifacts when they excavated the site in the nineteenth century. Almost all of them were transported to Paris through a diplomatic agreement and became the centerpiece of the Louvre's magnificent Ancient Near Eastern collection."

The security guard from the hallway strode in. *Steady*, Rune thought as she assessed the room with hawkish eyes.

"The griffins are made of siliceous bricks coated with bright glazes and set against a blue background. They lined the walls as part of the palace's architectural decor, but they weren't meaningless ornamentation. They had great symbolic value."

Rune's pulse spiked when an army of guards appeared out of nowhere and fanned out across the gallery. Visitors started to notice, including members of her group.

"What's going on?" asked a man in a pilling argyle sweater. There was a note of alarm in his voice.

"I'm sure it's nothing," replied the docent before resuming his lecture to an audience of zero.

The guards took up positions by the exits. Their eyes moved up and down from their phones to the crowd. Rune knew they were checking screenshots from the museum's surveillance footage against the women in the room. She also knew that her hasty costume change wouldn't withstand scrutiny. Her muscles tensed. She could stay where she was and hope for the best, or she could face the problem head-on. It wasn't like her to waffle, but recent events had taken a toll. Losing Lemaire's rubies. Madee stealing his ring. Kit breaking up with her. She wished, for the millionth time, that none of it had happened. The sight of the guards stopping women at random put an end to her pity party. "Do you mind if I borrow that?" she asked an almost handsome man fanning himself with a limp brochure.

"Be my guest."

Rune offered him a curt thank-you and made a beeline for a ruddy-cheeked security guard, the youngest of the bunch. "Excuse me!" she called out, waving the leaflet like a flag at a parade. Her heart thumped against her chest, but whether it was out of fear or excitement, she had no way of knowing. "Can you help me, please?"

The guard's face registered his surprise.

"I'm looking for the Mona Lisa."

His brow furrowed.

"We're here, right?" Rune jabbed her finger at a random spot on the ground plan. Her ploy worked. The guard looked down.

"That's the Denon Wing," he said in a tone that suggested she must be an idiot. "We're on the other side of the museum, in the Sully Wing."

"We are?" Rune gave a supersized pout. "How did that happen?"

The guard rolled his eyes. Lost tourists clearly ranked high on his list of people to avoid. "You're looking for *La Joconde*?"

Rune did her best bovine impression.

"The Mona Lisa, yes?"

"Oh, yes!"

"The painting is in Gallery 711. You have to go to the Denon Wing, then up one level to the first floor." He traced the route on the plan with the tip of his index finger.

"Aren't we on the first floor?"

"The first *French* floor. What you Americans call the *second* floor."

"I don't get it."

The guard gave an impatient cluck of the tongue. With a brazen thief on the loose, he had more important things to do than help a dimwit who couldn't read a simple ground plan. He pointed to the exit. "Go out that door and follow the signs to the Pyramid. Someone at the information desk can help you find the Mona Lisa. It's their job."

"That's a great idea!" Rune said, clapping her hands like a well-trained seal. "Thank you so much. You've been a huge help."

The guard stepped aside to let her pass.

She gave him a syrupy smile. Her smile broadened as soon as she was out of his sightline. By the time she reached the Pyramid, she was practically giddy.

Up the escalator . . . across the reception area . . . to the exit . . .

This was it. She was home free. She pushed the door open. A gust of unseasonably cold air lashed at her face. Her phone vibrated in her pocket.

Well?

Rune's shoulders drooped when she saw Lemaire's text. The spring in her step vanished. She deflated visibly. She may have gotten out of the museum, but any fool could see she was about as far from free as she could possibly be.

2

HÔTEL DE CRILLON, PARIS

"**T**here you are!" exclaimed Lemaire between bites of steak au poivre, the five-star hotel's signature dish. "I was beginning to think you'd run off with my prize."

"The Marie Antoinette Suite?" Rune replied. She glanced at the room with an arched brow. It was maddingly elegant. The dove-gray curtains matched the wall paint to a tee. The classical moldings and opulent chandelier looked spick and span after a 200-million Euro makeover.

She brushed past two churlish goons she recognized from her time in Bangkok and plunked herself at the dining table, directly across from Lemaire. Her forehead creased at the sight of the chinoiserie sideboard. The lines deepened when she noticed the bonbon-colored tapestry of music-playing Muses directly above it. She averted her gaze. She'd had enough old-world Frenchness for one day. "I didn't take you for a traditionalist."

"History, not tradition," Lemaire corrected her. He wiped his mouth with his napkin and straightened his already erect posture. He smoothed a strand of shiny brown hair that wasn't in need of smoothing. His angular face turned pedantic. "Did you know that Marie Antoinette took piano lessons in this room?"

That explains the tapestry.

"A few years later, she was guillotined by Revolutionaries in the plaza outside this very window."

Rune directed her attention to the terrace. It offered panoramic views of the Place de la Concorde, the largest public square in Paris. Traffic whizzed noiselessly behind the soundproof glass. The gold-capped obelisk, a gift from the Egyptian government, glittered in the afternoon sun. How ironic that a place now devoted to peace and harmony was once the site of terror and bloodshed. Then again, rewriting the past was a lot easier than owning it.

"You have something for me?" Lemaire said.

"Do I?" Rune knew she was testing his patience, but making him wait for the necklace was the only bit of control she had, and she planned to milk it for all it was worth.

"Perhaps we should start over." Lemaire's voice was even, but his pale eyes conveyed something else entirely. He brushed a piece of lint only he could see off his blazer.

Rune instantly regretted her mini revolt. Lemaire's gesture may have seemed innocuous, but she recognized it for what it was—a window into his mental state. After four months of being his peon, she knew better than anyone that the more displeased he was, the more exacting he became. She pulled the necklace out of her pocket and slid it across the table. As she did, she couldn't help but admire the massive step cut sapphires. Ten in total. The deepest blue she'd ever seen. The sparkly diamonds stringing them together provided just the right contrast. The necklace was magnificent. A gift worthy of an emperor.

"Ah," Lemaire breathed as he reached for the necklace and held it up to the light. "It's exquisite."

"If you say so."

"You expect me to believe you're not the least bit impressed? Surely someone with your background understands the value of this piece."

Rune bristled at the oblique reference to her father, a stalwart in New York's Diamond District and the person who taught her everything she knew about gemstones.

Tell me again, Rune. What are the Four Cs? her father would ask whenever she dropped by his office after school.

Color, clarity, cut, and carat, she would say, counting the words on her stubby fingers.

And where do the most valuable gemstones come from?

Rubies come from Mogok in central Myanmar, emeralds from Columbia's western belt, and sapphires from Elahera District in Sri Lanka.

Good. Now explain the difference between brilliant cut, step cut, and mixed cut gemstones.

"They're Ceylon sapphires."

Rune blinked.

"They're among the most sought-after gems in the world."

"I know what they are," Rune said. She quashed the urge to scream *Sri Lanka* at the top of her lungs. Leave it to Lemaire to cling to the country's colonial name.

"Each sapphire weighs over fourteen carats."

"So?"

"Now you're just being childish."

Rune shrugged. He wasn't wrong, but that's what happened to the powerless—they threw ineffectual jabs because they were incapable of inflicting any real damage. She brooded silently. She was being pathetic. It wasn't like her. It had to stop.

"You did good work," Lemaire said, throwing her a bone. "My buyer will be pleased."

"Who's your buyer?"

"That's above your pay grade."

It took a real effort for Rune to hold her tongue. She hated being Lemaire's lackey. She was done taking all the risks but reaping none of the rewards. The problem was, Lemaire wasn't going to let her go just because she asked. She needed a plan. It wasn't the first time the thought had crossed her mind, but the close call at the Louvre made ending their lopsided arrangement more pressing. She straightened her posture. If she showed weakness, he would eat her alive.

"If there's nothing else," Lemaire said.

Rune knew she was being dismissed. She deliberately missed her cue. She lowered her eyes to Lemaire's half-finished meal. The meat was red, like it had barely kissed the pan. It sat in a pool of scarlet-tinged liquid that looked disturbingly like blood. She reached across the table and grabbed a radish off the plate. "I wasn't kidding," she said, crunching loudly. "I want to know who your buyer is."

The shorter of Lemaire's men stepped forward. Lemaire raised his hand to stop him from pummeling her, then wiped his mouth with his napkin again and placed it neatly on the table. A wisp of displeasure crossed his face. It vanished after he moved the napkin so that it was perfectly centered with the plate. Only then did he address Rune. "So tell me, why the sudden interest in my clients?"

"It's not sudden," she replied. "I've been doing grunt work long enough. I want in on the business end of your operation. I've earned it."

"You stole rubies worth a quarter of a million dollars from me."

"And I made you that amount ten times over."

"That's beside the point."

"I did everything you asked. I did all the planning, took all the risks. We're even now. More than even."

"That's debatable," Lemaire said. He gave her a chilling look. "And then there's the small matter of the Kohl-Stromer ring."

"I gave that back," Rune said quickly. Her mind drifted to the shouting match she and Kit had after learning that Madee had stolen

Lemaire's ring. Kit could forgive many things—her impulsiveness, her brashness, her hairbrained schemes—but his kid sister following in her footsteps wasn't one of them.

You're a bad influence, Rune.

Look in the mirror, Kit.

None of this would have happened if it weren't for you.

Like I twisted your arm?

I swear, everything you touch turns to shit!

Kit had walked away after that. Like they were *nothing*. Like *she* was nothing. But she hadn't given up on them. What they had was real. A fight couldn't change that, no matter how explosive.

"You'd be dead if you hadn't returned the ring."

Rune fixed her gaze on Lemaire. She wanted nothing more than to dust off her Muay Thai skills and kick him right in the face. If he hadn't been so careless as to let a fifteen-year-old steal his ring, things would be exactly as they were before. She and Kit would be ripping off marks like the Robin Hoods they fancied themselves to be. Madee would be going to school like a normal kid instead of living in hiding. The three of them would still be a family. Sadness and anger percolated to the surface, threatening Rune's composure. She tamped it down. "The ring, the ring, the ring," she said, casting her eyes up in feigned exasperation. "Can you give it a rest already? Madee's a teenager. You think she understood what she was doing? And like I told you a million times, Kit and I had no idea she was going to take it."

Lemaire gestured to the taller of his goons, a frightful man with bloodless skin and dead eyes. The man stepped out of the room. He returned moments later with a large manila envelope and placed it on the table.

"Go ahead," Lemaire said. "Open it."

Rune didn't want to know what was inside that envelope, but she opened it anyway. The paper crinkled in her hands. She squeezed the metal clasp and pulled out a pair of glossy eight-by-ten photos. The first one showed Kit on a busy sidewalk, his motorcycle helmet tucked under his arm. There were lines around his mouth that weren't there the last time she saw him. His cotton candy-pink hair was dyed back to its natural color. The next picture showed Madee scrolling on her phone at a bus stop, looking taller and more mature than ever before. Seeing how much they'd changed—and how much she'd missed—made Rune want to burst into tears.

"They're back in Bangkok," Lemaire said. "He's working as a courier. She goes to school near the Chatuchak Market."

"That has nothing to do with me," Rune replied. She pushed the photos aside like they didn't mean anything.

"Doesn't it, though?"

She didn't take the bait.

"I don't have to tell you what will happen if you cross me."

Rune was seething now, but she kept her expression neutral. The less Lemaire knew about her true feelings, the better. She grabbed another radish from his plate and circled back to the subject of their arrangement. "I was serious before," she said, taking a bite. "I've proven my worth. And my loyalty. It's time to form an equal partnership."

Lemaire laughed in her face. There was something off about his laugh, like he understood the mechanics but not the emotion. Rune was about to tell him off when he stopped suddenly. The silence that followed was long and uncomfortable.

"You're obviously confused," he finally said. He gave a condescending shake of his head. "There's no *we* in this scenario. The arrangement is simple: You do as I say until I decide otherwise. Try anything and there will be consequences."

Rune's lips formed a tight line. Aside from the obvious problem this presented for winning back Kit, Lemaire essentially wanted her at his mercy for the rest of her life. She couldn't do it. It was killing her.

"Let me spell it out for you," Lemaire said, pushing his plate forward to make room for his elbows. His fingers formed a steeple as he studied her through arctic eyes. "Step out of line and the people you care about will suffer, starting with that little truant Madee."

Rune dropped her gaze to the steak knife on the table. Nothing would be more satisfying than sinking it deep into Lemaire's neck. He would bleed out before his men even knew what was happening. They would try to kill her, no doubt. The short, stocky one would probably take the lead. The tall one with the thinning hair always put on a good show, but he wasn't a true believer; she had a sense about these things. Her nerves pulsed with anticipation. It was an insane idea, but try as she might, she couldn't chase it away.

"One call and that ragtag family of yours will disappear." Lemaire smirked. "It will be like they never existed."

Rune formed a fist under the table. She could almost feel Lemaire's blood pump through her fingers. Thick. Warm. Sticky. Her calves tensed as she prepared to pounce.

Not yet!

Her hand loosened. Self-restraint snapped back into place. Now wasn't the moment to strike, but she wasn't prepared to roll over like a pet poodle either. She leaned forward and laced her fingers on the table. She kept her tone even, but her words were sharp as steel. "If you so much as touch Kit and Madee, you'll be the one to disappear, I promise you that."

Lemaire's men were on her instantly. The shorter one reached her first, just as she predicted. He grabbed her arm and yanked her out of her chair. The tall one was on her seconds later. His skeletal hand found her clavicle and squeezed. She let out a high-pitched squeak. It seemed she was mistaken about his commitment to his job.

"Enough," Lemaire said before the man could do any permanent damage.

He released his grip.

Rune slumped onto the floor.

"I don't know what's gotten into you," Lemaire said, looking down at her like the pitiful thing that she was. "But I'm willing to forget about this little episode and get back to business."

Silence.

"Unless you'd rather I leave you alone with these two." His eyes flicked toward his men.

Rune picked herself up and slid onto her chair, defeated.

"Don't look so glum. I hear Deauville is wonderful this time of year."

Dread mounted. Rune tried—and failed—to fend it off. "What's in Deauville?" she whispered.

Lemaire smile thinly. An inscrutable glint appeared in his eyes. He tapped the Bonaparte necklace with his forefinger and said, "The companion piece to this one."

3

CANAL SAINT-MARTIN, PARIS

The Comptoir Général on the grungy Canal Saint-Martin was an oddity in a neighborhood that was filled with them. Equal parts tiki bar, greenhouse, and art gallery, the cavernous space played host to young urbanites in search of strong drinks and an even stronger dose of escapism. Fronted by a graffiti-covered fence and an empty lot, no place in Paris was better suited for people who valued their anonymity.

Rune found herself transported to a different world the instant she walked through the door. The bar was packed with patrons who were drunker than they should have been given that the workday was not yet over. The high ceiling and exposed rafters gave the room a rustic appearance. The worn linoleum tiles spreading beneath her feet were peeling at the edges. Vines sprouting directly from cracks in the flooring trailed up to the ceiling, forming a lush, living canopy overhead. On one end of the room, she spied a cabinet of curiosities filled with animal skeletons and handcrafted tribal masks. On the other end was a bar shaped like a ship with a flaxen-haired siren affixed to the prow. The space was crammed with rickety tables and chairs, no two alike.

Rune climbed the staircase to the mezzanine level, passing a historic map of Africa and a tiger skin rug with a disproportionately large head. It was quieter and less crowded upstairs. She wove through displays of bric-a-brac no sane person would ever keep until she reached the back of the room. Her pulse quickened when she saw the person she was looking for: the brilliant Milo Ward. He was the sole occupant of a crushed velvet sofa that was on the wrong side of shabby chic. An empty bottle of Slash IPA sat on the coffee table in front of him. His brow was set in concentration as his fingers flew across his laptop like a practiced musician performing a dizzying solo. He must have sensed he was being watched because he stopped typing suddenly. His eyes found hers. He nodded once. It was her cue to approach.

"Hello, Milo."

"I wondered if I'd ever see you again."

"I've been busy."

"For two years?"

"You look good."

"Is that *really* what you want to say to me?"

Rune raised her shoulders. It was the truth. He wasn't traditionally handsome, but he'd gained weight in all the right places since she last saw him. His dark hair was curlier and more abundant than she remembered. The russet-colored flecks in his eyes seemed clearer, brighter. The old Milo was chronically overcaffeinated and under-slept. The new version seemed centered, self-possessed even.

"You look good too," Milo said grudgingly.

It was a lie, but Rune took his words as an invitation to sit.

"Something to drink?"

"Large."

"Obviously."

Rune watched Milo walk away. Several minutes passed. Then several more. If it weren't for the laptop on the table and the leather messenger bag on the floor, she might have thought he'd ditched her. Given their history, it wouldn't have been a stupid move.

Rune's phone buzzed in her jacket pocket. She reached for it thinking it might be Kit returning her call. She'd wanted to hear his voice after her meeting with Lemaire. The message she'd left him was long and artificially upbeat, but she hadn't said a word about getting back together. Pride had gotten in the way of that. It was humiliating to keep reaching out and getting nothing in return, but Kit was The One. The love of her life. The person who made everything okay. He'd forgive her eventually. He *had* to forgive her—all she had to do was keep trying. Hope surged when she saw she had a new voicemail. It vanished when she realized it was spam. She pushed her phone aside along with her hurt feelings.

"Here you go."

Rune looked up. Milo had materialized out of nowhere with a glass of white wine filled almost to the brim in one hand and a bottle of beer in the other. "Odysseus returns," she said as he sank down next to her. "I thought the siren lured you away."

"She tried, but I presented her with a compelling counterargument, so she let me go."

"Sancerre," Rune said after taking a sip. "You remembered."

"You're hard to forget." He gave her a pained smile, like it was the understatement of the century. "You've been well?"

"Oh, you know."

"What are you doing here, Rune?"

"I need a favor."

"The last time I did you a favor I nearly landed in federal prison."

Milo was referring to a scheme Rune concocted to rip off a Manhattan hedge fund analyst who crossed a line with her at a bar. At her urging, he hacked the guy's email, inserted a phishing attachment into a legitimate thread, and hijacked the personal data of nearly everyone at the fund. Everything would have been fine had it not been for an astute trader who noticed something was amiss and contacted the cybersecurity team, who, in turn, reached out to the authorities. Only a combination of luck and legal wizardry had saved Milo from a lengthy prison sentence. He'd kept Rune out of it. Out of loyalty, out of love. She heard through the grapevine that he'd come looking for her after the dust had settled, only to find her apartment empty and her phone disconnected. A mutual friend later told her that he'd moved to Paris to get on with his life. She'd moved to Bangkok not long after, looking for her own fresh start.

"I should have called," she said.

"You think?"

She didn't try to explain. What could she possibly say? That she took advantage of his obvious feelings for her? She didn't dare say that out loud, not because she feared his reaction, but because it would force her to admit she was *that* person. The kind who happened to people. The kind you had to work to forget. "Listen, Milo, I know you probably hate me—"

He took a long pull from his beer.

"And I'll completely understand if you tell me to get lost—"

The pull turned into a chug.

"But I'm in serious trouble and you're the only person who can help."

Milo set the bottle down. It emitted a soft clink when it hit the table. He angled his head slightly to one side. He was in the habit of doing that when he was making an important decision. "You're here, so talk," he finally said.

It wasn't great, but it was the opening she needed. She moved fast, before he could change his mind. "A man is threatening to hurt me and the people I care about. I need someone who can hack—"

"Let me stop you right there."

"But—"

He held up a hand to silence her.

"Milo—"

He put on his bomber jacket and slipped his laptop into his messenger bag. Across his torso it went. He walked away without another word.

Rune cast a longing glance at her wine before heaving herself up and following him downstairs. He sped away from her. She tried to keep up, but he had the tall man advantage. The crowd parted for him like Moses at the Red Sea. For her, not so much. She lost sight of him somewhere near the bar. It didn't matter. There was only one exit.

The air whistled when she opened the door. Sunlight exploded off the cracked sidewalk. She spied Milo walking along the canal. She caught up to him just as he reached a graffiti covered footbridge.

"Go away, Rune."

"Please, Milo. Hear me out. That's all I ask."

He stopped to face her.

Her next words came out quickly, before he could slip away again. "There's a man, his name is Charles Lemaire, he traffics in conflict rubies from Myanmar."

"The world is full of bad people, Rune."

"I work for him."

"Of course you do." Sarcasm dripped from his voice.

"Please don't be like that."

Milo looked contrite. Almost.

"The only reason I'm involved is because Lemaire threatened to hurt the people I love. One of them is a fifteen-year-old girl." She left out the part about stealing Lemaire's rubies and Madee swiping his ring. Those details would only muddy the waters.

"I'm sorry to hear that," Milo said. "But what's it got to do with me?"

"Lemaire does terrible things. And not just to me. He preys on desperate people who have no money, no options. They risk their lives in the mines. They risk their freedom smuggling gemstones across borders. He profits from their misery."

"It sounds like a job for the police."

Rune's lips tightened. She and the police didn't mix.

"Oh, I get it," Milo said with a knowing look. "You can't go to the police without implicating yourself in this guy's crimes."

A brisk wind whipped at Rune's hair. She smoothed it down, then stuffed her hands in her pockets.

"I hate to see you in a bind, Rune, I really do. But I'm not your guy. You burned that bridge a long time ago."

"Don't you want to help me stop Lemaire? He's dangerous. He's had people killed. I know that for a fact."

"Why should I care?"

"Come on, Milo. You're better than that."

His anger flared. "Oh, no you don't," he said, wagging his finger at her. "You don't get to do this. You don't get to waltz back into my life after two years and guilt-trip me into helping you. I heard you out and I'm saying no. Now leave me alone." He turned his back to her and stalked away.

"Milo! Wait!" Her words had no impact. She hurried to catch up.

"Leave me alone, Rune."

"All you have to do is help me get something on Lemaire. Then I swear you'll never hear from me again."

"Get something on Lemaire?" Milo echoed without breaking stride. "You mean do something illegal. I won't risk going to prison. Not for some random criminal who has nothing to do with me."

"Can't you put your feelings for me aside?"

"Not everything is about you, Rune."

"You can't just ignore this. You're a good person. I know you are."

Milo stopped walking and fixed his gaze on the canal. Silence quivered between them as a barge full of tourists navigated one of the locks. Only after it passed did Milo speak again.

"Did I ever tell you that my mother remarried when I was fourteen?" He kept his eyes trained forward. His words were a cold monotone.

Rune shook her head.

"My stepfather didn't want me around. Neither did my mother, for that matter. They sent me away to school. It was tough." His voice trailed off. He cleared his throat. "There was this kid I made friends with—Julian Tran. I told him I liked computers, and the next day, I found a coding book outside my dorm room. We spent hours on his PlayStation. The other kids picked on us, but Julian got the worst of it, by far." Another pause. "It was the week before Thanksgiving. I was pulling an all-nighter at the library when I ran into Julian on my way to the bathroom. He was holding a baseball bat. He looked straight at me, but he didn't say anything. It was like he didn't see me. Then I saw Nick Stratton, captain of the judo team and asshole extraordinaire. He was out cold next to the urinals. His pants were unzipped. His face was a mess. There was blood. A lot of it. He came to in the hospital the next day with a severe concussion and no memory of what happened."

"Jesus."

"I was called to the headmaster's office a few days after it happened. My mother and stepfather were there with a school counselor and two police officers. They asked if I knew who had attacked Nick. I told them no." Milo turned toward Rune, his face a mix of remorse and defiance. "I never told anyone about what I saw that night. I knew what Julian had done, but I didn't say anything because he was the only person at that school who ever showed me any kindness. I remember thinking that Nick probably got what he deserved. He was awful. All the boys at that school were." Milo let that sink in, then added, "I'm not the person you think I am, Rune."

She took a beat to digest his words. When she spoke again, it was with the compassion of someone who understood that the world wasn't black or white. It wasn't even gray, just blotchy, mottled. "We've all done things we're ashamed of," she offered gently. "There's not a single person on this planet who hasn't. It doesn't make you a bad person."

"People only see who they want you to be, not who you really are."

"I see you." She reached out and covered his hand with hers. His skin felt good, like it always had. "I *know* you."

He pursed his lip.

"Please help me, Milo. I can't do this without you."

"Why should I?"

"Because anybody else would be my second choice."

He looked at her pensively.

She gave him a half smile.

His resolve wavered, then slipped away. "Jerk," he murmured before pulling her into a tight embrace.

4

MONTPARNASSE, PARIS

Is there anything I can do to speed things along?" Rune asked. She cast a hopeful glance in Milo's direction. He was seated at a dining table big enough for ten people, twelve if the people were small.

"Yes, stop pacing," Milo replied. It was the first full sentence he'd uttered in an hour. Everything else had been a grunt.

"Have you made any progress?"

"Not since the last time you asked." He made a show of looking at his watch. "Five minutes ago."

"Can I make you some coffee or something?"

He leaned back in his chair and stroked his chin. Someone with a higher degree of self-awareness would have recognized the gesture as a self-soothing one, but Milo wasn't a navel-gazer. "Pestering won't help," he said. "You need to be patient."

Patience wasn't Rune's strong suit. How could it be when her freedom was at stake? She turned her back to Milo and appraised the apartment to keep herself occupied. Everything about it screamed expensive, from the herringbone floor to the sleek modern furnishings, Scandinavian, by the looks of them. Milo had cryptically said that the apartment belonged to a friend, but there was never any telling with him. He used to have a penchant for hacking into vacation rental websites and commandeering luxury homes. She'd learned about this habit when a homeowner unexpectedly came back one night to find them soaking in his hot tub. The man had been on the verge of calling the police when Rune convinced him that they'd all been duped by a crooked rental agent. The three of them ended up having dinner at a nearby restaurant, the kind with a raw oyster bar and a months-long waitlist, with the gullible homeowner picking up the tab. She smiled at the memory. One thing was certain, she'd met her match with Milo. It was one of the reasons things between them hadn't worked out. There just wasn't enough space in the relationship for both of their antics.

Rune walked to the window. The solar shades rose at the push of a button, rewarding her with sweeping views of the Montparnasse Cemetery, home to French luminaries like Simone de Beauvoir and Maurice Leblanc. A row of mature linden trees dotted with stubborn leaves marched down the length of the street. The stone wall surrounding the cemetery was shrouded with ivy that was surprisingly green given the lateness of the season. Under different circumstances, Rune might have been impressed. Instead, she imagined digging a three-by-eight hole in the middle of the cemetery and rolling Lemaire's lifeless body into it. Problem solved. The thought tugged at her lips. Then reality intruded and set off another round of pacing.

"Stop it!" Milo called out.

"Sorry," Rune said even though she wasn't sorry at all.

An exasperated sigh.

"I said sorry."

"If you can't sit still, at least make yourself useful. Tell me more about Lemaire."

"I've already told you everything."

"Tell me again. Any detail might help."

Rune plopped into the chair next to Milo's. She reached for his beer, ignoring the death stare he gave her when she drained half its contents. "Lemaire runs one of the biggest gemstone-smuggling operations in Southeast Asia," she said. She hiccupped loudly, then resumed. "He deals in all kinds of gems, but he built his business selling pigeon blood rubies."

"What are those?"

"Only the most expensive rubies on the planet. They cost more per carat than any other precious stone except colored diamonds." Rune paused to take another sip of Milo's beer.

"Can you save some of that for me?"

Rune continued as if he hadn't spoken. "Pigeon blood rubies are mined in Myanmar at a depth of nearly two thousand feet. They're hard to procure, on top of being extremely beautiful, which is why they cost so much. Consumer demand is huge, but reputable companies won't go near them. Cartier, Chopard, Van Cleef & Arpels, they all refuse to buy or sell pigeon blood rubies from Myanmar. They're not alone."

"For ethical reasons?"

Rune nodded. "The country's messed up. There was a military coup a few years ago. Thousands killed, millions displaced. But the problems go back decades. Genocide, gender-based violence, arbitrary detentions. You name it, they do it. No one wants to be associated with that regime. But Lemaire found a way to beat the system. He runs an end-to-end business. Miners, smugglers, lapidaries. He even has lab techs on his payroll. There's one right here in Paris, at the French Gemological Laboratory. I know for a fact someone there falsifies documents for Lemaire."

"I don't understand. Don't people know the difference?"

"No test is perfect."

Milo looked like he wanted her to say more.

"You can use lasers to determine the chemical composition of a gemstone. You can also study inclusions—the other things mixed into the stones. But not all gems have region-specific compositions or inclusions. The only thing science can tell us with certainty is whether a gem is natural or synthetic. Provenance is essentially a judgment call."

"I find that hard to believe."

"There's a saying in the business: Only a miner and God know for sure where a stone was extracted. If there's a problem with one country, traffickers can claim that gems come from somewhere else. No one's the wiser. And it's not just rubies either. The same thing happens with diamonds from Congo and emeralds from Afghanistan."

"Because there's nothing romantic about child labor and the stoning of women."

"Exactly."

"I take it you've tried getting at Lemaire through his associates?"

"I've approached the few that I know about. Discreetly, of course. They weren't receptive."

"So, he fosters loyalty."

"More like terror." Rune paused. "People aren't just scared of him. They need money. It's not like they have a ton of options."

"What else?"

Rune shrugged. "He stays at the Mandarin Oriental whenever he's in Bangkok. I met him recently at the Crillon. I don't know where he is the rest of the time. He sends me on jobs all over the world."

"Is that why you're in Paris? You're on a job?"

She took another sip of beer to avoid answering. She was relieved when Milo didn't press the issue.

"What about Lemaire's personal life?" he asked.

"What about it?"

"Can you think of anything that might be helpful?"

Rune started to shake her head, then stopped herself. "He owns a yacht. A big one." Her mind drifted to the day she woke up on Lemaire's yacht after being rescued from a human trafficking ring operating out of Bangkok's notorious Khlong Toei slum. Lemaire had come for her not out of the goodness of his heart but to recoup the rubies she and Kit had stolen from him. He'd threatened to throw her overboard when she finally admitted the stones were lost.

Hire me, she'd said in a desperate attempt to stay alive. *I'm really good at what I do. I'm one of the best. We can make a lot of money together.*

She'd been so bold. So persuasive. Now she wanted to eat her words.

"Do you happen to know the name of the yacht?" Milo asked. "Or better yet, the IMO or MMSI?"

"The what?"

"Ships have unique identifiers. The International Maritime Organization number, or IMO. And the Maritime Mobile Service Identity, or MMSI. They're usually displayed on the hull."

"I didn't notice any numbers."

"When were you on the yacht?"

"Last summer."

"Do you remember the date?"

"June 25th."

"And where were you docked?"

"At the Port of Singapore."

"That's good," Milo said, encouraged. "I'll compile a list of all the vessels in and around the port that day. Then we can try to figure out which one is Lemaire's."

"What good does identifying his yacht do?"

"All boats have transponders that provide real-time information. Position, route, speed, even ship type. They can be tracked with apps like VesselFinder, MarineTraffic, and SuperYachtFan."

"Yachts are trackable? Like Ubers?"

"Yup." Milo flashed her a smile. "People used the apps to narc on the Russian oligarchs trying to get around international sanctions in the early days of the war with Ukraine. If I can track Lemaire's yacht—"

"Then I can break in and look for something to use against him."

"Exactly."

There was an energy in Milo's manner. He could deny it all he wanted, but he enjoyed a challenge as much as she did, especially when it was laced with danger.

"The Port of Singapore, June 25th," he muttered as he typed the information into his laptop.

Rune forced herself to remain quiet.

"Hey, do you know anything about a raid on a Thai shipping container on June 25th?" Milo asked not long after. He angled his screen toward Rune. "It says here that the authorities rescued a bunch of trafficked girls from the Port of Singapore that day."

Rune erupted into a fit of coughing. She brought her forearm up to her mouth, not to be polite but to hide her face. She didn't want Milo to know she was among the poor souls trapped inside that horrible container. She didn't want to relive it. The hollow ache of hunger. The fetid bucket of puke and excrement. The fear that slithered around her neck and threatened not to let go. Lemaire had freed her, only to trap her in a different way.

"You okay there?" Milo asked when her coughing dragged on. He patted her firmly on the back and handed her what remained of his beer.

Rune pushed the memories aside and accepted the bottle, grateful to have someone so thoughtful—and so oblivious—by her side. "I'm good," she managed to croak after taking a sip. "Just look for the yacht."

Milo turned his attention back to his computer. A look of intense concentration crossed his face. Rune knew it meant. He was in his zone. He wouldn't emerge until he found what he was looking for. The only thing she could do now was shut up and wait.

Darkness had fallen when Rune awoke alone in an unfamiliar bed, her mouth dry and her head thick as cotton. She'd hit the booze hard while Milo accessed records from the Port of Singapore. It wasn't just the thought of what Lemaire would do to her if he learned about her plans that drove her to kill an entire bottle of wine unaided. Her impending trip to Deauville also weighed on her. Everything Lemaire made her do was risky, but the Deauville job was downright reckless coming on the heels of the Louvre.

Rune sat up with difficulty and rubbed her eyes with the heels of her hands. Her dreams had been sporadic, a disturbing patchwork of childhood memories and murderous fantasies. She didn't just feel unrested, she felt *unsettled*. But then, that's what happened when you drank yourself sloppy. She ran her fingers through her shaggy hair and checked her phone. Her heart sank when she realized she'd drunk-texted Kit. She flipped the phone over but not before seeing that he'd read her message and chosen not to respond. She swung her legs off the bed.

Why the hell am I pantless?

She turned her head, sending a jab of pain directly to her temple. Her jeans were draped over the back of an armchair. Her socks were on the seat, neatly folded in half. The sight was somewhat reassuring, but she still had questions. She got dressed at sloth-speed and went searching for Milo, no small task in the gargantuan apartment.

She found him exactly where she'd left him—in front of his laptop. There were three empty beer bottles on the dining table. In his hand was a wrap that looked bad and smelled even worse. "What is that?" she asked, pointing to the pungent offender.

"A sushirrito," he said. His jaw bounced up and down as he chewed. "It's a combination of sushi and—"

She raised her hand to interrupt. "I get it."

"Do you want a bite?"

Rune prided herself on being an adventurous eater, but nothing on God's green earth could convince her to ingest a sushirrito. She eased herself onto the sofa at half speed. Milo disappeared down the hallway and returned not long after with a glass of water and two white pills. She looked at him quizzically.

"Aspirin."

She muscled the tablets down without bothering with the water, then sat back and waited for the haze to lift. Milo fetched his dinner from the dining table and settled next to her. Her innards shot up. She pressed her fist against her lips. Only after she was sure the contents of her stomach would stay down did she speak. "Sooo," she began. "I wanted to ask you something." She tried to keep her tone casual, but there was a slight tightness in her voice. She opened her mouth to say something, then closed it again.

"Are you going to puke?" Milo asked.

"What? No." She chided herself silently. It wasn't like her to be at a loss for words. "I just want to clarify whether you and I—"

He angled his head.

"What I mean to say is, did we—"

"Spit it out already."

"Did we hook up?"

Milo looked offended. Or angry. Or maybe a bit of both.

"It's not a big deal if we did," she added quickly. "I just don't remember."

"Is that what you think I've been doing for the last two years? Waiting for a chance to jump back into bed with you?"

"It's a legitimate question," Rune said. "I woke up in your bed half naked."

"You left your pants on the floor like a big fat slob. I picked them up. I also turned you onto your side so you wouldn't choke on your own vomit. You're welcome, by the way."

Rune dropped her eyes, embarrassed.

Milo signaled he was moving on by taking a big bite of sushiritto. A glob of tobiko oozed out of the wrapper and slid down the side of his hand. He wiped it up, leaving a smear of neon orange on the napkin. It took all of Rune's willpower to keep the booze churning inside her from surfacing.

"You're sure you don't want any?" Milo asked when he saw her staring.

"I'm good."

"Suit yourself."

Silence fell between them. The sound of Milo's chewing filled the room.

"A big fat slob, huh?" Rune finally said.

Milo grimaced.

"You should see your face right now!"

"Worse than your passed-out face?" He rolled his eyes back and let his tongue loll to the side.

She burst out laughing. He joined her. Soon they were howling and exchanging verbal jabs just like they did when they were more than friends. Rune laughed from deep inside her belly. She laughed so hard tears streamed from her eyes. After the last miserable months, it felt good to let go.

"You have drool on your shirt!" Milo howled.

"I do not!"

"It's in your hair too!"

"Stop, it hurts!"

But he didn't stop. And neither did she. Their laughter continued until Rune broke into a coughing fit. Milo reached over and gave her a few firm pats on the back. Their laughter became less uproarious. Eventually it petered out and they both gave long, satisfied sighs.

"I found it, you know," Milo said when the moment of levity passed.

Rune tilted her head. "Found what?"

"Lemaire's yacht."

"Really? Why didn't you wake me?"

"I tried. Nothing happened."

She chose not to dwell on that.

"I made a list of all noncommercial boats that arrived in Singapore on June 25th. I eliminated the smaller vessels, then crosschecked that list with—"

"I don't care."

"Right." Milo nodded. He set down his dinner and reached for his laptop, angling it toward her.

Rune's eyebrows rose. The yacht looked like it belonged to a Bond villain. It was a striking vessel, yet she had almost no memory of being on it. In fairness, she'd been locked in a dark container for three days and not at her sharpest.

"It's an Oceanco. Top of the line. Dutch-made," Milo said. There was an excitement in his voice. His admiration for Lemaire's yacht was coming through loud and clear. "The thing is huge, nearly three hundred feet. It has a private owner's deck, an outdoor pool, a hammam, a sauna, a fully equipped gym—"

"How do you know it's the right yacht?" Rune asked, putting an end to the infomercial.

"Look at the name."

She followed Milo's finger. It directed her to the yacht's stern, where a single word was written in bright red letters. *Ruby.*

"The yacht sails under the UK flag, but it's registered to a company in the Caymans. For tax purposes, I'm guessing. The IMO is 1013066."

"Where is it now?"

"Palma."

Mallorca. A two-hour flight from Paris.

"What's the plan?" Milo asked when she didn't react.

"There's no plan."

He shot her an incredulous look. "You expect me to believe that?"

"There's no plan *yet*," she amended.

"Well, I wouldn't wait too long. It won't be there indefinitely. Most yachts that size spend the winter in the Caribbean or the Indian Ocean."

Rune made a noncommittal sound.

"You know that getting caught breaking the law in the EU is better than in other parts of the world, right?"

"I know."

"I don't understand. You practically begged me for help. You made it sound urgent."

"It *is* urgent. But I have some things to take care of first. Personal things."

"Whatever you say." Milo shrugged, then reached for what remained of his sushirrito.

"Wait." Rune put her hand on his arm. It was time to get to the other reason she'd approached Milo, the more immediate reason. She tried to be casual, but inside she was tense. So much was riding on what happened next. "Listen, Milo, I know we agreed to one-and-done, but since I'm here, would you mind doing me another small favor?"

He looked at her with well-deserved suspicion, but he didn't say no.

"I need information about someone."

"Who?"

"Her name is Margot Steiner. She and her husband will be in Deauville next weekend."

"Does this woman have something to do with Lemaire?"

"She was one of his marks," Rune said. She offered the information knowing it was just a matter of time before Milo figured it out. "I'm following up on a hunch." She cringed internally. She didn't like lying, but she knew Milo wouldn't help if he knew the truth about Deauville, and she needed someone with his skillset to pull off her next job. She held her breath. She could practically see the gears in his mind turning.

"Margot what?" he asked after what felt like eons.

She exhaled silently. "Steiner. Margot Steiner." She scooted closer, no longer put off by the stench of Milo's meal.

"What do you want to know?"

"Absolutely everything."

5

CASINO BARRIÈRE, DEAUVILLE

T he town of Deauville on the coast of Normandy in northern France
was a playground for rich and fabulous Parisians. The drive from
the capital to the seaside resort was a smidge over two hours, making it
a go-to destination for Paris' upper crust. Some referred to Deauville as
the Parisian Riviera. Others called it the 21st arrondissement. In addi-
tion to its expansive beaches and enchanting Art Deco architecture,
the town was home to an annual film festival, a thoroughbred racing
series, and international polo events, all of which imbued it with an aura
of old-world glamour. Unlike its less affluent neighbors, which turned
to ghost towns come the fall, Deauville attracted visitors year-round,
including adrenaline junkies in search of their next big rush.

Gambling had been central to Deauville's identity since its famous
casino opened in 1912. The beachfront property housed nearly three
hundred slot machines, as well as dozens of blackjack, poker, and punto
banco tables. Roulette, boule, and craps were also on offer. With its
stately facade, Michelin-rated restaurant, and glittering chandeliers, the
sprawling casino was an apt symbol of the luxury lifestyle Deauville
peddled to the ultra-rich.

Rune walked into the casino looking like a woman with money to burn. She was dressed impeccably in separates from Balmain Atelier, not the ready-to-wear collection. A high-waisted skirt hugged her body in all the right places. Her silk blouse had a scandalously low neckline. Come-hither boots and a copper-colored wig completed the package. She declined a silent invitation from a sugar daddy with an oversized paunch and surveyed the gaming floor. It was exactly what she expected, full of flashing lights and carnival-like sounds, festooned in crimson and gold. She resisted the urge to adjust her wig and zeroed in on a boisterous group of gamblers at a roulette table. A spot opened minutes later, but she didn't take it. It wasn't nerves holding her back. She was just waiting for the right moment to make her move. She ordered a glass of Sancerre from a freckled waitress to pass the time.

She was halfway through her second glass when a dapper man with enviably thick hair left the table. She slid onto his empty stool before anyone else could claim it and glanced at the croupier, a pale-skinned woman with eyes as mercurial as the Norman sky. Her name was Magali, according to the tag pinned to her lapel. She acknowledged Rune with a misanthropic nod, as the French were wont to do.

Rune toyed with her hair as Magali sent the wheel spinning. She picked up five chips and slid them onto the 1 to 18 box knowing it was a cautious bet that would, at best, yield a small payout. Magali waved her hand over the table as the wheel began to slow, indicating an end to the betting. The ball bounced around several times before landing on 35 black. Rune said nothing as Magali swept away her chips. After losing three times in a row, she leaned over to her neighbor and murmured, "You seem to be better at this than me. What's your secret?"

Her seatmate looked to be a recent prep school graduate. Like most of the men in the room, there was an overconfident air about him, the kind you could only get from a boarding school education and a lifetime of privilege. He was clean-cut and nice to look at, if you were into double-breasted blazers and classic bucks. His hair was a fetching shade of warm caramel, his teeth artificially white from overpriced treatments at the dentist's office. He locked eyes with Rune before letting his gaze move down to her décolleté. She didn't have much in that department, but what she had, she knew how to use. She leaned forward to give him a better view. He brought his eyes back up and answered her question with an admission that was surprisingly self-deprecating. "There's no secret. Roulette is one percent strategy and ninety-nine percent luck."

"Then you must be luckier than I am," Rune said. She shook her head ruefully. Her copper locks swayed across her shoulders.

"I don't know about that." He grinned and toyed with his chips, cutting them like he would a deck of cards. "I'm Maxime, by the way, but everyone calls me Max."

"No way! I'm Maxine with an *N*. I go by Maxie."

"Are you serious?"

"Yesss!"

"What are the odds?"

"Worse than winning at roulette?"

Max bared his super white teeth.

Rune leaned a bit closer.

"Where are you from, Maxie?"

"California. It's my first time in Deauville. You?"

"I live in Paris."

"Nice."

Max made a face. "Paris is a disaster. I barely recognize it anymore. I'm just lucky my parents keep a place up here."

Rune matched Max's expression. "LA is the same. *Blech!*"

Emboldened, Max launched into a well-rehearsed diatribe about Paris going to the dogs and the chinless globalists tripping over themselves to drag it there. Rune interjected with well-timed "uh-huhs" and nods of agreement. She could keep Max talking forever now that she knew which way he leaned.

And talk they did over the roulette table for the next hour, only ceding their seats after Rune lost all her chips. She looked on with genuine admiration as Max cashed in. He'd done well for himself.

"Where to next?" she asked, tucking her hand in the crook of his arm.

"Your hotel?"

Her bottom lip jutted out in fake disappointment. "I'm staying with a friend."

"Oh."

"What about your place?"

"My parents are home."

"That's too bad." This time her disappointment was real.

"They're driving back to Paris after dinner though. Do you want to hang out here until then?"

"I'd like that."

"Should we try the slots?"

She pretended to think about it. "I bet you're good at poker. Will you teach me how to play?" The compliment had exactly the effect she anticipated. Max's chest expanded. He stood slightly taller. "Pretty please?" she added to seal the deal.

"Sure, why not?" He smiled down at her, drunk on the feeling that came with having a grown woman on his arm. He slid his hand around her waist and pulled her close. "Who are you, anyway?" he murmured into her hair.

She looked up at him from under her lashes and said, "Whoever you want me to be."

An hour or so later, the smile had been wiped from Max's face and replaced by an impassive expression. He sat at a no-limit poker table with a buy-in of ten thousand Euros. The game was Texas hold 'em. There were five other players. A buxom British woman with big hair and an even bigger voice occupied the seat immediately to the left of the goateed dealer. The next three players were interchangeable in Rune's mind: Frenchmen who looked like they'd spent their lives sucking on Gitanes. She nicknamed them the Three Musketeers; though, admittedly, they lacked the floppy hats and distinctive facial hair of Dumas's title characters.

The last player was the one Rune had her eye on and not because she was any good at poker. Sitting beside Max was none other than Margot Steiner dripping in enough diamonds to give De Beers a run for its money. She looked remarkably composed for someone who'd recently been robbed of a priceless heirloom. Her security guard was nowhere in sight, presumably fired after the debacle at the Louvre.

Rune stood behind Max, her weight on one leg, her hand resting on his shoulder with cultivated nonchalance. She'd hoped to be at his parents' place already, but this wasn't a bad way to pass the time. The British woman was especially entertaining to watch. She was an inscrutable player with an uncanny ability to know when her opponents were bluffing. She also happened to be the big winner so far. *I think I'm in love*, Rune thought as she gazed at the woman's chips.

The dealer removed the cards from the shuffling machine, cut the deck, and placed it on the table. The action began before any cards were dealt, starting with the British woman, who placed a small blind bet of five thousand Euros. Her neighbor, Musketeer #1, raised to six thousand, making that the minimum bet of the game. The dealer then dealt each player two cards. The preflop round ensued starting with Musketeer #2. He raised. The remaining players called, bringing the action full circle.

The crowd leaned closer. Their hushed voices sliced through the tension. With a small fortune on the table, it was hard to keep the gawkers away.

The dealer revealed the flop: the Five of Spades, the Jack of Diamonds, and the Ten of Hearts. Musketeer #2 raised again during the second round of betting. Max and the British woman called, while Margot and the two remaining Musketeers folded. The dealer shared the turn—the Jack of Hearts. Betting continued until the dealer turned over the final card—the river. Rune perked when she saw it: the Queen of Hearts, her lucky card. She wasn't at all superstitious, except when it came to poker.

"All in," the British woman said with a wave of her hand. Murmurs rose from the crowd as she pushed her chips to the center of the table.

"Your action, sir," the dealer said to the last Musketeer standing.

The man toyed with two of his chips, clicking them together like a metronome set at sixty beats per minute. Beads of sweat dotted his hairline. His nostrils flared. Rune knew at once that he had a weak hand. He shifted in his seat, then said, "Fold."

It was Max's turn. He sat stock-still for what seemed like an eternity. Rune could understand his hesitation. His hand was good but by no means a slam dunk. She did the math in her head. There was almost a quarter million in the pot. She squeezed Max's shoulder reassuringly, giving him just the dose of courage he needed to make his move. It was easy to be brave when it was someone else's money on the line.

"Call," he said. He moved what remained of his chips to the middle of the table.

"Sir, ma'am, showdown, please," the dealer replied.

Max turned his cards over, revealing the Jack of Clubs and the Five of Diamonds. He leaned back in his chair. Rune gave his shoulder another squeeze.

"Jacks full of Fives," the dealer announced.

Everyone turned to the British woman, eager to see her hand and her reaction. Showing no emotion, she set down her cards: the Nine of Hearts and the King of Hearts.

"Straight Flush," the dealer said. "Ladies and gentlemen, we have a winner."

And just like that, the game was over. Max looked dejected. Rune could hardly blame him, but she couldn't muster up any real sympathy either. This wasn't something anyone had done to him. He'd lost his money all on his own. Still, she was surprised when he clung to her like a wounded animal as they walked out of the poker room and into the main gaming hall.

"What am I supposed to do now?" Max whined.

Rune was about to respond when Margot Steiner strode past with her husband, Rolf, CEO of Steiner Pharmaceuticals, a behemoth in the German pharmaceutical industry. Margot snapped her fingers at a waiter, ordered a drink—no "please" or "thank you"—and pointed to the high roller room. Only after they were out of earshot did Rune direct her attention back to Max.

"Do you want to take me to your place now?" she asked. She ruffled his hair like she would a pet or a small child.

He looked at his watch, a pricey Omega with a titanium case.

"Are your parents still there?"

"No," he said. "But they don't like it when I bring strangers to the house."

His candor surprised Rune. She didn't know many men who would infantilize themselves like that. But then, Max had barely crossed the threshold into manhood. "What if you broke the rules just this once?" she said with a coquettish tilt of her head.

Hesitation.

She rose onto her tiptoes and drew him toward her. Their mouths met. If the prospect of bedding her didn't change his mind, she didn't know what would.

"Let's go," Max said hoarsely.

Rune's lips unfurled. She kissed him again. Then she grabbed his hand and led him toward the exit.

6

DEAUVILLE

The air smelled different in Deauville. It was sharp. Briny. It was also cold. So cold it penetrated Rune's coat and settled deep inside her bones. So cold it sucked the air out of her lungs. The weather was all anyone could talk about. The city was on track for its coldest autumn in decades. If that wasn't bad enough, a low-pressure system had dumped an unprecedented amount of rain on the region, causing basements to flood and businesses to shutter their doors. Some blamed climate change for the extreme weather. Others said it was an act of God. Doomsdayers of all persuasions warned that the worst was yet to come.

Rune hugged her coat against her body as she hurried toward her parking spot, taking care not to step in the lake-sized puddles dotting the pavement. Her nose scrunched when her rental car came into view. A Mercedes EQS sedan was what she'd wanted. A compact Renault with a rattle in the engine was what she got. Flashing headlights caught her attention as she slid into the driver's seat. It was Max in a red Porsche with custom rims and a rear wing. It was so cliché she could hardly suppress an eyeroll.

He revved his engine. She reached for her seatbelt. He peeled away, tires squealing.

"What the hell," she muttered. She pressed the ignition button and threw her car into gear. She did her best to keep up, but her clunker wasn't up to the task. She watched Max cut off a minivan and blow through a red light. A barrage of honking followed. She tightened her grip on the steering wheel and prayed no one had to die just because Max wanted to flex for her.

She caught up to him at the next light and leaned on her horn. He must have gotten the message because the rest of the drive was uneventful. They reached the outskirts of town about ten minutes later and pulled into a gated driveway. Relieved, Rune killed the engine and peered out the window.

The centuries-old mansion with sea views stood fifty feet from its only neighbor, two lonely outposts in an otherwise densely built area. It was a grand house with a steeply pitched roof and sturdy wood beams crisscrossing the exterior. Rune was surprised by its weathered state. The white stucco was in serious need of scrubbing, like a porcelain tub discolored by age and use. The old timbers were black from exposure to the elements. The house needed work, yet it outshone all the other properties they'd passed.

"Nice place," Rune said after joining Max at the top of the driveway.

"It's been in my family for over two hundred years. It has real character, not like the new condos cropping up everywhere." He said the words with obvious pride, like he was personally responsible for the age and excellence of the house. His keys jingled when he pulled them out of his pocket. He opened the door and stepped aside like a gentleman.

The interior of the house was unexpectedly well-kept given the state of the exterior. The wide-plank floors and tasteful furnishings were in pristine condition. The white marble fireplace added a touch of grandeur that was entirely appropriate for a place like Deauville.

Rune glanced at the staircase leading to the second story, to the family's private quarters, before turning her attention to Max. "Who do these belong to?" she asked, inclining her head toward a shelf full of trophies and ribbons.

"My parents own racehorses."

Of course they do. She pointed to a picture of a chestnut-colored horse with a white star between its eyes.

"That's Clovis," Max said. "He's a two-time winner of the Deauville Grand Prix. His stud fee is more than what most people in this country make in a year."

Rune arranged her face to look like she cared, then picked up a photo of a smiling couple posing with said pony.

"My parents." Max took the frame from her hands and put it back on the shelf. "But we're not here to talk about them."

"No, we're not."

He led her to the living room and lowered her onto the couch. "Oh, baby," he breathed. His tongue wormed into her ear. "I want to eat you for breakfast, lunch, and dinner."

What?

"Nom, nom, nom."

Noooo!

He pawed at her shirt with clumsy fingers. The seam tore at the collar. She pushed him away with both hands.

"Slow down!"

He stopped. Color stained his cheeks. "Sorry."

She softened her tone. "Let's start over, okay?"

He nodded, eager for a second chance.

"How about offering me a drink?"

"Right. Of course. What would you like?"

"Surprise me." She kept her eyes on him as he walked to the bar and fumbled with a pair of tulip-shaped glasses. He poured two generous helpings of Calvados. *When in Rome,* she thought after he handed her a glass. She waited for him to place his drink on the coffee table, then said, "Can I get some water?"

He might have protested if she hadn't reprimanded him moments before.

"With ice, please," she added sweetly.

He returned to the bar. She reached for the vial of GHB in her handbag. Into his glass it went. A quick stir with her index finger ensured it would go undetected. By the time Max returned, Rune was sitting pretty and sipping her Calvados.

"To you," he said after lowering himself next to her.

"To us," she replied. She wet her lips with the cloying liquid. He threw his back in one go. She wanted to pump her fist in the air. Instead, she said, "Mmmm, that's tasty."

"You're tasty."

She braced herself for more yum-yum sounds, but he seemed to have gotten that out of his system.

He took the glass out of her hand and set it on the table. His face came within inches of hers. "May I touch you?"

Rune relaxed. It seemed Max had learned from his previous misstep. She was genuinely happy for him and his future lovers, but bedding him wasn't on the agenda. A disappointed grunt rose from his throat when she pulled away. She tugged on his hand and guided him to an antique wing-back with floral upholstery and dark green piping. She raked her fingers through his hair and nipped at his lips. "You don't have to do anything," she said in a husky voice. "This is all for you." She turned out the lights and stepped into the silvery beam of the moon streaming in from the window. She turned to face him, her body scarcely more than a silhouette.

Max wore the expression of someone who couldn't quite believe his good fortune, like hitting the jackpot with her made up for losing a fortune at the poker table. He fumbled with his belt and stuck his hand down his pants. Rune removed her shirt with deliberate slowness. Her skirt came off next, pooling gracefully at her feet. She watched Max's reactions as she reached back to unhook her pretty lace bra. His eyes were hooded with lust, his hand moved vigorously over his crotch. She approached slowly, her hips swaying with every step. His eyelids fluttered once. Then a second time. A smile played on her lips. Her smile grew when his hand started to slow.

Five . . . four . . . three . . . two . . .

He was out before she reached one.

<hr />

Rune was naked under her coat when she dashed outside to fetch the supplies from the trunk of her rental car. The duct tape was in her hand before she reached the front door. She ran her thumb over the roll until she found the end and taped Max's torso to the back of the chair. She repeated the procedure with his legs, making sure they were good and tight. Some might have called it overkill given the drugs in his system, but Rune hadn't gotten this far in life by taking shortcuts. She stood back to admire her handiwork.

Hmm.

She ripped a small piece of tape with her teeth and pressed it over Max's lips. On a whim, she brought her mouth to his, leaving behind a cherry-red lipstick mark.

Perfect!

She smoothed Max's hair over his forehead with something approaching tenderness, then turned her attention to the task at hand—stealing Margot Steiner's earrings.

They're part of Napoleon's sapphire parure, Lemaire said during their meeting at the Crillon. A parure, it turned out, was just a fancy word for a set.

On the surface, the Deauville job seemed easy. All Rune had to do was break into the Steiners' house, grab the earrings, and get the hell out of dodge. The problem was, the Steiners were sure to be on high alert after the incident at the Louvre. Waiting a few months for their guard to come down would have been the smart move, but that wasn't an option. Lemaire had made that perfectly clear. The only thing giving Rune solace was knowing that, with Milo on her side, the Deauville job might be her last. And with Lemaire out of her life, everything could go back to the way it was. Her nightmare would be over. She let her imagination take flight. In it, she zipped through the crowded streets of Bangkok on the back of Kit's vintage Ducati Scrambler. The sun caressed her skin. The wind carried the sound of their laughter. The image was so real she almost felt like her old self again. Bold. Free. Fearless. She savored the feeling. She needed it to pull off this job.

Where to start? she asked herself, tapping her thigh with the palm of her hand. She could almost hear Kit's answer: *At the beginning.* With that in mind, she rummaged through her bag for a change of clothes. The next few hours demanded a practical outfit, not the racy ensemble she'd worn to seduce Max.

Rune padded across the living room a short time later donning black jeans and a fitted black sweater. She took off her wig and scratched her head as she made her way to the back of the house. She padded down a hallway decorated with antique plates and found the kitchen. The refrigerator caught her attention. She was about to reach inside for a snack when the angel on her shoulder reminded her to stay on task. She fished around in her bag for her binoculars and planted herself by a window overlooking the backyard.

The house behind Max's belonged to the Steiners. The couple was in Deauville for a charity function benefiting sick children. Or orphaned children. Or sick orphaned children. Whatever the case, the event, scheduled for the following night, warranted bringing out the family jewels. It was no accident that Rune had befriended Max at the casino. His was the only house that provided discreet access to the Steiners' property. The fact that he was there in the off-season was just bad luck.

Rune squinted through her binoculars. The Steiner house was dark and, if everything went according to plan, it would stay that way for a good long time. She was tense but not excessively so. The casino's high roller room had more than enough games to keep Margot and Rolf occupied. Still, it never paid to dillydally. With that in mind, she grabbed the black hoodie from her bag, zipped it up, and headed out the backdoor.

She approached the Steiner property like a huntress. The dead grass, squishy after days of rain, muffled her footsteps. She advanced until she reached a barren hedge. At over six feet, it was clearly built to safeguard the privacy of the homeowners. Rune squeezed through the branches, dousing herself in ice-cold water. "Splendid," she muttered when a large drop landed on her head and trickled down her neck. She brushed it away as best she could, then gazed at the chain-link fence hidden behind the branches. It wasn't the worst thing she'd ever climbed, but there wasn't much room to maneuver and her hands were already stiff from the cold. She rubbed her palms together, then reached for the top of the fence and hoisted herself over.

The Steiner's backyard was empty. The house lay in shadows. It looked to be the same vintage as Max's, but Rune didn't waste time admiring it. She ran across the yard, the sodden grass slippery beneath her feet. She skidded to a stop at the back door. A quick tug confirmed it was locked. No big surprise. She pulled out her picks and got to work.

Locks were not usually a problem for Rune, but this one wasn't cooperating. "Dammit!" she said when the metal hook she was using to jiggle the pins fell out of her hand. She bent to retrieve it and wiped it on her jeans. She was about to get back to work when she happened to look up and see a tab above the door. It was innocuous to the untrained eye, but Rune recognized it immediately as a motion sensor. Had she succeeded in opening the door, a silent alarm would have alerted the Steiners' security company, which, in turn, would have alerted the cops. She blamed Lemaire for the gaffe. Everything was always a rush with him. Then she got over it and pulled out her phone.

"Pick up, pick up, pick up," she said with a note of urgency in her voice. The longer she was outside, the greater the chance of discovery.

"Yeah?" Milo grumbled after the third ring.

"I need your help getting past a security system," she said, cutting straight to the chase. A lighter touch might have won her brownie points, but she didn't have time for niceties.

"I'm fine, thanks for asking. And you?"

"Give me a break, Milo. This is an emergency."

"Your whole life is an emergency."

He wasn't wrong. Rune ignored the jab. "I think I have a lead on one of Lemaire's associates. I need your help getting past their security system." The lie poked at her but not enough to make her regret it.

"You think or you know?"

"I won't know for sure until I get into the house. Will you help me or not?"

There was silence on Milo's end of the line. Rune bit her lip to keep from saying anything. Knowing when to push and when to ease off was an art she'd perfected long ago, but it didn't come easily.

"What's the address?"

Rune silently thanked her lucky stars. "24 Rue des Lais de Mer, Deauville."

"Your accent is awful."

"Thanks for the feedback. Is there anything else you'd like me to work on?"

"24 Rue des Lais de Mer," he repeated in perfect French. "That's the address of the woman you asked me about the other day, isn't it?"

"Uh-huh."

"Margot Steiner, right?"

"Yup."

"You think she was in on it?"

"Maybe."

"Was it an insurance scam?"

"I won't know until I get inside."

Silence.

"Come on, Milo. Help me out."

"Fine," he grumbled. "But only because they're Big Pharma."

Milo's words gave Rune pause. She wondered if he knew something about the Steiners she didn't or if he just didn't like giant corporations. She didn't ask. She didn't want to interrupt whatever it was he was doing.

"The Steiners just replaced their home security system," Milo said after a few minutes.

Rune knew exactly what had prompted the upgrade.

"There's a doorbell camera on the back door. Luckily for you, it doesn't have advanced sensing capabilities."

"Meaning?"

"It won't activate unless you ring the doorbell." He paused. "You haven't, have you?"

"I'm not stupid."

"Calm down, I never said you were."

Calm down? Rune suddenly remembered why things hadn't worked out between them. "Just tell me how to get in. I see a sensor on the door."

"There are sensors on the ground floor windows too. And inside the house. You'll have to get in from the second floor and disarm the alarm."

"Okay."

"You'll have sixty seconds. Any longer and the alarm will go off."

She peered up. The house suddenly looked impossibly tall. "I can do it," she said with more certainty than she felt. "Can you get me the code?"

"Probably."

"Can you, or can't you?"

"I guess I can."

Milo was being wishy-washy on purpose and Rune knew it, but whatever anger he still had toward her needed a place to go, so she cut him some slack. It wasn't as if she had a choice. She couldn't pull off this job without him.

"You're just standing around waiting for me to come up with the code, aren't you?" asked Milo.

How does he know?

"Your time would be better spent looking for a way in."

"Right."

"I'll call when I'm ready."

Rune wanted to ask how long it would take, but the connection was already severed. She took a quick look around. A gnarled oak tree was within reach of the second-floor balcony, but she wasn't convinced she could climb it. She rejected the gutter for the same reason. That only left one solution: a ladder. She squinted through the darkness until her eyes landed on an A-frame shed near the fence. Back across the yard she went, her feet squelching with each step.

"Of course," she muttered when she saw it was padlocked. She reached for her picks, then changed her mind. She gave the door a hard kick. The wood splintered. A second kick produced a hole big enough for her to get through. Using her phone as a flashlight, she panned around the shed until she spotted a three-rung step stool. It wasn't a ladder, but beggars couldn't be choosers. She lifted it off its hook and trotted across the yard. She'd almost reached the house when she felt her phone vibrate against her thigh.

"I have the code," Milo said without preamble.

"That was fast."

"You sound surprised."

"I guess I forgot how good you are."

Milo didn't respond, like he was embarrassed by the compliment.

"Well?" she pressed.

"It's 2468."

"As in, *who do we appreciate?*"

"Yes, but Margot is French and Rolf is German, so that probably wasn't the intention."

"How sure are you?"

"About the code? A hundred percent."

Rune's confidence rose. In all the time she'd known Milo, he'd never overinflated his abilities. If he sounded cocky now, it was for a reason. "Great," she said. "I'll call if I run into any trouble."

"Please don't."

"You love this, Milo. Admit it."

"Yeah, yeah."

Rune could tell he was pleased. Knowing that pleased her too, for reasons she didn't want to dissect. "Thanks. I owe you."

"Yes, you do."

The phone went black before she could respond. She slid it into her pocket and carried the step stool over to the balcony, adjusting it twice before getting on. It wobbled under her weight. She stretched her arms as far as she could and jumped. Her hands gripped the bottom rail. She hung for a moment, then she swung her leg and hooked it around a post. From there, getting onto the balcony was easy.

It took Rune seconds to reach the sliding glass door. A few more and she'd picked the lock. She put her hand on the pull.

Wait!

She paused. Once she opened the door, she'd have exactly one minute to locate the security panel and enter the code.

Voices rang out nearby. A car alarm sounded. It was the push she needed. She yanked the door open and catapulted into a spacious bedroom, moving so quickly she nearly tripped over her own feet. Her hip caught the edge of a dresser. She grunted in pain, but she didn't stop to cry about it. Four strides took her to a long hallway. Four more and she reached the top of a staircase. The front door lay directly ahead. She sprinted toward it.

"2, 4, 6, 8," she panted as she punched the code into the flashing panel.

The flashing stopped. A green light came on. She pressed her forehead against the wall to catch her breath, then set off to search for the Bonaparte earrings.

They'll be in the house, Lemaire had assured her.

How do you know?

Margot wears them to all her charity events. She thinks she's a royal benefactress, a modern-day Josephine.

Rune hadn't asked how Lemaire knew all this. There was no point. It wasn't as if he'd tell her. In all the time she'd known him, he'd never divulged more than what was strictly necessary. Not about work and certainly not about his personal life. She sometimes wondered what he did in his down time. If he had friends or a family or a pet. It wasn't idle thinking. She'd use anything—and anyone—if it meant breaking free of him.

The house was dark, but Rune didn't switch on the overheads, nor did she use her phone to light the way. She moved swiftly knowing it was just a matter of time before she found the Steiners' safe. She started in the most logical place: the study, a ponderous room with wood paneling that looked like it concealed secret passageways. It only took a few minutes to determine that the safe wasn't there. Option two was the primary bedroom. Rune was on her way there when she happened upon the kitchen. Her eyes landed on the fridge. She resisted the urge to sneak a peek.

The stairway was decorated with family photos she hadn't noticed when she'd raced down moments before. Near the bottom step was a picture of Margot and Rolf in their younger days, him with a hunting rifle, her with a fur-lined trapper hat. Next to it was a picture of a very blond man with a square jaw and the prominent brow of a cave dweller, presumably their son. He towered over an impossibly beautiful brunette with bow-shaped lips and sad eyes. In front of them, wearing matching lederhosen, were two sweet-faced boys. One looked to be eight or nine, the other no older than twelve.

Rune walked up the steps, passing black-and-white photos of the Steiners' long-dead ancestors along the way. She was nearing the top of the staircase when she heard muffled noises coming from outside the house. She froze. One breath. Then a second. She was about to dismiss the sound as a figment of her imagination when she heard the distinct jangling of keys. She scrambled up the remaining steps just as the lights came on in the entryway. She ducked into the closest room, a kid's bedroom with twin bunkbeds and a striped rug. She blanched when she realized the alarm was disarmed, then she reminded herself that people explained this kind of thing away all the time. What was more likely? A break-in or forgetting to turn on the alarm?

Footsteps sounded below. Rune strained toward the sound. She assumed it was Margot and Rolf but realized almost instantly she was wrong.

"Ab ins Bett Jungs." *Off to bed, boys.* The woman's voice was high and melodic. Her accent was stilted, like German wasn't her mother tongue.

"Noch fünf Minuten, Mama!" *Five more minutes, Mom!*

"Bitte, Mama!" *Please, Mom!*

"Je vais compter jusqu'à trois." *I'm going to count to three.* The woman's lilt melted away along with her German. The French that replaced it was clipped and Parisian. Rune deduced she was the Steiners' daughter-in-law and that the boys were their grandchildren.

A man's voice sounded. Loud. Angry. Rune didn't understand the words. It didn't matter. His yelling frightened her. The woman and children must have felt the same way because they fell silent. Their reaction was enough to make Rune pull the plug on the job. Lemaire wouldn't be happy, but that was a problem for another time. The Steiners' son, if that was indeed who it was, didn't sound like someone she wanted to cross.

She stepped out of the room. Her foot hadn't yet hit the floor when she heard a strange jingling nearby. She retreated and looked for a place to hide, but there were no closets in the room, just a child-sized armoire she couldn't possibly squeeze into.

Think!

She dove under the bed. She'd barely made it under when a shaggy dog the size of Mr. Snuffleupagus bounded in, metal tags clinking like discordant castanets. It let out a throaty bark.

"Go!" Rune said, shooing it away with a flick of her wrist.

The barking grew louder, more persistent.

"Brioche!"

Rune broke into a sweat when she heard the woman's voice. She sounded like she was close, maybe halfway up the stairs. Her tone was a mix of exhaustion and desperation. The dog took a swipe at Rune with its giant paw.

"Go!" she repeated, more desperately this time.

"Brioche!"

The woman was almost at the door. Brioche grew more agitated. Short on options, Rune thrust her arm out from under the bed and gave the dog a quick scratch. Her arm retracted just as the lights came on. The dog snorted and shook its massive head, sending slobber in all directions.

"Villain!" *Bad dog!* The woman grabbed Brioche by the collar and showed him the door. "Au lit!" *To bed!*

The dog clinked away. The woman muttered something under her breath, then called out to her children. "Venez les garçons!" *Come, boys!*

Stomping feet. A chorus of *nos* and *pleases*.

"Pyjamas! Allez!" *PJs! Let's go!*

Pants fell to the floor. Socks and sweaters followed. Rune tensed. She was done for if the woman bent to retrieve them. The ladder creaked as the boys climbed into bed. The mattress above her head sagged. She looked up. It was then that she noticed the large white envelope tucked under the bedframe.

"Schlaf gut, meine Lieblings. Ich habe euch liebe." *Sleep well, my darlings. I love you.* The lilt in the woman's voice was back. So was her German. She hit the light switch, plunging the room into darkness.

It must have been warm and cozy under the sheets, but with the mother gone, sleep took its time coming. Rune lost track of how long the boys chattered. Despite the circumstances, she couldn't help but smile. She understood not a word of what they were saying, but the conspiratorial whispering told her they were close as can be.

A maternal shush sounded outside the door some time later. Another came soon after. The boys' voices ebbed and eventually went silent. Rune let out a long, slow breath. She needed to find Margot's earrings, but with the extended family in the house, a difficult task had become nearly impossible.

—

Rune waited until the boys' breathing was deep and regular before making a move. The first thing she did wasn't to crawl out from under the bed but to pull the mysterious white envelope from the frame. She lit it with her phone. The recipient was Romy Steiner, the sender a Paris-based lawyer. She pulled the papers out, taking care not to crumple them. It was a divorce petition, if she was decoding the French correctly. It looked like Romy planned to leave her husband, Alaric, and take custody of their two children. Rune frowned in the darkness. Romy was hiding this from her husband, which meant she was scared of him and how he'd react. Given the yelling downstairs, Rune couldn't say she blamed her. She slid the papers back in the envelope and wedged it under the frame. She felt for Romy, but the family drama was none of her business.

Rune rose from her hiding spot with more grace than expected given the stiffness in her limbs. A well-loved pink elephant lay discarded on the rug. She scooped it up and placed it next to the boy in the top bunk, the younger of the brothers. The door was steps away. It creaked when she opened it, but the kids were too far gone to notice.

Alaric's voice boomed downstairs. Romy hissed something in response. There was a dull thud, then the sound of muffled crying.

Part of Rune knew what was going on down there. Part of her wanted to step in and put Alaric in his place. But the other part—the practical part, the selfish part—told her to stay out of it. She had her own problems. Romy would just have to fend for herself.

A hushed voice filtered from below. "Bitte. Bitte. Bitte." *Please, please, please.* The crying stopped, then the TV came on. The sound reassured Rune. Watching TV meant that the fighting had stopped, that the couple's attention was elsewhere, and that she didn't have to bail on the job after all. With luck, they'd be glued to the screen long enough for her to find Lemaire's earrings.

Rune made her way to the primary bedroom, the room she'd crossed coming in from the balcony. She froze when she stepped on a creaky floorboard but only for a moment. Margot and Rolf wouldn't stay at the casino forever. If they came home, the house would be full and she could kiss the earrings goodbye.

She opened the door to the walk-in closet and lit the interior with her phone. What she saw put Lemaire's perfectionism to shame.

Hanging exactly one inch apart were dresses from the best couture houses in France. The organization of shirts was just as precise. There was a whole rod of them, short sleeved on one side, long on the other. As for Margot's impressive collection of handbags, they were arranged on shelves by type, size, and hue. Rune was about to swipe a pair of diamante slingbacks from the Great Wall of Chanel when she realized they were two sizes too big for her. Feeling a bit like Cinderella, she returned them to their spot and directed her attention to the cabinets.

The safe was behind the first door she opened. She clucked her tongue at the Steiners' carelessness. If you could afford expensive jewelry, you could afford to store it properly. Safe deposit boxes were the best option. There were some who balked at the inconvenience, but adhering to bank hours was a small price to pay for peace of mind. Luckily for Rune, most people didn't go through life thinking like thieves.

The Steiners' safe was a Müller, a thousand-pound hunk of steel made by Germany's best and brightest. The couple had opted for a luxury model with a reinforced body and a blast-proof door. Rune wasn't worried. She'd cracked trickier safes under more trying circumstances. She took a moment to center herself, then rested her cheek against the cold metal and got to work.

The safe held her at bay for just thirty minutes, a record even for her. She gave the dial a few spins before entering the combination. She puffed with pride, then deflated. Kit had once remarked that the more jobs they pulled off, the bigger her ego got and the more reckless she became. She'd brushed him off, but in hindsight, he wasn't entirely wrong. She'd always been the adventurous one in the relationship, Kit the prudent one. They were opposites in every way and not just about this. For the first time, she entertained the possibility that their differences were insurmountable, that they would never get back together, no matter what she did or how much she loved him. The corners of her lips tugged down. Maybe what they had wasn't what she thought it was. Maybe they were destined to implode, with or without Lemaire.

The sound of shouting chased away Rune's melancholy. Alaric was back on the warpath. Glass shattered. Expletives in two languages followed. She blocked out the mayhem and turned her attention to the safe.

The contents were as orderly as the rest of the house. Rune sifted through them carefully, making sure to put everything back in its original place. She opened box after box of high-end jewelry: a diamond encrusted watch from Cartier's Panthère collection, a vintage choker with an emerald as big as a robin's egg, and a total of six Tiffany bracelets, including a platinum cuff covered in rare pink diamonds. She reached for the last box. It shook in her hand. What if Lemaire was wrong? What if the Steiners kept the Bonaparte earrings in a safe deposit box after all? She was good at what she did, damn good, even, but she didn't stand a chance against a bank vault. She lifted the lid.

"Oh!"

The earrings were splendid. She lifted one from the cushion and held it up. Sixteen old cut diamonds encircled a sapphire stud that was the size of a nickel. Beneath it, surrounded by more diamonds, dangled a pear-shaped sapphire twice as big as the stud. The gems were a rich, saturated blue and more luminous than any she'd seen before, except the matching necklace. A feeling of intense satisfaction swept over her as she slipped them into her pocket and placed the box back in the safe.

Rune had broken into the Steiners' home with the best intensions. She'd planned to take the earrings and quietly leave the way she came. Maybe it was a desire to recapture her past, or maybe she just didn't like the Steiners. Either way, she suddenly had a terrible case of the gimmies. One by one, she opened Margot's jewelry boxes. One by one she pocketed the contents—the Cartier watch, the emerald choker, and all six Tiffany bracelets. Her heart was galloping, not because she feared getting caught but because she was finally doing something for herself and not for Lemaire. It felt good to stick it to him, even if he didn't know it was happening, and it felt equally good sticking it to the Steiners.

Rune was putting the last box back in the safe when she spotted an envelope under a pile of folders. She reached for it thinking it was full of cash. What she found instead were the Steiners' passports. She flipped through each one, placing them back in the envelope as she went. The first two belonged to Margot and Rolf, the third to Alaric. The next two belonged to the boys sleeping down the hall: Sebastien, aged twelve, and Jonas, aged nine. Rune opened that last passport. A credit card fell out. The name on it matched that of the passport holder: Romy Steiner, Alaric's unhappy French wife.

A door slammed downstairs. Rune started at the sound. The shouting stopped, and new voices came from the ground floor. They belonged to Margot and Rolf, home early from the casino.

Time to go!

Rune closed the safe and gave the dial a quick spin. Then she wiped every surface she'd touched with the sleeve of her jacket and hurried out of the closet. She stopped in the middle of the room and cast a look back. Only after she was satisfied everything was in order did she move toward the balcony.

The glass door slid open noiselessly. Rune ignored the sting of the cold on her cheeks and hurried to the railing. She leaned over. The step stool taunted her from below. A light came on behind her. It was all the encouragement she needed. Over the edge she went, dangling from her fingertips until she mustered the courage to let go. Elation swelled when her feet hit the top of the stool, only to vanish when it toppled over. She hit the ground with a thud, bruising her thigh along with her ego.

The gaff didn't slow Rune for long. Step stool in hand, she sprinted across the yard to the shed with the busted door. Minutes later, she was over the fence and inside Max's house. All she had to do now was untie him, mess up his bed so he'd think they had a spectacular night, and get out of Deauville. She was fetching her binoculars from the kitchen when a strange sound caught her attention. She stopped to listen.

Creak, creak, creak.

The sound was faint. It came from the other end of the house.

Creak, creak, creak.

There it was again. Soft but distinctive. She walked toward it slowly, her movements silent, her footfall light. The sound grew louder as she moved through the kitchen, past the dining room, and down the hallway. By the time she neared the living room, it was downright urgent.

Creak! Creak! Creak!

She paused. Her body buzzed with nervous anticipation. Her hands were shaky and damp.

Go already!

She didn't move. It was like she was cemented in place.

Just go!

She turned the corner. Her breath caught. Her eyes widened. Rocking back and forth on the antique wingback was Max looking more alert—and significantly more upset—than he did when he lost his money at the poker table.

7

PALMA, MALLORCA

L ong before Mallorca became a prime destination for international partygoers, the picturesque island in the western Mediterranean was best known for its secluded coves and languorous way of life, earning it the nickname *la isla de la calma*—the island of tranquility. Through much of the twentieth century, Mallorca's population hovered somewhere around half a million, annual visitors numbered in the mere tens of thousands, and local industry centered on agriculture and fishing.

When change came, it came quickly. The expansion of Palma's airport in 1974, alongside the rapid development of Mallorca's coastline, drew sun-starved Europeans to its shores in increasingly large numbers. Upwards of 16 million visitors now flocked to the island each year, bringing with them much needed Euros.

But every boon had its downside. Although residents of Mallorca were grateful for the influx of cash, they complained endlessly about the type of tourist their island attracted—Europe's answer to the American spring breaker. Fed up with the noise and the pervasive smell of urine, local politicians restricted the sale of alcohol, decreased the number of tourist beds, and introduced strict quotas for cruise ships. The changes barely made a dent, prompting a group of local restauranteurs to take matters into their own hands. Their solution? Banning shirtless revelers and anyone in a soccer jersey. The policy didn't target specific nationalities per se, but Brits and Germans were disproportionately affected.

The tsunami of tourists that descended on New York and Bangkok every year had prepared Rune well for the conditions she encountered in Mallorca. Even in the low season, the island teemed with visitors eager to let loose and live their best lives. Rune tightened her hold on the strap of her duffel as she slalomed through the crowd loitering outside the airport and joined a taxi line that was growing longer by the second.

The cabbie was older, in his sixties, and eager for attention. He tried chatting Rune up as he placed her bag in the trunk of his car, first in Spanish, then in Catalan, and finally in English. She pretended not to understand. Her face rumpled with confusion when he asked where she was from. He mimicked her expression when, in halting English, she gave him an address in Son Gotleu, a neighborhood few tourists to Palma ever visited. He shot her strange looks from the rearview mirror as he drove away from the airport and onto the freeway.

Rune lowered her head to avoid the driver's gaze. When that didn't work, she turned to the soulless landscape outside the window. The view reminded her of a trip she took with her parents the summer before second grade, her first to Europe. She didn't sleep a wink on the overnight flight from JFK to Fiumicino Airport. Short on patience, her mother insisted that she take a nap while her father wove in and out of Rome's abominable rush hour traffic. Rune remembered stealing glances out the window while she pretended to sleep. As it turned out, she should have listened to her mother. The autostrada and industrial parks outside the Eternal City were so vastly different from the gladiators and charioteers of her imagination that she cried all the way to

71

the hotel. And now, sitting in a cab on the outskirts of Palma, she couldn't help thinking that driving from the airport was the worst introduction to a new city. Urban sprawl was urban sprawl, even in the most beautiful places.

Rune cracked the window, sending warm air whooshing into the cab. It felt good after the damp cold of Normandy, but it wasn't the only thing soothing her soul. Being out of France was also doing wonders. She'd been off her game for months, but the Deauville job put a spotlight on it like never before. Part of her still couldn't believe how badly she'd messed up. Max had regained consciousness earlier than expected. Worse, he'd seen her without her disguise. A knot formed inside her stomach as she pictured him walking into a police station and describing her to a sketch artist.

She rolled the window all the way down and angled her face toward the sun, craving more of the comfort it was providing. It helped until she remembered that underdosing Max wasn't the only mistake she'd made in Deauville. If only. She'd been so rattled by Margot and Rolf's arrival that she'd fled their house with more than just their jewelry. She was already halfway to Paris to meet Lemaire when she discovered Romy Steiner's credit card and passport in her jacket pocket. By that point, it was too late to turn around. It wasn't a big deal in the grand scheme of things, but Rune felt bad creating problems for a woman who already had her fair share.

The cabbie exited the freeway without signaling. The car behind narrowly avoided rear-ending them. Honking followed, then a rude gesture. The near miss stopped Rune from ruminating about things she couldn't change.

The cab stopped in front of a restaurant advertising the world's best kebabs in two languages. The driver pointed to the meter and muttered something unintelligible. Rune gave him twenty-five Euros and indicated he should keep the change.

The smell of grilled chicken hit her even before she stepped inside the restaurant. The man behind the counter wiped his hands on his stained apron and greeted her gruffly. In broken Spanish, she explained that she'd rented the apartment next door for the night and that the owner had directed her to the restaurant to pick up the keys. Unlike the cab driver, who was openly curious about her, the kebab man reached into his cash register and pulled out the keys without batting an eye.

Rune sized him up as she accepted them. He seemed like a discreet sort, the kind who knew not to ask newcomers questions about where they were from and what had brought them to this place. She was with him on that. In her experience, knowing what lay beneath the surface rarely yielded anything good. She mumbled her thanks. He acknowledged her words with a nod, then turned his attention back to his chicken.

Thirty minutes later, Rune exited her squalid Son Gotleu flat looking unrecognizable in a wiry gray wig and plain black shirt, worn untucked and rolled at the sleeves. Foundation thick as spackle aged her smooth skin. Tinted glasses masked her unusual eyes. The kebob man with the don't-ask-questions attitude didn't even look up when she passed his open door and set off on foot for Palma's glitzy port with a walking cane in hand. No one on the street looked her way either. She was invisible, like all women society deemed to be past their prime.

Son Gotleu was a far cry from the well-heeled neighborhoods Rune usually frequented when she was on a job, but as she walked through its streets incognito, she was struck by the beauty that existed amid the decay. A woman hanging laundry from a sagging balcony caught her attention. Her clothesline stretched across the width of the street, creating a dynamic tableau of flapping white linens against the cloudless sky. Directly below, a group of elderly men sat in a miasma of smoke at an outdoor café decorated with cerulean-blue tiles, the most vibrant she'd ever seen. Her ears perked at the low, melodic hum of the Muslim call to prayer, the second of the day. The sound came not from a domed mosque with showy minarets but from an apartment building that looked like all the others on the block. Across the street was an equally modest building, an evangelical church dedicated to brotherly love.

Maybe it was because of her own mixed background, but Rune found it comforting that the two coexisted on an island that was otherwise thoroughly Catholic. Growing up, she often felt like she wasn't enough. Not White enough or Asian enough. Not important or authentic or even whole enough. It took a lifetime to shake off the feeling that she was somehow deficient. To focus on the *and* of her identities, not on the *or*. Some places made it easier than others. Palma was one of them.

Rune's cane scraped against the sidewalk as she walked toward the port. It was only a couple of miles away, but she was moving at old lady speed, so it took the better part of an hour to get there. The look of the city changed the closer she got to the coast. The first big shift came when she reached Pere Garau, an area with a high concentration of Asian immigrants. Rune slowed her pace to a virtual crawl when she caught a whiff of sizzling ginger coming from a Chinese restaurant. The smell made her belly rumble and her heart ache for Bangkok.

Things got livelier when she crossed the ring road and entered the city center. This was Palma's tourist hub and economic lifeblood, where five-star hotels and fashionable boutiques stood shoulder to shoulder with knickknack shops and dive bars. She followed the signs to Santa María de Mallorca, a Gothic cathedral known to locals simply as La Seu—the See. She reached the cool shadow of the building within minutes. Directly ahead, palm trees swayed in the gentle breeze. Beyond, the turquoise waters of the Mediterranean glistened under the midday sun. She descended a stone staircase and followed a road that was so close to the sea she could practically touch it.

The Port of Palma was as large as one would expect for an island capital, stretching uninterrupted for almost two miles along the west side of the Bay of Palma. With its state-of-the-art facilities and impeccable safety record, the port drew thousands of vessels to its docks each year, ranging from small fishing boats and graceful catamarans to luxury yachts and gargantuan cruise liners. The port was so popular that it operated at or near capacity twelve months out of the year. Although there were fewer visitors to Palma in the fall and winter, the city's port remained chock full of boats that were either waiting out the shoulder season or heading to the nearby shipyard for repairs. Thanks to Milo, Rune knew that Lemaire's yacht was moored at the Marina Club de Mar on the port's west end, at Dock 3, Berth 64, right next to the cruise terminal. No one noticed when she hobbled past the unmanned gate and into the area reserved for boat owners and personnel. On the far end of the dock, a group of workers in fluorescent vests unloaded crates from a majestic sailboat with a soaring mast. Closer to her were two sun-kissed boys scrubbing oil stains off the dock with stiff brushes. They didn't object when she walked past. No surprise there. Children were programmed not to question adults, especially those who looked and acted like they belonged.

Rune paused when she reached the first yacht, a monstrosity of a thing with no fewer than four decks. A quick scan of the marina revealed three other possibilities. Rune kicked herself for not paying closer attention when Milo showed her pictures of the *Ruby*. To her untrained eye, all big boats looked the same. She checked the first yacht's stern and saw the name *Serena* splashed across in black letters. One down, three to go.

The next yacht she approached was smaller—a mere tri-deck—but it had a helipad on the bow and a golf tee on the main platform. Rune thought it looked promising until she noticed the blue and gold Bahamian flag atop the mast. The *Ruby* sailed under a UK flag, at least that was what Milo had said. She checked the yacht's name just to be sure. Her lips turned up. *Pier Pressure.* She appreciated a billionaire with a sense of humor.

The next yacht was moored about fifty feet away, in the last berth before the dock made a ninety-degree turn. It was a sporty looking vessel with clean lines and sleek white balconies, but its most notable trait was its silhouette. Instead of being top-heavy, like the typical yacht, this one featured a low superstructure made entirely of dark glass. Capping it was a black mast that bore an uncanny resemblance to a dorsal fin. The contrasting play of light and dark, combined with the yacht's low center of gravity, made it stand out among all the others at the marina. Rune spied the Union Jack fluttering above the stern. She was too far away to read the yacht's name, but she could see that the letters were a deep shade of red. Her head bobbed. This was the *Ruby.* She was sure of it. She walked toward it as quickly as she could without attracting attention.

She was about halfway there when she sensed she was being followed. Call it a sixth sense. Or a well-developed intuition. Whatever it was, it had saved her from many sticky situations in the past and today was no exception. Without slowing her pace, she drew her phone from her handbag and brought it up to her ear. She heard three rings, then a subdued "Hello?"

"Did you forget about me?" Her voice was loud, like she was angry or extremely hard of hearing.

"Why are you yelling at me?" Milo replied in a confused tone.

"I'm at the marina. There's no one here."

"What?"

"You were supposed to call the security company so I could get on the yacht."

"I see," Milo said, finally cluing in. "Someone's listening?"

"Yes." Rune turned. A mustached official was nearly on top of her. He started to say something. She held up her index finger to shush him, then pointed at her phone. Her fake tirade continued. "I reminded you yesterday. How could you forget?"

"Is there anything I can do?" Milo asked.

"I didn't say next week. Why would I say next week? I need to get onboard today. Now."

"I'm standing by."

"I know but my flight leaves in three hours and I need my papers. Hold on." Rune lowered her phone and looked at the official as if she was surprised that he was still there. "What?" she said.

"This is a restricted area, señora," the man replied. His eyes were black and bottomless. His nose looked like it had been broken at least twice. He put his hands on his hips to assert his authority. "I'll need to see some identification."

Rune gave him a look that was at once uppity and exasperated. "I'd love nothing more than to show you my ID, but my wallet is locked inside this yacht and my scatterbrain nephew forgot to contact the security company, so I have no way of getting on." She brought the phone back up to her ear to address Milo. "A dock worker is harassing me. I told you to avoid Palma. You never listen to me. You need to call Pablo and get this sorted straight away."

"Señora—" the official interjected.

Rune glared at him.

"Por favor, señora—"

She lowered her phone again and widened her eyes at him. "Do you have any idea who I am?" She gave his name tag a long look, as if committing it to memory, then she met his gaze. "Well? Do you?"

Uncertainty flashed in the man's eyes. His mustache twitched.

Rune wanted to whoop in triumph. "This yacht belongs to my nephew. His name is Charles Lemaire. Perhaps you've heard of him?"

The official had. His mustache was dancing now.

"Charles is contacting his security company. They'll send someone over to clear this up."

The man blinked rapidly, like he was on the edge of making a decision. All he needed was one more push.

"Go ahead. Ask him if you'd like." Rune thrust out her phone as if daring him to take it. She knew Milo would play along if the man called her bluff.

"That won't be necessary, señora," he said, raising both hands in surrender. His features softened. His manner turned deferential. "May I recommend a place for you to wait? The club's restaurant is unfortunately closed today, but Palma has many excellent cafes within walking distance of the marina."

"You expect me to walk all the way over there?" Rune squawked, shaking her cane at the shore. "Absolutely not! I'm staying right where I am. If you have a problem with that, I suggest you take it up with your superior."

The man opened and closed his mouth without saying anything.

Rune relaxed. The battle was over, and this hapless official wasn't the victor. The time had come to throw him a bone. She shifted her weight from one foot to the other and grimaced like she was in pain. She reached for the man's arm, giving him the opportunity to rescue her.

"Are you alright, señora?" he asked, offering her his hand.

"It's my sciatica. It acts up when I'm stressed."

"Let's find you a place to sit."

Rune put on a brave smile. "I wouldn't want to impose."

"It would be my pleasure."

"Perhaps you could help me get on board?"

The man hesitated.

Rune moaned softly and worked at a knot in her lower back. She was putting on a good show, but even she was surprised when the man held out his arm and walked her onto the yacht. He kept a steadying hand on her elbow as she hobbled up two flights of stairs to the main deck. "Would you mind?" she said, motioning to an L-shaped couch that was tarped and trussed for the season.

"Not at all," he replied. He eased her onto the couch.

She patted the spot next to hers. "Why don't you keep me company? Pablo lives on the other side of the island. It will take him at least forty-five minutes to get here. An hour if he can't find parking."

Maybe it was the fear of taking an unsanctioned break, or the thought of having to converse with an old biddy for an unspecified amount of time, but the man looked positively mortified.

"That's very tempting," he said, his eyes bouncing around the deck like they couldn't find a comfortable place to land. "But I'm afraid I have to get back to work."

"I'm sure no one will mind. The marina is so quiet at this time of year."

"As much as I'd love to, I don't think my supervisor will allow it."

"There's nothing I can do to convince you?"

"I don't make the rules."

Rune smiled as the man made a hasty retreat. Her smile spread after he stepped off the yacht and hurried toward the shore. She sank deep into the couch, pleased to have the *Ruby* all to herself. She took a satisfied breath and savored the moment. Sometimes when you wanted something, all you had to do was convince others it was what they wanted too.

○═══╋═══○

Rune didn't bask in her victory for long. Within moments of the official leaving, she was twisting the top off her cane and tipping out her lock picks. She dropped the cane into the water and scanned the main deck.

It was a thing to behold, even with the yacht moored for the season. A black tarp covered a plunge pool fitted with what looked like a waterfall feature. Behind it was an alfresco dining area large enough to accommodate a battalion of friends. Beyond, behind a wall of dark glass, was the salon, the largest enclosed common area of the yacht.

Rune knew the *Ruby* was equipped with a top-notch security system complete with digital deck sensors and a vast CCTV infrastructure. The security company's website advertised advanced intruder detection capabilities, covert recording, and rapid information-sharing with land-based authorities in emergency situations. It also touted an intuitive interface that gave yacht owners complete control of their vessels from anywhere in the world using their handheld devices.

Rune and Milo had hashed out a plan to break into the *Ruby* back in Montparnasse. Self-confidence was not a quality Milo lacked, but he'd balked at the idea of hacking a security company.

Not possible, he'd said with case-closed finality.

He'd used words like database permissions, pattern checking, address space layout randomization, and others Rune didn't understand. That didn't prevent her from coming up with a solution though. She understood instantly that the convenience of Lemaire's security system—the ability to control it remotely—was also its weakness. If Milo could access Lemaire's phone, physical locks were all that would stand between her and the interior of the yacht. Milo had been quick to embrace the plan.

Make sure your Bluetooth is on and put your phone near his. I'll do the rest.

It can't be that easy.

It isn't. I'm just that good.

Despite Milo's assurances, Rune worried things might go terribly wrong when she met Lemaire at the Crillon to hand over Margot Steiner's earrings. Thankfully, her concerns were misplaced. He barely noticed when she placed her phone face down on the table in the Marie Antoinette suite. If her inane babbling about the value and beauty of the sapphires raised any red flags, it certainly didn't show. To prolong the encounter, she'd once again broached the subject of altering their business arrangement. It was an exercise in futility, and she knew it, but her goal wasn't to change his mind. What she wanted was to buy Milo enough time to work his magic, which was exactly what he'd done.

Rune's confidence was a nine out of ten when she approached the door to the *Ruby's* salon with her trusty picks. Her recent troubles in Deauville had triggered some soul searching, but they hadn't dented her faith in her ability to pick a lock. It helped that she had all the time in the world. Milo had already hacked the yacht's security system and set the cameras on a loop.

She reached for the lock. The bolt retracted. She jumped back, fully expecting to see Lemaire and his men charge through the door. They didn't. Her pocket vibrated.

"Pretty cool, right?" Milo said before she could get a word out.

"That was you?"

"It turns out you can control *everything* remotely. The sensors, the cameras, even the locks."

Rune heard the bolt extend and retract again. She reached for the handle. It clicked shut. "Cut it out."

"I see you!"

She raised her middle finger at the camera above the door.

"The system is ingenious," Milo said, unbothered. "The locks are simple solenoids, but they were designed specifically for marine environments. The lock body and bolt are made of V4A stainless steel and—"

Rune hung up on him mid-sentence. Milo could geek out on his own time, she had other things to do. She softened the blow by forming a heart with her hands and raising them toward the camera. The lock clicked open. She blew him a kiss, then slid the door open and stepped inside.

Restrained luxury was one way to describe the salon. Deathly boring was another. Everything was colorless, unless beige counted as a color. Rune turned her nose up at the room, but the fact was, she was envious. Correction. She was angry *and* envious. Lemaire had all the money in the world. He wanted for nothing, yet he chose to take away everything she had—her family, her livelihood, her freedom. And for what? So that he could get even richer? She resisted the temptation to trash his precious yacht. Today was about the long play, not immediate gratification.

The yacht was neat as a pin, just as she expected. Everything had its place—the cushions on the couch, the knickknacks on the shelves, the black-and-white photography books artfully arranged on the coffee table. Even the dedicated games area with its chessboard and Scrabble set looked like it was there for show and not for fun.

Rune had no idea what she was looking for when she started her search. Evidence of Lemaire's illegal activities was probably too much to ask. Then again, hubris made smart people do stupid things.

She went through the salon with a fine-tooth comb. Zilch. Her search of the dining room produced the same result. She gazed at the crystalline water to clear her mind. The floor-to-ceiling windows had no color enhancers, nothing to reduce glare. The complete transparency and absence of seams between the panes created the sensation of being suspended midair. She soaked in the view knowing she was safe from the prying eyes of the dockworkers. The *Ruby's* windows might look transparent from the inside, but from the outside, they were practically black. Whoever designed them understood perfectly well the value Lemaire placed on privacy.

The distant sound of yelling prompted Rune to lean closer to the window. She craned her neck and watched as two workers argued about how best to move a large crate off a pontoon and onto the dock. Her peace shattered, she directed her attention to the bar.

Five minutes later, Rune padded upstairs with a glass of Veuve Clicquot rosé in her hand. She hadn't pegged Lemaire as the pink champagne type, but she admired that he was secure enough in his masculinity to keep a fridge full of the stuff. She'd also found cases of top-shelf bourbon and fizzy water, but the champagne seemed more appropriate given the setting.

The staircase led directly to the owner's deck, a space so breathtaking she couldn't even pretend to poo-poo it. A grid of glass provided an unobstructed view of the sky. Below was a bedroom, a sitting area, an ensuite, and a study. Outside, on the bow of the yacht, was a ten-person jacuzzi. On the stern was a terrace fitted with a rotating sofa designed to highlight sunsets. Rune chugged her champagne and got to work.

It took more than an hour to search the owner's deck. Rune opened draws and cabinets and cupboards. She peaked under the furniture and even lifted the rugs. All she had to show for her efforts were stiff shoulders and a sore back. She scratched at her itchy gray wig and flopped onto the bed. Hard work didn't always pay off, no matter what people said.

It was the call of nature that got Rune off the comfy mattress and into the bathroom. The sight of it drew a low *wow* from her lips. Black marble. Gold fixtures. She eyed the soaking tub longingly. She wanted more than anything to hop in and splash around like Shamu. Instead, she did her business, slipped a miniature soap bar into her pocket with a silent *take that Lemaire*, and headed back to the study.

She'd already searched Lemaire's desk, but she couldn't shake the feeling that she'd missed something. Her eyes swept across the room, past the damask wallpaper and heavy panel curtains. Her gaze lingered on a school of fish made of Venetian plaster and resin drops meant to look like sea spray. No detail had been spared in the design of the

Ruby. It was so pristine—so sanitized—she started to feel like she was wasting her time. She sighed, resigned.

And that's precisely when she noticed it. Hanging behind the desk. A framed drawing of a sailboat rendered in charcoal and ink. She hurried over and lifted it off the wall.

Bingo!

The safe's steel door winked in light. Rune rested her cheek against it and curled her fingers around the dial. Then muscle memory kicked in and she did the thing she did best.

8

PALMA, MALLORCA

The sun was dipping toward the horizon when Rune finally closed the safe. She hadn't found anything incriminating inside, but that didn't mean she'd wasted her time. For one thing, it was where Lemaire kept the yacht's paperwork, including the registration and safety certificate, both issued in the Caymans. Potentially more useful was the transit log, a record of past trips and passengers. Aside from the crew, only four people had been on the yacht recently: Lemaire, his two henchmen, and someone identified only as C. Vidal. It wasn't a lot to go on, but Rune wasn't mad. Extracting herself from Lemaire was going to take time and effort. Not all days would yield flashy results.

Movement below snuffed out Rune's optimism. Someone was on board. She listened closely. Correction. Two people. Men, if the heaviness of the footfalls was any indication.

She gave the safe a quick wipe with her sleeve and hurried down the staircase to the main deck. She knew the way out was to the right, through the salon and past the pool. She peeked around the corner. Panic.

The men were outside, just a few feet away from her. One spoke into a handheld radio, the other was coiling a rope. Rune expected them to rush inside and grab her, but they didn't move. She exhaled sharply. The dark glass. It was her invisibility shield.

The men directed their attention outward, like they were talking to people on the dock. Rune started forward. With luck, she could slip off the yacht without them noticing.

She slinked through the salon to the sliding glass doors, the same doors Milo unlocked a few hours before. She was about to open them when she saw three more crew members, including a man in a white shirt with striped epaulets. The captain was on board. The yacht was leaving port.

The captain walked out of sight, but the other two crew members remained on the main deck. Rune watched them go through their departure checklist. The passerelle was brought in, hatches and gates were locked, lines were pulled in from the dock. The process took forever. The sunlight dimmed. Eventually it vanished.

Engines hummed to life down below. The vibration sparked a fresh rush of anxiety. Rune wanted to hurl herself off the boat, but the men wouldn't leave. She felt movement soon after. The yacht was inching away from the dock.

No!

Rune whipped her head from side to side looking for another way off. There wasn't one. She was stuck until they got to Monaco or Mykonos or wherever. Her pulse was racing now. How long could she go unnoticed? How long could she go without food?

The men on the deck disappeared. Rune didn't wait to see where they went. She dashed through the salon and out the door, past the pool and down the stairs. She reached the swim platform on the stern. The dock was fifty feet away. She could swim that easily, but it was pitch black out there and she was scared.

The yacht picked up speed. The water frothed in response. The window of opportunity was closing.

Jump!

She hit the water hard. Her head dipped beneath the surface. Her muscles contracted in the frigid water.

Swim!

She came up sputtering and disoriented. She kicked her legs frantically, terrified hypothermia would set in and that her limbs would stop responding. She spun around. In one direction, the *Ruby* glided soundlessly into the night. In the other lay the twinkling port and its promise of safety. She swam toward it. One stroke. Then another. Eventually she reached the *Ruby's* empty berth.

Exhaustion set in as soon as she pulled herself out of the water. She lay on the pavement, spent. She would have loved to close her eyes and rest, but she was sopping wet and someone could walk by at any moment. She struggled to her feet and wrung out her shirt. The water had washed away her old lady makeup and wig, along with her granny glasses and one of her shoes. She took the other one off and dropped it in the water. Walking around with no shoes was less conspicuous than wearing just one.

The marina gate was locked and unmanned. Rune squeezed through and trudged toward town, leaving wet footprints on the pavers. She winced when she stepped on an overturned bottlecap. Then the shivering started—from the cold, from relief she'd reached the shore in one piece.

She passed a boarded-up booth advertising sailing and snorkeling trips. Next came Pepe's Charter Boat Tours, also closed. Her ears perked when she heard soft voices and tinkling utensils. The sounds came from a row of restaurants across the street. She waited for a break in the traffic and hurried toward them. In a place like Mallorca, where there were restaurants, there were clothing stores.

She chose a shop displaying beachwear on outdoor racks, a staple in every European port town. She grabbed a black sarong, a beach bag, and a pair of flipflops and walked away without paying. She emerged from a dark side street moments later, hair slicked back, sarong knotted into a cross-neck dress. Her underwear was still damp, but she wasn't inclined to go commando.

The old town lay directly ahead. Rune passed the cathedral and continued north through Palma's winding streets. She'd just stepped into the Plaça Major when her phone vibrated in her bag. How it had survived her impromptu swim, she was at a loss to explain. She rejected the call when she saw it was Milo. He could wait. What couldn't was her grumbling stomach. She directed her attention to the menus displayed outside the restaurants lining the plaza. All of them offered tourist fare at tourist prices, but she was a visitor to Mallorca and there was no sense pretending otherwise. She chose a seat at an outdoor tapas bar and ordered a glass of sangria from a flirty waiter with a mop of black hair. She had nothing on until her flight in the morning. She couldn't think of a better way to spend her time.

Her phone buzzed on the table. It was Milo again. She would have answered, but her sangria appeared along with a delicious looking plate of *pan con tomate*. She rejected the call and reached for a slice. Seconds later, her phone emitted a soft ping.

CALL ME!!!!

For most people, an all-caps text with multiple exclamation marks would warrant immediate attention, but Milo was prone to histrionics, so Rune took a bite of *pan con tomate* instead. The Spanish couple at the table next to hers giggled when she moaned out loud. She offered them a sheepish smile. Containing her enthusiasm for food had never been her strong suit. She was raising the bread to her mouth again when her phone pinged a second time. The screen lit up.

LE MONDE!!!!

Rune froze midbite. *Le Monde* was one of France's oldest and most respected newspapers, with a broad readership at home and internationally. Something in it had obviously triggered Milo. A link appeared below his message. She tapped it with her pinky and drew closer.

Braquage Bonaparte! *Bonaparte Heist!* the headline screamed. Below were two fuzzy pictures of her, one taken from a security camera at the Louvre, the other from the Casino Barrière. She grabbed her phone with a shaky hand.

"What does it say?" she demanded as soon as Milo picked up.

"It's bad, Rune."

"Tell me." She willed herself to stay calm. *You're okay. Everything is going to be okay.* She lowered her head. The wigs she wore for the Paris and Deauville jobs looked nothing like her natural hair, but her face was still her face.

"It's about the Bonaparte jewels," Milo said.

"How much do they know?"

He translated the article. "The judicial police of Paris has issued an arrest warrant for an unknown woman suspected of stealing two pieces from a parure commissioned by Napoleon Bonaparte."

"Crap."

"Crap is right." He cleared his throat. "A sapphire necklace valued at about 12 million Euros was stolen from Margot Steiner, a senior member of France's former imperial house, during a private tour of the Louvre Museum last week. Two days ago, earrings from the same set went missing from Steiner's vacation home in Deauville, along with jewels worth an estimated 7 million Euros. The victim did not respond to *Le Monde's* requests for comment."

"It could be worse," Rune said, ignoring the tightness in her chest.

"There's more."

The tightness turned into a stabbing pain.

"Unnamed sources close to the investigation confirm that a single individual committed the thefts," Milo said. "Twenty-year-old Maxime Saint-Yves, a witness who was assaulted during the Deauville robbery, described the suspect as a dark-haired American woman between the age of twenty-five and thirty-five."

Rune's brow shot up. *Assaulted?* She wouldn't have put it quite like that. She cursed herself once again for mis-dosing Max.

"Police are asking anyone with information to come forward. The Steiner family has offered a fifty thousand Euro reward for information leading to the recovery of their jewels, many of which are family heirlooms of both sentimental and historic value." Milo's words tapered off. The sound of his breathing filled the emptiness.

"That's it?" Rune finally said.

"That's not enough?"

She exhaled slowly. Her initial panic was subsiding. Level-headedness was in sight. That was a good thing. She'd need it if she was going to get out of this mess. "It's okay," she said, sincerely hoping that what she was saying was true. "They don't know my name. And the pictures they published are blurry. They could be anyone."

"I don't know," Milo said. His voice was full of uncertainty. "The cops probably know more than what's in the article."

"I was careful."

"What about the witness? He obviously got a good look at you."

Rune's fingers tensed around her phone. The look in Max's eyes when she'd walked into the living room after robbing the Steiners was seared in her memory.

"I can't believe you assaulted a kid. What were you thinking?"

"Give me a break, Milo. It wasn't a kid. And I didn't assault him. I just slipped him a little GHB." The words sounded worse out loud than they did in her head.

"Jesus, Rune! You could have killed him!"

"There's no need to catastrophize. I barely gave him any. I should have given him more, clearly."

"That's not the point. You can't keep treating people like they don't matter. It isn't right."

Rune didn't know if Milo was talking about what she did to him or what she did to Max. She chewed her lip. There was nothing she could say or do to change the past so instead she changed the subject. "Listen, Milo. I know this is asking a lot, but can you find out what the cops have on me?"

Static.

"Please."

"I guess I can try."

Rune didn't like how uncertain he sounded. She knew it wasn't because he doubted his abilities, but because he had doubts about her. She spoke her next words softly. "I wouldn't have stolen those jewels if Lemaire hadn't forced me. You know that, right?"

"I know."

"I didn't have a choice. It's not just about me. He knows where Kit and Madee live. He has my parents' address."

"Is Kit your boyfriend?"

Rune closed her eyes when she heard the hurt in Milo's voice. She felt like a truly horrible person. "Kit's not my boyfriend. Not anymore." She said the words to comfort Milo. She choked back a sob when she realized they were true.

"I think you should get out of sight for a while," Milo said quietly, like he knew he'd struck a nerve.

"Agreed."

"Will you stay in Palma?"

Rune thought about it for a moment. She'd planned to go back to Bangkok in the morning, but maybe it was better to stay put for a while. The residents of Son Gotleu weren't the type to meddle in other people's business. Then again, it was a small neighborhood where new faces stood out. The fifty-thousand-Euro reward was another factor to consider. No one in Palma needed money more than the low-paid immigrants who lived in Son Gotleu.

Indecision gnawed at Rune. In all her years as a thief, she'd never been on the police radar. Never had she feared officers coming to her door. A sickening feeling settled over her. It took her a moment to realize that what she was feeling was fear. "I stand out in Mallorca," she finally said. "And I don't speak the language."

"So, you're leaving?"

"I think so."

"When?"

"I don't know."

"Will you come back to Paris?"

"I don't know!" She took a shaky breath. "I'm sorry, Milo. I-I have to go. I need to figure things out."

"It's okay. I understand."

"Thanks for the heads up."

"Of course."

"I mean it."

"Just promise me you'll be careful."

"Always."

Everything felt different after Rune ended the call. The waiter was no longer flirty but intrusive. The Spanish couple at the adjacent table was not so much charming as nosy. She tucked a few Euros under her plate and jumped to her feet. Her chair scraped loudly against the pavement. It felt like everyone's eyes were on her—the waiters balancing plates of *patatas bravas*, the patrons throwing back pitchers of sangria, even the busker singing an Ed Sheeran song in slanted English. She hurried away from the restaurant, seeking out the shadowy arcade of the Plaça Major.

Darkness enveloped her. With it came relief, but the feeling didn't last. The arcade ejected her onto a packed street that was so brightly lit it might as well have been daytime. The crowd around her was thick enough to feel threatening but not so thick as to offer anonymity. She squeezed past a group of belligerently drunk twenty-somethings who said things to her in Russian she instinctively knew were vulgar. She tried to ignore them, but a young man with coarse hair and the beginnings of a potbelly grabbed her by the arm and pulled her close. His skin was red from too much alcohol or not enough sunscreen. His breath stank of last night's gyro. He bent down to kiss her, but she twisted out of his grasp and speed walked away to the sound of his laughter.

A stone church with a stumpy bell tower appeared up ahead. The *Basílica de Sant Miquel*, according to a sign on the front. Below, in smaller letters, was the word *santuari*. Rune didn't need to know Catalan to know it was a safe place. She gave the panhandler near the entrance a wide berth and wrenched the door open.

It was colder and darker inside the church than it was outside. The air smelled humid, like centuries of rainwater were trapped inside the walls. The sound of a pigeon cooing from an invisible perch broke the hushed silence.

Rune was hypervigilant as she walked down the aisle. Her eyes darted from side to side, sweeping past the woman lighting a candle in a side chapel, the tourist admiring the towering organ, and the elderly caretaker mopping the floor. By the time she slid into a pew near the chancel, she was so focused on plotting her next move that she barely noticed the church's showpiece—a large altarpiece with spiral columns framing gilded statues of saints.

Rune ignored the dense ball in her stomach as she typed three words into her phone's browser—Napoleon, jewel, and heist. There were only two hits, both several years old. The first was the theft of a Napoleonic ring valued at 1.7 million Euros from an unlocked car in Paris' 6th arrondissement. The second was a heist at the musée Hébert near Grenoble, where thieves made off with jewels that once belonged to Princess Mathilde, Napoleon's Italian-born niece.

Rune redid the search using the same terms, this time in French. *Le Monde* was the only paper running her story, but that did little to ease her mind. It was just a matter of time before other media outlets caught on. Once that happened, nowhere would be safe. There would be no place to hide.

Clack!

Rune's head spun to the side. The caretaker had dropped his mop and was struggling to pick it up. She rose to help, not because it was the right thing to do but because not helping would draw more attention than lending a hand. The man thanked her in raspy Spanish. She acknowledged him with a nod and went back to her pew.

The quiet of the church brought Rune clarity. Although it was tempting to hunker down, a touristy island was the last place she wanted to be if the situation deteriorated. Better to return to Son Gotleu, pack her things, and get out of dodge. Content with her choice, she returned her attention to her phone. A few keystrokes were all it took to set up the necessary alerts. Now, if her name or anything related to the Bonaparte parure appeared online, Google would be sure to tell her about it.

9

PALMA AIRPORT, MALLORCA

S on Sant Joan was large for an island airport. With its four boarding modules and dual runways, the two-and-a-half-square-mile airport was the third largest in Spain after Madrid and Barcelona. Despite its considerable size, however, Palma Airport was always crowded, no matter the season or time of day. This was certainly the case when Rune strode into the departures hall in her forgettable black outfit, her duffel bag slung over her shoulder.

She squinted at the screens, then glanced at her watch. It was nearing midnight. If she hurried, she might catch the last flight to Europe, a redeye to the French city of Marseille. The destination gave her pause. Instinct told her not to step foot in France ever again, but her fear of being stuck in Mallorca superseded that concern. She brushed her misgivings aside. Marseille was an international port city full of tanned faces—not a bad place for someone like her to disappear. Spain, Monaco, Italy, and even Switzerland were within easy driving distance. And unlike the other destinations on offer at this late hour, Marseille was an inter-European flight, which meant security on both ends would be relatively lax. Feeling good about her decision, she set off in search of the Ryanair counter.

The line at check-in was long, snaking through rows of stanchions that seemed to go on forever. Frustrated travelers huffed and har-rumphed as they inched forward with their overstuffed suitcases in tow. Rune kept her cool. Getting upset over things she couldn't control was a waste of energy. Besides, the wait was almost certainly not as bad as it looked.

She wasn't quite so equanimous by the time she reached the front of the queue. A thrumming headache was starting to take hold, in no small part because of the group directly behind her, an assemblage of six adults and nearly twice as many children, all of them feral. She wasn't unsympathetic to parents traveling with young children, but this particular set had abdicated all responsibility for their overstimulated, under-slept offspring. She cringed when a crusty nosed toddler reached for her with his grubby hands. Only the ticket agent waving her over saved the parents from getting an earful.

Rune was halfway to the counter when her phone buzzed against her hip three times in rapid succession. She glanced at the screen. Her knees weakened.

She didn't know French, but she understood enough. *Le Monde* had released new details about the Bonaparte heists. She scrolled down and saw a picture of herself leaving the Louvre. No disguise. Face fuzzy but recognizable.

How's this possible?!

She pushed the question aside and scanned articles from two other French outlets: *Le Figaro* and *Le Parisien*. Both summarized *Le Monde's* original piece connecting the Louvre and Deauville jobs. Neither included the new photo, but it was only a matter of time. Fear crept through her body, seeping from her pores and leaving her skin clammy and cold. What if Milo was right? What if the police knew more than they were letting on? What if they already had her name and just hadn't released it to the press?

"Señora, pase por delante, por favor." *Please step forward, ma'am.*

Rune was so fixated on her phone that she didn't hear the ticket agent calling her.

"Por favor, señora." *Please, ma'am.*

"It's your turn," came an impatient voice from behind.

Rune turned to the speaker, the father of the unwashed child who'd wiped his paws all over her. His vexed expression knocked the stasis right out of her. Her mind raced as she started toward the counter. It was imperative that she get off the island, but she didn't know if it was even possible at this point. How did law enforcement work in the EU, anyway? Was she already in some shared database, or was it just the French authorities she had to worry about? Either way, she couldn't risk traveling under her own name.

"Buenas noches, señora." *Good evening, ma'am.*

Shit!

Señora?

Romy Steiner's passport!

Rune didn't think through the idea, she just ran with it. "I'd like to buy a ticket," she said, channeling Lumière from *Beauty and the Beast.* If the agent had questions about her fake French accent, he didn't let on.

"Where do you wish to go?" he asked.

"Marseille. Tonight. It's an emergency."

The agent turned his attention to his computer and began typing. The typing went on much longer than seemed necessary given the simplicity of the task.

What on earth is he writing?

"You want one ticket for flight 5200 departing Palma de Mallorca at 1:40 A.M. and arriving at Marseille Provence Airport at 3:00 A.M., yes?"

It's the only plane going to Marseille tonight, you jackwagon! "Yes, that's correct."

"The flight is quite full. The only available seats are in business class. Is this acceptable?"

"Yes, that's fine."

"Passport, please."

It was the moment of truth. Rune handed the man Romy's passport and tried her best to look normal. It wasn't that hard. She and Romy had a lot in common. They were both brunettes—thank goodness—and both had hazel eyes. Romy was almost a decade older and a good three inches taller, but numbers were harder to gauge than visuals. As for their complexions, women always left Mallorca with a good tan.

Rune's impromptu decision to use Romy's ID paid off. The agent didn't notice that the woman in the picture wasn't the woman in front of him. He pounded at the keyboard with laser focus. People in the queue started to get restless as the transaction dragged on. There was a snitty comment here, a long-suffering sigh there. Rune didn't care. She hadn't complained when a pair of influencers repacked their suitcases at the counter to avoid overweight fees, or when a group of Value Fare passengers exercised wishful thinking by insisting on free upgrades.

"Will you be checking a bag?" the agent asked. His eyes were fixed on Rune, but nothing suggested he was onto her.

"All I have is this." She shifted her body so he could see her duffel.

"Very well. Your total is nine-hundred-and-seventy Euros."

For a one-hour flight? Rune couldn't keep her eyes from widening. Airlines had free rein to gouge passengers, but she was the one who was a criminal?

"How will you be paying?"

She'd planned to pay in cash, but she hadn't banked on the ticket costing more than her rent. Short on options, she reached into her bag and pulled out Romy's credit card. Had the agent been paying closer attention, he would have noticed the slight tremor in her hand when she gave it to him. She hoped with all her might that it hadn't been canceled.

The agent swiped the card. Long seconds passed. Rune's body stiffened when she saw ridges form between his eyebrows. This was it. The card was about to be declined. She'd have no choice but to make excuses and run before he called the cops on her.

Put me out of my misery already!

The machine beeped. The printer spit out the receipt.

"Your flight boards at one o'clock at Gate 31," the agent said. He handed her Romy's card and passport and circled the gate number on her boarding pass. "Security is on level 4."

"Thank you," Rune said, relieved.

The feeling was short-lived. She'd made it past one hurdle, but an even bigger one awaited. The strap of her bag dug into her shoulder as she walked up the stairs to the security hall. It was packed, but this time, the wait really did look worse than it was. She silently thanked the powers that be for not forcing travelers to take off their shoes as she placed her belongings in a plastic bin. She passed through the metal detector without incident, but the security agent selected her for secondary screening. He directed her to a table manned by a sallow skinned official with facial hair that did nothing to hide his weak chin. There were three people in front of her. Then two. Then one. Before she knew it, she was at the front of the line.

Stay cool.

"Is this your bag?" the man asked.

"Yes," she replied, pronouncing the word as she imagined a French person would.

He opened her duffel, gave the contents a disinterested look, then held out his hand. "Passport, please."

She gave him Romy's passport. He opened it to the picture page and held it up. His eyes toggled from the photo to her face.

Rune's pupils dilated. Her breathing came in short, shallow spurts. Any second now she would be taken to the dreaded back room. She would be handcuffed and questioned for using a stolen passport. How long before they figured out it wasn't the only thing she'd stolen?

"Here you go."

The agent held out the passport. Rune's body shook as she accepted it. How he'd failed to notice it belonged to someone else—or that she was on the verge of a nervous breakdown—was a mystery for the ages. She zipped up her bag and threw it over her shoulder.

Something profound occurred as Rune walked away from the security area. It happened naturally, without conscious thought. Her posture drooped slightly. Her pace slowed to a relative crawl. Her face took on a more somber expression. By the time she reached her gate, the transformation was complete. Rune Sarasin had disappeared. RIP. Good riddance. For better or worse, she was reborn as Romy Steiner.

PART 2

10

MARSEILLE, FRANCE

I t was the middle of the night when Ryanair FR 5200 touched down at Marseille Provence Airport. Rune was first in line when the cabin door opened. That alone justified the cost of the business-class ticket. But that was easy to say when someone else was footing the bill.

The time Rune gained being first off the plane she lost waiting for the shuttle to the train station. What should have been a five-minute journey took more than thirty, but she was so relieved to have gotten out of Mallorca that she hardly cared at all.

She stepped off the shuttle at Vitrolles Station in a heightened state of alertness. The platform, though nearly empty, wasn't as creepy as she expected given the predawn hour. She got on a regional train heading east to Saint Charles Station in the center of Marseille. What she'd do when she got there was unclear. She knew nothing about the place except what she'd learned from a cursory Google search. It was the oldest city in France and the country's biggest port. Its residents hailed from all over the world. The region was blessed with three hundred days of sunshine per year.

None of these fun facts were at the front of Rune's mind during the twenty-minute ride to Saint Charles. Never in her life had she been more on guard. Then again, she'd never been hunted by the authorities either. She ran through her options. Turning herself in and hoping for the best seemed like a terrible idea, but the thought of living on the run unleashed a wave of despair so intense she felt ill. She wanted her old life back. It was all she'd ever wanted. To have another obstacle thrown in her path made her want to curl into a ball and weep. She might have done exactly that if she hadn't been surrounded by strangers. Instead, she pulled herself together and texted Lemaire. It was his fault she was in this mess. It seemed only fair that he get her out of it.

911!

Rune wasn't optimistic about getting a response at this time of night, but she was way too keyed up to wait. Her typing resumed.

Have you seen the headlines?

She waited a few seconds, then she did the crazy ex thing and sent three more messages in rapid succession.

What should I do?

Well?

HELLO???

She was about to send another text when the "read receipt" appeared below her last message. She calmed somewhat. Lemaire had money and power and connections. If anyone could fix this, it was him. She waited for the blinking ellipsis to appear to indicate he was responding. It never came. She resumed screaming via text.

IF I GO DOWN, YOU GO DOWN!

Her thumb was on top of the Send arrow when a cold fear crept in. She deleted the message. She couldn't antagonize Lemaire. She was a loose end, the one person who could tie him to the Bonaparte thefts and serve him up to the authorities. If he questioned her loyalty, she was done for. He'd get rid of her like everyone else who jeopardized his operation. Reality hit. She didn't just have to hide from the cops, she had to hide from Lemaire.

Her phone buzzed. It was him. She rejected the call.

Can't talk, she wrote. *Not safe.*

The ellipsis appeared. Her leg bounced waiting for his response.

Where are you? I'll send someone.

She stared at the message. Was his offer genuine or a ruse? She didn't know, but her gut told her not to trust him.

I'll come to you, she typed.

How soon can you get here?

Not sure. Tomorrow?

Meet me at the usual place.

She gave him the thumbs-up and reread her words. She knew they wouldn't hold him off for long. It didn't matter. A head start was all she needed to disappear.

The train rattled around a turn. Rune looked up and saw the couple across the aisle scooch closer together. They exuded youth and happiness, but it was their easy intimacy that caught her eye, the way they gazed at each other like there was no one else around. They reminded her of the person she used to be, of who was when she was with Kit. She wanted more than anything to call him, to hear him say he forgave her and that everything would be okay. But she didn't call. She knew reaching out now would only confirm all the awful things he thought about her. Tears pricked at the back of her eyes. *Don't cry, don't cry, don't cry*, she intoned silently. It was easier said than done.

The train pulled into Pas-des-Lanciers, a tiny station in the middle of nowhere. A lone passenger waited on the platform. He took his time climbing aboard and lowering himself into a rear-facing seat. Rune watched him take a metal thermos out of his backpack and unscrew the cap. The smell of fresh coffee filled the air. Rune took a deep breath. Her mind cleared. She called the one person she knew could help her.

MAILAN DOQUANG

"Do you have any idea what time it is?" Milo said. He spoke slowly. His voice was thick and full of sleep.

"Sorry, I know it's late." Rune glanced around nervously, then whispered, "Have you seen the headlines?"

"I was sleeping."

"Look now."

Silence.

"Are you still there?"

"I'm here." Milo sounded wide awake now. "Where are you?"

"Marseille. I just got here."

"France? Is that a good idea?"

"It was the first flight out of Palma."

"What can I do?"

Rune was relieved he hadn't made her ask. If anyone knew how much pride she had, it was him. "I need a place to lie low for a while. Do you still do that thing with the vacation rentals?"

"Of course." He chuckled softly. "You thought that place in Paris was mine?"

The comment made her smile. She heard footsteps, then the sound of a chair sliding on hard flooring. She pictured him sitting at the dining table of the fancy Montparnasse apartment in soft pants and a hoodie. It was a nice image.

"Is there a neighborhood you had in mind?"

"A place where people don't ask a lot of questions. I was thinking a cité."

"A cité?" he echoed incredulously. "Do you have any idea what it's like to live in public housing in Marseille?"

Rune made a vague sound, but she wasn't completely clueless. Like all major French cities, Marseille had its fair share of housing projects, called cités, as if a glamorous name could make up for crappy living conditions. The cités were part of a government effort to create an ideal urban environment for all citizens of the Republic, combining rationally laid out apartment blocks, lawns and playgrounds, and a variety of stores that made daily excursions to the outside world unnecessary. What they actually created were insular, disaffected communities of people with no money and few prospects. Gang activity was rampant in France's cités. People who didn't live in them steered clear, even the police. And that was precisely why they appealed to Rune. What better way to avoid the cops than to plant herself in a neighborhood they never stepped foot in? "I know it won't be the Four Seasons," she said. "But I think it will be a good place to blend in."

"If you say so."

Rune ignored the skepticism in Milo's tone and directed her gaze to the coffee drinker. She idly wondered what kind of job required getting on a train hours before sunrise.

"Do you have a particular cité in mind?" Milo asked.

"Not really."

"How about Parc Bellevue?"

"Tell me about it."

"Parc Bellevue is the official name, but people also call it Félix Pyat after the street name, or the 143 after the numerical address. It's the gateway to Marseille's northern districts."

"What are those?"

"Only the poorest neighborhoods in France. Parc Bellevue is arguably the worst of them. Fifty percent of residents live below the poverty line."

"Maybe pick a different one."

"You're sure? It's in the 3rd arrondissement, near the city center. The others are far from everything."

Rune thought for a moment. "Will I fit in at Bellevue? Demographically, I mean."

"No."

"Then why did you propose it?"

"None of the cités have the right demographics. You're not French."

"I could probably pass."

He snorted. "It's not just the language barrier. Most people in the cités are second- and third-generation immigrants from former French colonies. Algeria, Tunisia, West Africa."

"That works."

"I hate to break it to you, but just because you're not quite white doesn't mean you'll blend in in a French cité."

Milo had a point, but Rune wasn't ready to let the idea go just yet. People had mistaken her for things she wasn't her entire life—Latina, Turkish, Native American, Jewish. Rarely did they guess she was Asian and white. Why would a French cité be any different? "I can blend in," she reasoned.

"If you say so."

"And the police stay out of the cités, right?"

"I guess."

"Let's go with Parc Bellevue, then."

"Okay."

Rune heard Milo's fingers tapping against the keyboard. She chewed on her lip to keep herself from distracting him.

"You're in luck," he said after a few minutes.

"Tell me."

"Someone vacated a one-bedroom at Parc Bellevue last week. It only showed up in the HLM system yesterday."

"HLM?"

"It's the French acronym for low-income housing. I can create a profile and bump you to the top of the waiting list."

Rune didn't answer. It didn't feel right taking someone else's spot.

Milo sensed her hesitation. "There's no other way," he said.

"Fine." She shook off the guilt. "Can you create a profile under the name Romy Steiner?"

"Steiner? As in the family you robbed?"

"Yup."

"They're going to want to see some ID."

"I've got that covered."

If Milo had questions, he had the good sense to keep them to himself. Rune pulled out the stolen passport and fed him the information he needed. Full name: Romy Melodie Steiner. Date of birth: May 12, 1990. Place of birth: Paris. Current address: Berlin. Milo made up a social security number.

"What happens now?" she asked after they finished.

"You go to Parc Bellevue to sign the lease. The management office is in Building A2. It opens at 9:00 A.M."

Rune glanced at her watch. Morning was hours away. She didn't relish having to kill time in a dark unknown city.

"Is there anything else I can do for you?"

The question surprised Rune. It was the kind of thing a customer service rep might ask. Accommodating but impersonal. It didn't sound at all like Milo. "I'm all set for now," she said slowly.

"That's good."

"Is everything okay?"

Milo waited a long time before answering. When he finally spoke, he did so firmly, like he was afraid of being talked out of whatever it was he needed to say. "You know I care about you, right, Rune?"

"I know."

"And I think you care about me too."

"Of course."

"Then I need you to do something for me."

"Anything." She meant it. Milo had gone above and beyond. She owed him so much.

"I need you to stop calling me."

"What?"

"I took the fall for you once. I won't do it again."

Rune opened her mouth to protest, then closed it before any words could come out. She suddenly understood that this call was Milo's farewell gift to her. He'd helped her one last time before closing the chapter on them once and for all, something he never got to do when she pulled her Houdini act on him years ago. Part of her wanted to beg him to reconsider. But she knew he would, and she didn't want to be the person who broke his heart a second time. She knew how it felt to want someone who didn't want you back.

"I understand," she said softly. She struggled with her next words, knowing they might be the last she ever said to him. "Thanks, Milo." It was the best she could come up with. Her voice dropped to a whisper. "And I'm sorry. For everything."

"I know, Rune."

The phone went silent. The screen turned black. A sob rose in her throat. She turned to the window for distraction, but out there, everything was black as well.

11

PARC BELLEVUE (FÉLIX PYAT), MARSEILLE

Building A2 in Parc Bellevue was as unimaginative as its name. The fifteen-story tower was cast in the same mold as the others in the compound. Tall. Rectangular. Free of any embellishments. The white concrete was stained with decades of soot and guano. All manner of junk spilled from the balconies. The walls were cracked to the point of looking unsafe. Here, about three thousand people—mostly of North African descent—were squeezed into an undesirable parcel of land hemmed in by clogged motorways.

Rune was on edge as she approached the building. It seemed she'd been misinformed about the relationship between the police and the cités. Cops didn't avoid the area. Quite the contrary. There was a police station right next to the complex. Her teeth sank into her bottom lip. Her eyes flitted from side to side. Knowing the police were close was unnerving, but she had a more immediate problem—her meeting with the building manager. She could pass for many things, but Milo was right. A French woman wasn't one of them.

Rune perked at the sound of laughter slicing through the morning air. It came from a trio of college-aged women wearing jeans and brightly colored hijabs. Cell phones in bejeweled cases dangled from their manicured hands. Leather bookbags hung casually from their shoulders. Their voices petered when they passed a group of young men lounging on a soiled couch in the otherwise deserted parking lot. The contrast couldn't have been greater. The women looked like they were going places. The men had already reached their destination.

The intercom for Building A2 was a relic from a bygone era, with rusted call buttons and a beaten-up speaker plate. The front door was scratched, like a large dog went to town thinking dinner was on the other side. Rune rang the manager's office. A garbled voice responded. She replied with Romy's name, knowing her words would be equally unintelligible. The door buzzed open.

The walls of the hallway were ravaged by moisture. The air smelled stagnant and musty. A lightbulb hung from an exposed wire in the ceiling. If this wasn't a building code violation, Rune didn't know what was. She gave herself a silent pep talk before knocking on the manager's door.

"Entrez!" *Come in!*

The man behind the desk didn't deign to greet her when she entered his office. He had the harried look of a new parent, with a misbuttoned shirt and purple half-moons under his eyes. The plaque on his desk identified him as Claude Barbeau. He made a brusque motion for her to sit. She lowered herself into the only seat that hadn't been repurposed as storage. The chair creaked under her weight.

"Madame Steiner?" Claude said.

She nodded.

"Papiers, s'il vous plait." *Papers, please.*

Rune understood that he was asking for her ID. She handed him Romy's passport. He barely looked at it before turning to his computer and typing in what felt like slow motion. She noticed a dark stain on the carpet and tried not to imagine what had caused it.

The printer came to life. Claude swiveled in his chair and waited for it to churn out a multipage document she assumed was the lease agreement. The wait was a long one. The printer, like the computer, was practically an antique.

"Voila," Claude said as he spun around to face her.

Rune accepted the stack of papers and watched him paw around for a pen. He located one surprisingly quickly given the state of his desk. He scribbled on an envelope to make sure it worked.

"Voila," he said again, wielding the pen like a fencing foil.

Rune brought it to her chin and pretended to read the lease. She kept up the pretense until she reached the last page, then signed on the blank line and handed the papers back.

"La date, s'il vous plaît." *The date, please.*

Rune scrawled the date next to her signature. "Voila," she said, repeating his favorite word.

Claude prattled on and on as he made a copy of the lease. His words were impenetrable, except the part about a six-hundred-Euro deposit. Rune counted out the cash and traded it for a copy of the lease and three keys.

That went well, she thought as she slipped everything into her duffel. She rose from her seat and thanked Claude in something approximating French. Then she patted herself on the back and set off to find her new home—Parc Bellevue, Building A6, Apartment 703.

○━━●

Traversing the cité for the second time was not so much scary as it was depressing. Busted sidewalks and overflowing trash bins spoke of the neighborhood's poverty and neglect. Laundry strung from every other balcony suggested that residents couldn't afford dryers. The roar of traffic from a nearby interchange was inescapable. The five minutes it took Rune to reach her building had her cursing out the geniuses who thought it was a good idea to build a housing complex near two major highways.

Building A6 required a key to enter. Not a fob or a code, an actual key to a lock that looked like it dated from the 1950s. Seafoam tiles of the same vintage covered the vestibule. Rune set her qualms aside and looked for the elevator. She found it at the end of a hallway, past a mailroom that was littered with cigarette butts and takeout containers. She gave the call button a firm jab.

She'd been waiting a good five minutes when a woman emerged from a ground floor unit. She looked to be in her mid-to-late twenties, with intelligent brown eyes and skin as lustrous as a new penny. A black-and-white scarf with a bold floral pattern covered her hair and neck. A cocoon coat shrouded the rest of her body. Her look struck a balance of modest and modern.

The woman said something in rapid French.

Rune smiled and nodded. She hadn't understood a word.

"The elevator is broken," the woman said in slightly accented English. "It's been like that for months."

"Really?" Rune was shocked. It was a fifteen-story building. Didn't France have accessibility laws? "Has anyone told the building manager?" she asked.

"Claude is a do-nothing. Un vrai feignant."

Rune didn't know what a *feignant* was, but it didn't sound good.

"You can complain if it makes you feel better, but it's not going to accomplish anything. In the cités, nothing ever gets fixed."

Terrific.

"On the upside, you'll save money on a gym membership."

"I thought French women didn't go to the gym."

"They don't. But you're not French." That was apparently a good thing because the woman held out her hand to introduce herself. Her perfectly shaped nails were painted a timeless nude hue. A silver and coral wrist cuff peaked out from the sleeve of her coat. "I'm Leila Habib. I'm in 106."

"Romy . . . from 703. I'm new to Parc Bellevue."

"Poor you."

Rune couldn't tell if Leila was joking or not.

"Be careful in the stairwell. It's where the dealers keep their weapons."

"Seriously?"

"Their drugs too."

"Should someone call the cops?"

Leila scoffed. "The police are more dangerous to the people here than the dealers."

Rune gave her a dubious look.

"Don't believe me? Read the papers. Every week there's something."

Heat crawled up Rune's cheeks. What did she know about the relationship between the French police and the marginalized residents of the cités? She grew up solidly middle class. Her experiences were nothing like theirs.

"I have to go to work," Leila said. Her keys jingled in her hand. "It was nice meeting you."

"Likewise." Rune smiled. "I'm sure I'll see you around."

Leila made a move to leave, then turned back. "I hope you don't mind me saying this, but you strike me as someone who doesn't want to draw attention to herself."

Rune's smile froze.

"If you want to fit in here, stop smiling. Only Americans smile at strangers."

Her smile wilted. She assumed a neutral expression.

"Better."

Rune nodded, grateful for the crash course in how to look French.

"And another thing, only politicians and journalists call this place Parc Bellevue. To everyone here, its Félix Pyat."

Feh-leex Pee-yat. Milo had tried to tell her. "Got it."

"If you need anything, feel free to knock on my door."

"Thanks, Leila. I will."

"See you later, Romy from 703."

Rune shifted her duffel from one shoulder to the other and headed to the stairway. Her plan had been to keep to herself, but as she opened the dented metal door, she couldn't help thinking she'd be smart to befriend a local. She and Leila had only briefly spoken and already she'd received valuable information about life at Parc Bellevue. Correction. Félix Pyat.

She started the long ascent to her seventh-floor apartment. Her pace was brisk at first. She slowed at the halfway mark. By the time she reached her floor, she was practically crawling. She pushed the door open.

The hallway was downright offensive. The stench of dirty carpet and burned meat shot up her nostrils and lodged itself at the back of her throat. The rat-a-tat of video game gunfire needled at a spot directly behind her right eye. Dogs barked maniacally from at least three units. She located her apartment, jammed the key in the lock, and gave it a firm turn. The deadbolt didn't budge. She twisted the key a few times until she heard a click. All she could think when she closed the door was how relieved she was that it was thick.

The apartment was no better or worse than Rune expected. It was small and boxy, with bad lighting but no obvious signs of vermin. The previous tenant had left behind a scarred coffee table and a faux-leather sofa with tears in the seat cushions. The kitchen, if it could even be called that, was equipped with a two-burner cooktop and a leaky faucet.

Black dots radiated from clusters of blistering paint in the miniscule bathroom. Rune hit the light switch in the bedroom, illuminating a double bed with a sagging mattress. Another switch controlled a ceiling fan that vibrated loudly with every turn.

Rune set her bag on the bed and checked the time. It was barely ten o'clock, way too early to start drinking. Still, she returned to the kitchen and opened the mini fridge hoping against all hope to find a cold bottle of wine. What she got instead was a face full of old fridge smell. She slammed the door and swore never to open it again.

Out she went to the balcony. Dingy concrete towers like the one she was in extended as far as the eye could see. Between them were parking lots and vacant tracts planted with trees so scrawny they emphasized the lack of greenery. Someone leaned on their car horn. Someone else revved their engine. Other aggressive sounds followed—a thunderous shouting match, an explosion of glass, music set at earsplitting levels. Rune swallowed hard as the reality of living in a cité set in. She took a deep breath. Then she straightened her shoulders. Like it or not, Félix Pyat was home for the foreseeable future.

12

OLD PORT, MARSEILLE

Marseille was a place of contrasts. Centuries of maritime trade and conquests had left their mark on the city, dotting it with quaint fishing havens and imposing stone fortresses. The modern metropolis had burgeoned around the historic sites. Grittier but more laid-back than Paris, France's "Second City" was now the country's largest port and an important center of commerce and culture. The city also boasted an outstanding local cuisine as well as hot summers and mild winters. Civic authorities spent millions advertising Marseille's virtues. Tourists hardly needed convincing. They came for the beaches and the bouillabaisse. Museums, churches, and forts topped every itinerary. They spread across every inch of the city, but nowhere were they more numerous than in the storied Old Port.

Hotels ranging from luxury to barebones were scattered across the port. Of these, the Auberge du Monde was firmly on the low end. It wasn't a bad hotel per se, it just wasn't any good. The common areas were long overdue for refurbishment. The rooms were tiny and uninspired. Mold and mildew were taking root in all the bathrooms.

Guests had started to notice and were leaving negative reviews on various websites.

Torn bed sheets! Fraying towels! TO AVOID! shrieked Florenz Brecht from Tübingen.

Noisiest hotel ever, declared Zane Johnson from Tacoma.

Meh, opined M.J., no location.

The hotel's shortcomings were not at the front of Rune's mind as she gazed at the boats bobbing lazily in the Old Port six stories below. Her hair, dyed an unremarkable shade of brown, was tucked under a wide headband. Dark contacts toned down her striking eyes. A baggy gray button-down concealed her lithe figure. Those who knew her before she went into hiding would surely have mistaken her for someone else.

The Auberge du Monde left a lot to be desired, but in Rune's opinion, the location more than made up for it. The building stood on the eastern extremity of the port, at the end of the famed Canebière, Marseille's answer to the Champs-Élysées. The main tourist attractions were all within sight. To the right, beyond the colorful Panier neighborhood, was the Fort Saint-Jean, an old fortress incorporated into a modern museum of Mediterranean culture. To the left, in the distance, the basilica of Notre-Dame de la Garde and its golden Madonna watched over the city from a craggy peak. And straight ahead, on a small island just offshore, lay the massive Chateau d'If, a former prison made famous by Alexandre Dumas's *Count of Monte Cristo*. Rune inhaled slowly. The air smelled of sea spray and thick-cut fries. Directly above, seagulls circled languorously in the cloudless sky.

"Keep this up, Romy, and I'll have no choice but to dock your pay."

Rune shuddered at the sound of Philippe Moreau's nasal voice. She gave the port a final look before reluctantly stepping into the room. The glass door squeaked when she slid it shut. She removed her rubber gloves with a combative snap and flexed her stiff fingers. They felt bare without nail polish and rings, but adornments of any sort were against hotel policy. "Pay?" she said with an arched brow. "Is that what you call the pittance you give me at the end of each week?"

Philippe's mouth pinched with displeasure. He didn't enjoy having his cheapness brought to his attention. His official title was Head of Housekeeping, but he insisted on being called *Director* Morel, like people couldn't see through the inflated title. Men like Philippe didn't like the Runes of the world. They were too willful. Too mouthy. Impossible to control.

"How many times do I have to tell you?" Philippe said. "If you're not happy with your pay, you know where the door is." He straightened his doughy body to its full height and stuck out his chest to the point of absurdity. What he said next sounded almost like a dare. "There are plenty of people who would be grateful for this job. *Extremely* grateful."

Rune gave him a disinterested shrug.

"You know, you could make a lot more money if you learned French."

"I'm working on it."

"I'd be happy to give you lessons."

Rune wanted to wipe the wolfish smile right off Philippe's face. He liked hitting on the housekeepers, almost all of them *sans papiers*—undocumented immigrants. Her coworkers had two choices when he harassed them or docked their pay for no reason other than to jerk them around. They could either take it like champs or find another job. Most of them took it. Romy's papers offered Rune some protection, but her nonexistent French severely limited her employment options. She often daydreamed about going back to her old ways. Stealing was easier than cleaning, not to mention more lucrative. She never went through with it though. She couldn't risk getting arrested. The stakes were simply too high. Still, she kept her skills sharp by breaking into in-room safes and locked suitcases whenever she had the chance. It was all perfectly harmless. She never stole anything expensive, just unopened toiletries and the odd piece of clothing. Guests noticed when cash and jewelry went missing from their rooms. They didn't think twice when they couldn't find their La Mer face cream or Hermès scarf.

"What do you say about the lessons?" Philippe asked. His expression had gone from lewd to something bordering on pathetic. He shifted his considerable body weight onto one leg. "We can start tonight. At my place."

Rune knew she should let him down easy. But knowing something and doing it were two completely different things. She spoke her next words with blunt finality. "Get real, Philippe. It's never going to happen."

He reacted as if she'd slapped him. Then he did what he always did when he felt emasculated. He punished her. "I finished the schedule for next week," he said with undisguised smugness. "We're overstaffed. I cut your hours. You're down to five days."

Vindicative son of a—

"It was either that or letting someone go. You wouldn't want that, would you?"

He studied her to see if his words hit their mark. They had, but Rune wasn't about to let him know. She bit the inside of her cheek to keep from telling him off.

"You'd best get back to work," he said when it was clear she wouldn't be baited. "The toilets aren't going to clean themselves." He gave her an ugly smirk before turning his back to her and ambling away.

Rune waited until she heard the elevator ding down the hall before unleashing her fury. She kicked a chair over and tore the sheets off the bed. Then she flung herself on the mattress and screamed into a pillow. It accomplished nothing, but God it felt good to rage.

13

OLD PORT, MARSEILLE

R une stood in a long line of commuters waiting for the number 89 bus. Two had gone by without stopping. One was out of service, the other too packed to fit any more bodies, despite vociferous complaints from the angry masses. Cigarette smoke crept up her nostrils. Car exhaust blew in her face.

"Romy!"

Rune tore her eyes away from the crack in the pavement she was studying. Leila was coming straight for her, looking chic as ever in her cocoon coat and floral headscarf. Her nails were perfectly manicured, her makeup exactly right. Just being in her presence made Rune self-conscious. She curled her hands into fists to hide her ruined nails and leaned in for the requisite cheek kisses.

"Je ne m'attendais pas à te voir ici!" *I wasn't expecting to see you here!*

Rune gave her a pained look. "English, please."

"Bad day?"

"You could say that."

"Is it serious?"

"Just work." Rune had been in Marseille long enough to know that sharing details about her workday was neither necessary nor desirable. Growing up, work was often the main topic of conversation. Things were different here. Rune and Leila had chatted many times in the last four weeks, mostly when they crossed paths in their building but also at a café not far from the cité. Rune knew that Leila was born in France to a Polish mother and an Algerian father, that she had a younger sister named Myriam, and that she drank her coffee with sugar but no milk. She knew all this, but she hadn't the faintest idea what Leila did for a living, where she went from nine-to-five each day, or how she paid for her understated but obviously expensive wardrobe. It never came up. It wasn't important. The adage about the French working to live and Americans living to work appeared to be right on the money.

"Where are you going?" Leila asked with an inquisitive cock of her head. Her expression turned horrified. "Not home, I hope."

"Yes, home. I'm tired."

"But it's Saturday."

"I know what day it is."

"Well, then?"

"I don't see the point."

"Mais, ça va pas dans la tête?" *Are you out of your mind?*

"In English."

"You're young and beautiful. Only the old and ugly spend their weekends alone at home."

"That's very mean."

"Bof." Leila gave a gallic shrug before brightening noticeably. "I'm meeting a friend for an apéro. You *must* come."

Apéro—short for apéritif. The tradition of pre-dinner drinks was practically sacrosanct in France. In Marseille, it was synonymous with pastis, an anise-flavored spirit typically served in a highball glass alongside a pitcher of water. Purists drank it without ice. Everyone else knew to add the water *before* the ice to prevent the liqueur from crystalizing. Rune had always thought of herself as a wine drinker, but her time in Marseille had convinced her of the merits of pastis. She mulled over Leila's invitation, then she reminded herself that rent was due and that despicable Philippe had cut her hours. She had Romy's credit card, which miraculously hadn't been canceled, but she reserved it for emergencies and drinks with Leila didn't qualify. She gave a firm shake of the head. "I really can't."

"Come on. It will be my treat," Leila said, reading her mind.

Rune hesitated. It wasn't just a money thing. She wasn't keen on being around people, of showing her face to every true crime fanatic and citizen detective in the city, not to mention the cops.

"The place has great mezzes."

She felt her resolve waver. She'd been in Marseille for over a month with no issues. What were the chance of something happening now? "Maybe just one drink," she said, throwing caution out the window.

Leila let out a celebratory cheer. Rune allowed herself to be pulled away from the bus stop. She'd resisted the invitation, but the fact was, she *wanted* to join Leila for a drink. Her social life had been dismal since leaving Bangkok. She missed having company. She missed having fun. But more than anything, she missed the feeling of just being normal.

14

NOAILLES, MARSEILLE

L eila hooked her arm through Rune's and led the way to the Cours
Julien in the lively Noailles district. The neighborhood was only
fifteen minutes away from the Old Port—most of it uphill—but it
looked and felt like a different planet. In contrast to the port, which
was scrubbed and sanitized for the cruise ship crowd, the Cours Julien
could only be described as the real Marseille—rundown, edgy, and
full of character. Occupying the site of a former fruit and vegetable
market, the pedestrian esplanade and adjacent alleys were home to a
cross-section of Marseille. Longtime Jewish, Christian, and Muslim
residents rubbed shoulders with young creative types whose numbers
had ballooned in recent years. The area was known for its street art,
with graffiti covering virtually every wall, door, bench, lamppost, and
mailbox in the neighborhood. Mom and pop shops reigned supreme in
the Cours Julien, providing an important counterpoint to the international chains besetting the rest of the city. Best of all were the neighborhood restaurants specializing in food from the four corners of the
world. French, Syrian, Japanese, and Mexican were well represented.
So was just about anything the stomach desired.

As pleased as Rune was to discover a gem like the Cours Julien, she couldn't help but wonder what the appeal was for Leila. The area was hipster-punk, while Leila seemed like the kind of person who painted within the lines. She was about to ask when Leila pointed to a bar with a busy outdoor terrace illuminated by colored strings lights. It was on the cusp of too cold to sit outside, but none of the patrons seemed to mind. Still, Rune was relieved when Leila walked to the front door, where a tall man with straight teeth and a head of thick black hair greeted her with very sexy cheek kisses. Leila's affinity for the Cours Julien now made perfect sense.

"Isa, this is Romy. Romy, meet Isa. He owns this place."

Rune inhaled as she kissed Isa's smooth cheeks. He smelled like a god.

"Nice to meet you, Romy."

"Ravie." *Delighted.* She glanced around the bar. It was full of tattooed youngsters, strait-laced old-timers, and everything in between. "I love the vibe here," she said in English, having exhausted her knowledge of French. "It's so laid-back."

Isa seemed pleased by the compliment. He pointed to a black-and-white mural of a turbaned man in the middle of the room. "That's Ibn Khaldun, a fourteenth-century thinker from Tunis." His tone was full of admiration and deference. "Khaldun wrote about the concept of asabiyyah. It's Arabic for solidarity, or social cohesion. His ideas are the inspiration for this bar. Muslims, Christians, and Jews, young and old, rich and poor, socialists and conservatives—everyone is welcome here, as long as they respect others." He turned to Leila. His voice became soft. "Come, I saved you a table."

Leila batted her lashes and smiled. Rune suddenly understood that when a French person smiled, it was because they really meant it.

Isa led them to a table near the bar. He helped Leila out of her coat and pulled out her chair. Rune managed on her own.

"What can I get you?" he asked.

"I'll have a pastis," Rune said. *When in Rome.*

"Diabolo menthe," said Leila.

Isa left to get their drinks. Rune stared at Leila in disbelief. "You begged me to go out for a drink and all you're having is peppermint soda?"

"I don't drink alcohol."

Rune knew not to ask why hanging out in a bar and kissing a man who was obviously not a relative was okay but drinking alcohol and showing her hair were not.

"Everyone cherry-picks when it comes to religion," Leila said, once again reading Rune's mind.

How does she do it?

Leila erupted in laughter. "You really need to work on your poker face."

Rune crossed her eyes, which made Leila laugh even harder. They settled into an easy conversation. Soon after, a freckled waitress with strawberry-blond hair and eyes as clear as the Provençal sky arrived with their drinks.

"I'm glad you could join me," Leila said after the waitress departed. "It's nice to see you outside the cité."

"I'm glad too." Rune poured water into her glass and watched it turn cloudy as it hit the pastis. She gave it a quick stir and brought the glass to her lips. It tasted good, like cold black licorice or fennel.

Leila took a sip of her drink and sat back in her chair.

"No one should ingest anything that green," Rune remarked.

"Have you ever tried it?"

"No."

"Then how do you know you don't like it?"

"It's mint syrup and lemon soda. I don't have to taste it to know it isn't delicious."

Leila pushed her glass across the table. Rune obliged and took a sip. "Well?"

"I'll stick to pastis."

"Suit yourself, Romy from 703."

Leila was teasing, but Rune could tell there was something behind her words. No surprise there. She'd been tight-lipped about her identity, for obvious reasons. She made the spontaneous decision to take away some of the mystery. It was a risk, but nothing piqued people's curiosity more than unanswered questions. "Steiner," she said before taking another sip of pastis.

"Excuse me?"

"My surname is Steiner."

Leila nearly spit out her drink. "Sorry but you don't look like a *Steiner.*"

"It's my ex-husband's name," Rune said quickly. She lowered her gaze. Spinning tales was nothing new, but it didn't feel good lying to Leila. She fiddled with her stir stick. Leila was the closest thing she had to a friend in Marseille. In fact, she was her *only* friend. She searched for a way to end the conversation. "I never changed my name back after the divorce. It was too much trouble."

"Ah." There were questions in Leila's eyes.

"We were young. We grew apart. Blah, blah, blah."

The questions vanished.

Rune saw an opportunity to pivot and took it. "But enough about that. Tell me about Isa. I want to know *everything.*"

It was all the invitation Leila needed. She gushed about Isa's drive and intellect and values. The mere mention of his dimpled chin and long lashes made her blush. Rune encouraged the conversation with well-timed interjections and an endless supply of encouraging nods. It was calculated, there was no denying that, but that didn't make it any less genuine. She'd never had a close girlfriend, not as an adult, anyway. Her relationships with women had always been colored by the horrible bullying she'd experienced as a teen—the gaggle of mean girls, the weeks of debasement at a picture-perfect summer camp. Women sensed her reticence. They steered clear of her. They didn't open up.

But things were different with Leila. Becoming Romy had allowed Rune to shed parts of her identity that were no longer serving her. She held back, of course—her name, her history, the truth about what brought her to Marseille—but she was emotionally available in a way that was entirely new, at least in her interactions with women. She felt connected. She liked the feeling.

Maybe it was the budding intimacy between her and Leila that prompted Rune to let her guard down, or the glasses of pastis Isa kept sending to their table. Either way, the line between conversing and oversharing was impossibly blurred by the time the clock struck midnight.

"You expect me to believe that you've given up on romance?" Leila asked after Rune balked at the idea of a blind date with one of Isa's friends.

"I don't have time for romance," Rune said, waving her hand like she was dispersing cigarette smoke.

"You have to *make* time. Otherwise you'll wake up one day and find that your whole life has gone by and that you missed out on a big part of it."

"All romance ever brought me is heartbreak."

"Heartbreak means you're trying. You're too young not to try."

"Oh, trust me. I've tried. I texted Kit a billion times."

"Kit? Is that your ex-husband?"

"Husband? Noooo! Kit was my boyfriend." Rune realized her mistake even before she stopped speaking. She sobered instantly.

"What happened with him?"

Rune wanted to backpedal, but she was buzzed and thinking was hard.

"It's okay," Leila said, sensing her hesitance. "We don't have to talk about it if you don't want to."

But she did. Because she needed a friend. Because saying nothing would turn it into an even bigger thing. "I screwed up. He left me," Rune said simply. It was easier to tell the truth than to keep track of lies.

"You're sure it's unfixable? Not so many things are deal-breakers, you know."

"That's what I told him."

"Maybe that's the problem. Maybe he thinks you're minimizing. Maybe he's waiting for you to take accountability."

Leila's words irked Rune. She seemed to be taking Kit's side. Weren't girlfriends supposed to ride or die with you?

"Or maybe he's an unforgiving jerk and you're better off without him."

That was better. Rune nodded vigorously.

"A toast, then," Leila said, raising her glass of green liquid. "To new friends and new beginnings."

"To new friends and new beginnings," Rune repeated. She clinked glasses with Leila. Then she downed her drink, hoping it would wash Kit out of her system once and for all.

The conversation shifted to lighter topics—to fashion and music and movies. Isa pulled up a chair and waved over two of his buddies. Vodka shots and snacks appeared. Rune let herself get swept up in the fun, like the close call with Leila never happened. She was so focused on her new friends that she didn't notice the freckle-faced waitress with the blue eyes scowling at her from across the room.

15

PARC BELLEVUE [FÉLIX PYAT], MARSEILLE

I t was the insistent buzzing that lured Rune out of her dreamless sleep the next morning. Her body was stiff and uncomfortably cold, like the heater was on the fritz again. Her mouth was so dry it was hard to swallow. She opened one eye and pawed at the bedside table until her hand found her phone. "Hello?" she rasped.

"Where the hell are you?"

The nasal voice on the other end of the line was full of righteous anger. The drum inside her head pounded. She pinched her temples with her thumb and middle finger and tried to figure out who it was.

"Your shift started twenty minutes ago!"

"Mr. Morel!" She sprang into sitting position. Her face contorted in pain. It felt like someone had used her skull as a punching bag.

"You've been late twice already this week! This is unacceptable!"

"I'm really sorry, Mr. Morel. I'm on my way."

"*Director* Morel."

Rune didn't respond. Late or not, she wasn't playing that game.

"Give me one good reason not to fire you."

She was wracking her brain for an excuse she hadn't already used when the alcohol she consumed the night before threatened to come up. She pressed her free hand to her mouth. Only when she was sure she wouldn't throw up did she speak again. "I'm on the bus. Traffic is terrible."

He exhaled loudly. "How much longer?"

"Ten minutes."

"Ten? You're sure?"

Rune understood his dilemma. On the one hand, it pained him to let her tardiness go unpunished. On the other hand, a tour group was scheduled to arrive that afternoon—the biggest since the end of the summer—and he needed to be fully staffed. "I'm sorry, Mr. Morel. But you know how it is with public transit." Rune winced, anticipating more yelling.

"Fine," he muttered.

Her face relaxed.

"I'll let it slide this time. But don't think there won't be conse-quences. You'll stay late today and come in early on your next shift."

"No problem," Rune said, grateful he wasn't going to make her beg. "I'll be there in twenty minutes, thirty tops." She hung up before he could object, then fell back onto her pillow.

"Good morning, beautiful."

"Jesus Christ!"

"I'm really not."

Rune stared at the attractive man lying naked in her bed. She grabbed the sheet and yanked it up to cover her own naked body. "Wh-who are you?" she sputtered.

"Djamel. I'm Isa's friend." He angled his head to one side in an extremely charming way. "We met last night. You don't remember?"

"Of course I remember," Rune said even though she had no idea who he was. She thought hard, but everything after the first round of vodka shots was fuzzy. She glanced at the man, hoping to jog her memory. He had the physique of a professional tennis player, with well-formed pecs and washboard abs. A trim beard covered his angular jaw. His skin tone was warm like the Sahara. It never felt great to wake up next to a stranger, but even in her current state, Rune knew she could have done worse. "Well, Jameel. It was very nice meeting you, but I have to go to work now."

"It's Djamel."

"Right."

"I'll go. No problem."

Rune watched him get up and retrieve his clothes. He moved with swagger, completely comfortable with his nakedness. With a body like that, who could blame him?

"Are you going to the gym or on a trip?"

Rune took her eyes off Djamel's backside long enough to see him looking at the duffel she kept by the bedroom door. It was her go-bag, the only thing she had to grab should the need to make a quick exit arise. "Neither. I was in Paris last week. I never unpacked."

"Oh."

She didn't wait to see if Djamel bought her story. She had to get to work. With that in mind, she heaved herself out of bed and hurried to her tiny bathroom.

Hurrying proved to be a terrible mistake. Her queasiness came back with a vengeance. Her stomach seized up as waves of nausea rolled over her. "Don't throw up, don't throw up, don't throw up," she whispered like an incantation. She waited for the moment to pass, then bent to drink directly from the tap. "Ouch!" she cried when she smacked her lip against the spout.

"Are you okay?" Djamel called out.

"I'm fine! Just go!" She draped her torso over the sink and lapped at the water like an injured kitten. She managed a few sips before dragging herself to the shower stall. The water came out as a lukewarm trickle. She lathered up as quickly as she could in her condition, but she was too slow. The water went ice-cold. A lesser person might have gotten upset, but it happened so frequently that Rune barely flinched. She stepped out of the shower more alert than she was when she went in and grabbed a towel. By the time she padded into the bedroom, she almost felt like herself.

Djamel had left a note on the dresser asking her to call him. She crumpled it up and tossed it in the trash without an ounce of regret. Hot as he was, she didn't need that kind of complication in her life. She scanned the room for her work shirt and found it hanging from the ceiling fan. She tried to imagine how it had gotten up there. Each scenario was more absurd than the last. No wonder Djamel had left his number. She stepped onto the bed to retrieve it and brought it up to her nose. It wasn't great, but it would do. On it went over a more or less clean pair of pants. She checked the time as she put on her socks. Breakfast was out of the question.

The stairwell was empty when Rune trotted down a few minutes later, her freshly shampooed hair leaving wet marks on her jacket. She burst through the door and hurried past a group of young men posturing in the lobby. One made a snide remark. The other sucked his teeth. She was nearing the exit when an elderly neighbor flagged her down. She greeted him politely but in a way that didn't invite further discussion. She'd bumped into him enough times to know that he liked to hold court, even with someone who clearly didn't understand what he was saying. She normally didn't mind letting him talk at her. Sometimes, to his delight, she even learned a word or two. But she was late for work as it was.

"Votre courrier, Mademoiselle Steiner!" *Your mail, Ms. Steiner!*

Rune accepted the postcard he thrust at her. The mail carrier often got things wrong at Félix Pyat, leaving it to residents to sort things out among themselves. She glanced at the glossy image of Montparnasse cemetery and flipped the card over. It was blank. She knew instantly it was from Milo. Her features softened knowing this was his way of saying there were no hard feelings. She folded the postcard in half and slid it in her pocket. "Merci, Monsieur," she said. *Thank you, sir.*

"Très bien!" *Very good!*

Rune smiled before she could catch herself.

The man smiled back. His eyes twinkled through his cataracts.

"I have to run now," she chirped. "Au revoir!"

"Au revoir, Mademoiselle."

Rune couldn't help but laugh as she ran to catch her bus. The man had been around the sun eighty times. If her smiles brightened his day, she was more than happy to oblige.

16

OLD PORT, MARSEILLE

Rune breezed into the Auberge du Monde exactly one hour after she was scheduled to be there. She gave the front desk clerks in matching navy pants and tie-neck shirts a polite nod. They turned their noses up at her in response. The hierarchy at the hotel was no joke. Liberty, Equality, Fraternity—France's beloved national motto—seemed to not extend to housekeepers.

Most hotels had breakrooms where employees could stash their belongings. The Auberge du Monde was not among them. The clerks were allotted cupboards in the reception area and the restaurant staff had individual lockers by the kitchen. As for the housekeepers, they were stuck with open cubbies next to the boiler room. It was an awful setup. The previous week, a cell phone charger had gone missing. The week before that, a metro pass. Nothing precious or terribly expensive was ever stolen, but for women who were barely scraping by, it was the world.

Rune circumvented a group of Japanese tourists and made her way to the elevator. The doors dinged open. She stepped inside and pressed the button to the basement. The doors had almost completely closed when a dimpled hand made them retract. In lumbered Philippe, doughy as ever. He made a show of looking at his watch. She pretended she cared.

"Good of you to join us this morning, Romy."

"Sorry, Mr. Morel. The bus was *really* slow."

Philippe pursed his lips.

"I can stay late, if you want." She wasn't being generous. She'd already agreed to do that. Her words seemed to placate him.

"Go straight to the fifth floor," he said sternly. "The school group from Lille just checked out. I need the rooms as soon as possible."

Rune groaned inwardly. Cleaning up after guests was never fun, but it was infinitely worse when the guests were teenagers. The last time a school group stayed at the hotel, she and a coworker had spent hours wiping gunk off the walls and scraping gum from under the furniture. If it were up to her, the Auberge du Monde would be an adults-only establishment. She didn't share her thoughts with Philippe. "Fifth floor. Sure thing."

"What are you waiting for?"

"Nothing. We're in the elevator."

There wasn't a trace of snark in Rune's voice, but that didn't stop Philippe from taking offense. It was always like that with him. He blamed others for everything, even the stupid things that came out of his mouth.

"You'll work an extra two hours today," he growled to cover his embarrassment.

The math didn't add up, but the doors opened and spared her from saying as much. She stepped out of the elevator and headed toward the cubbies.

"Make it three hours, just so you learn your lesson!" he called out after her.

She raised her hand to indicate she'd heard him.

The boiler coughed like an asthmatic. She ignored the sound and slipped out of her jacket, folding it neatly before placing it in the last available cubby. As she walked back toward the elevator, she swore never to give Philippe more time and energy than was absolutely necessary. He controlled her work schedule and her paycheck. Nothing more. If she let him get under her skin, she had no one to blame but herself.

The fifth floor was more disastrous than Rune anticipated. The school group had turned eight adjoining rooms into a veritable landfill, covering every available surface with food containers and half-empty soda cans. Slimy bars of soap clogged the already sluggish drains. Towels were left sopping wet on the carpet, creating dark rings that were sure to leave a stain. For hours, Rune dusted and vacuumed and scrubbed. For hours, she changed sheets, folded towels, and replaced miniature shampoo and conditioner bottles. She was a machine. The rooms had to be spotless, otherwise she'd have to sit through another of Philippe's interminable lectures. The backbreaking work was not without its upsides though. By the time she finished, she was all caught up on her favorite podcast.

Rune was reorganizing her cart when a ponytailed coworker poked her head in the room and said something she didn't hear. The woman had a name, but everyone called her *casse-couilles*—ballbreaker—because she enforced Philippe's rules in exchange for better hours and marginally higher pay. Either she was unfamiliar with divide-and-conquer managerial tactics, or she just didn't care.

"Sorry, what did you say?" Rune asked after pulling out her earbuds.

The coworker's nose wrinkled, like she'd caught a whiff of something rotten. "Those aren't permitted," she said, eyeing the buds.

"I forgot." Rune replied with a straight face even though she knew full well what was and wasn't allowed. She waited for the woman to get on with it, but all she got was a disapproving look. "Was there something you wanted to speak to me about?"

"Farrah needs help on the sixth floor."

Rune bristled. The sixth floor was home to the premium suites, such as they were. They attracted highly entitled people who expected VIP treatment at bargain-basement prices. Guests of the sixth floor had a reputation for being demanding, which would have been more tolerable if they weren't also lousy tippers.

"You better get going. Farrah's dragging her feet. I bet she's pregnant again."

Rune's mask slipped.

The ball-breaker noticed. She smirked, then flipped her ponytail over her shoulder and sauntered away.

Don't. Say. Anything.

It was a big ask. She wanted to curse the woman out for spying on her coworkers, for enforcing Philippe's stupid rules, and for being an all-around asshole. Instead, she gave her cart a hard push. She heard a crack. One of the casters had snapped. She rested her head on her forearms. What else could go wrong on this already crappy day?

Farrah was nowhere in sight when Rune got to the sixth floor, nor was anyone else. She pushed the cart down the hallway, the broken wheel sliding instead of spinning over the carpet. She turned a corner and saw a do-not-disturb sign hanging from the first door on the right—Room 600. She parked her cart outside the adjacent room—602—and knocked gently.

"Ménage." *Housekeeping.*

No one answered. She knocked slightly harder, listened, then opened the door with her master key.

The room was neater than she expected. Its occupant was a lone man or a tall woman, if the imprint on the bed was any indication. Whoever it was knew how to hang a towel and use a wastebasket. Rune reckoned she could tidy up in fifteen minutes, ten if she hurried. She put on a fresh pair of gloves and tackled the bed, pulling the sheets so tightly every crease vanished. Pillow fluffing came next. A long blonde strand went airborne. The guest was a woman, if she had to guess.

A bottle of liquid foundation on the bathroom counter confirmed her assessment. Beside it was a brand-new Lancôme lipstick in a shade not so different from her favorite cherry hue. Rune tried to resist, she really did, but the devil on her shoulder was very persuasive. She gave her lips a swipe, pressed them together, and checked her reflection. *Not bad*, she thought with an exaggerated pout. Only after sliding the tube into her pocket did she give the shower a quick rinse and wipe the fingerprints off the mirror. She then dumped blue cleaner into the toilet and called it a job well done. The gloves came off. She was ready for some me time.

She started in the closet, like she always did. Her eyes landed on the safe, then dropped to the silver carry-on nestled on the luggage rack. She immediately recognized it as a pricey Rimowa, a brand she rarely saw at the Auberge du Monde. She hesitated but only briefly. Who could resist a Rimowa?

The suitcase was locked. That was hardly a problem. Rune bypassed the combination mechanism and focused on the two TSA key locks flanking the handle. She pulled a pin out of her hair and popped the first lock with an adept twist. The second was just as easy. She opened the suitcase, eager to discover its hidden treasures.

The heater came to life. The clonking drowned out all other sounds—the dinging of the elevator, guests' footsteps in the hallway, the arrival and departure of room service four doors down. The heater was so loud that Rune failed to hear the guest at the door until it was too late. The card reader beeped. The doorhandle jiggled. She slammed the Rimowa shut and jumped to her feet.

The woman who stepped into the room was tall and blonde. A rash of acne showed through her makeup. Her mouth and eyes formed surprised *O*s. "What are you doing in here?" she demanded.

American. Thank God! Rune gave her a look that was both meek and contrite. "Cleaning. I'll get out of your way." She made a move for the door.

"Not so fast!"

Dread rose. She tried to fend it off as she met the woman's gaze.

"Didn't you see the sign?"

"I didn't. Sorry." She apologized even though she knew for a fact the do-not-disturb sign wasn't on the door.

The woman eyed her suspiciously, like she was trying to decide whether to escalate. "Well, are you finished?" she finally said.

Rune nodded.

"Fine, you can go."

Her muscles relaxed. She started forward.

"Your gloves," the woman called out.

Rune turned. Her eyes found the rubber gloves draped over the bathroom doorknob. She caught a glimpse of her reflection when she reached for them.

The lipstick!

She wanted to wipe it off, but the woman had already seen it. She shoved the gloves in her pocket.

Say something normal!

"I'm sorry for disturbing you," she mumbled. "Have a good afternoon."

"Humph."

Rune took that as a dismissal. She stepped out of the room. The lock clicked behind her. She pushed her cart to the elevator as fast as the broken wheel would allow and pressed the down button. The doors took forever to open. When they finally did, she found herself face-to-face with the ball-breaker.

"Finished already?" the woman asked.

"I'm taking a break," Rune replied.

"Have you been working for six hours?"

"I have." *More or less.*

The woman made a show of looking at her watch.

Rune wanted to flatten her with her cart. She needed to get off this floor. She needed to get rid of the stupid lipstick in her pocket before the blonde put two and two together. "Do you mind?" she said. "You're eating into my break."

The woman stepped aside, unprepared to challenge France's hallowed labor laws. Rune shoved the cart into the elevator and punched the button for the ground floor. Her nerves thrummed. The blonde would eventually notice that her lipstick was gone. No biggie. The problem was the suitcase. She hadn't had time to lock it. One thing was easy to ignore. Two was a big ask. What if the woman complained? What if Philippe fired her? What if he called the police?

Over a tube of lipstick?

Reason prevailed. Her paranoia was just the hangover talking, the product of too many shots and not enough sleep. She got off the elevator and parked her cart in an empty hallway, then she dropped the lipstick in a trashcan and stepped outside. The Marseille sun beamed down on her. She turned to face it. Deep breath in, hold, release. Rinse and repeat. A few of those was enough to get her head straight.

A bus pulled up to the hotel. Tourists disgorged, noisy and stinking of BO. Rune lamented the loss of her peace and quiet and hurried inside to avoid them.

"That's her!"

The shrill voice sliced through the lobby. Rune turned in time to see the blonde from the sixth floor pointing an accusatory finger at her. Next to her was Philippe looking thoroughly pissed off. He motioned her over.

"What's up?" she said, playing dumb.

"That's her," the blonde repeated. "She's the one who came into my room!"

Philippe cast a worried eye at the tour group pouring into the lobby. "Ma'am, if you'll come with me, I'm sure we can resolve this in my office."

The first rule of hospitality: The guest is always right. The second: Even if the guest is wrong, refer to the first rule.

"I'm not going anywhere with you," the woman shrilled. "I want this handled here. Now!"

Philippe turned to Rune for an explanation. "Were you in this woman's room?"

"Yes," Rune said. "I cleaned it. Like I was told to."

"She stole five-hundred Euros from my suitcase."

What?

"I'm certain this is a misunderstanding," Philippe said quickly. "Please, if you'll just follow me."

"It's not a misunderstanding. She stole my money. You need to call the police."

Shit!

"Empty your pockets, Romy," Philippe said.

"Seriously?"

"Don't make me ask you again."

"This is bullshit." Rune glared at the blonde and turned her pockets inside out. Then she widened her eyes at Philippe as if to say, *see?*

"She must have hidden it somewhere," the woman said.

Rune couldn't believe it. The woman was doubling down. Why?

"Did you check your things?" Philippe asked her. "Perhaps the money is in a jacket pocket or in a different bag."

"Are you calling me a liar?" The woman's voice had gone up a notch. People at check-in turned to stare.

"Of course not," Philippe backtracked. He clasped his hands in a conciliatory manner. "What can I do to make this right?"

"You can start by finding my money."

"What if your stay at the hotel was on us? Two nights, correct? That roughly equals the amount you lost."

Rune glanced at Philippe. He looked pained, but from his perspective, comping a stay was better than the police getting involved.

"That won't do," the woman said. She crossed her arms and lifted her chin. The raking light accentuated her acne.

Philippe tried again. "I can also offer a complementary meal at our restaurant."

She remained unswayed.

"Perhaps a gift certificate for a future stay?"

Rune read the satisfaction in the woman's eyes. This was what she'd wanted all along, to milk as much free stuff out of them as possible. Rich people didn't stay at the Auberge du Monde. The Rimowa. The Lancôme lipstick. They were for show, to make her scam more believable.

"Fine," the woman said. She narrowed her eyes at Rune. "But I want her fired."

There was a moment of awkward silence. Philippe looked at the woman, then at Rune. "Get your things," he finally said. "Your pay will be mailed to you."

"But—"

"My decision is final."

Rune turned to the blonde. The woman glanced purposely at her lips. Her expression turned smug. She knew about the lipstick. As for Rune, she understood that she'd been bested, and she had no choice but to live with the punishment.

17

PARC BELLEVUE (FÉLIX PYAT), MARSEILLE

"**R**omy! Wait!"

Rune pretended not to hear Leila calling. She transferred her bag of cheap wine from one hand to the other and kept walking toward her apartment. Marseille's famous sunshine, uplifting on most days, was no match for her funk.

Two days had passed since the disaster at the hotel. She'd spent all that time inside with the blinds drawn, drinking herself to oblivion. A shortage of alcohol was the only reasons she was out in the world.

"Romy!"

Rune cringed. She was sick of being Romy Steiner, downtrodden and weary and stuck in a cité with all the other forgotten people. The problem was, being herself wasn't an option either. Every day since leaving Mallorca, she'd scoured the news for information about the Bonaparte thefts. Every day she'd wondered if law enforcement knew things they simply weren't sharing with the press. The media might have dropped the story, but that didn't mean the police had. And then there was Lemaire to think about. As long as he was out there, she would never be safe.

"Are you deaf?"

Rune let out a silent breath and turned to greet Leila. "Hi," she said, leaning in to accept her friend's kisses.

"I've been calling," Leila scolded. She smoothed her hijab with a manicured hand. "Where have you been?"

"Oh, around."

"If I didn't know better, I'd think you were avoiding me."

"I've been under the weather."

"Under the—?"

"Weather. It's an expression. I've been sick." Day drinking did that.

A troubled look passed over Leila's face. "Is the heater in your apartment working? The entire twelfth floor has been without heat for days. It's criminal to let people freeze like this."

Rune couldn't bring herself to pay attention when Leila droned on about starting a petition and staging a protest. She knew it would come to nothing. Leila knew it too. What was it she'd said the day they met? *In the cités, nothing ever gets fixed.*

Leila changed the subject, as if sensing Rune's apathy. "So, tell me," she said. "What happened with Djamel the other day?"

"You'll have to ask him."

Leila's well-shaped eyebrows shot up. "What does that mean?"

"It means I drank too much and woke up with him in my bed. I don't know what happened, but I can venture a guess." Rune normally censored herself around Leila, but that, too, required more energy than she was willing to expend. Silence dangled between them.

"I've been hearing things about you since that night," Leila said. "Just so you know, I'm here if you need to talk."

"I'm good."

"You're sure?"

"Yup." Rune didn't care if people were gossiping about her sex life. And she wasn't going to pretend to be hurt or damaged by a one-night stand. Part of her felt bad for shutting Leila out, but what was she supposed to do? Whine and cry about a guy she didn't even know? She had real problems to worry about. Anger swelled just thinking about what her life had become. It was directed primarily at Lemaire, but Milo and Kit weren't immune. They'd pretended to love her, but they'd abandoned her when she needed them most.

"Nathalie is saying crazy things."

Leila's words put a stop to Rune's stewing. "Who?"

"You met her the other night. She's the waitress at Isa's bar."

Rune didn't remember her. But then, so much about that night was fuzzy.

"She's convinced you're a thief and that you're hiding out at Félix Pyat. She says you stole jewels that belonged to Napoleon."

The bag of booze hit the pavement. The bottles broke on impact. Rune dropped to her knees.

"Just leave it," Leila said, thinking Rune was trying to clean the mess, not realizing that her legs had buckled. She gestured to the trash on the ground. "Really, it's what everyone else does."

Rune managed to stand. Her body shook terribly, but Leila didn't notice. She tried to think of an appropriate response to the Nathalie bombshell. She didn't have one. "A jewel thief, huh?" She forced a chuckle. "I wish." It was weak, but it was the best she could do under the circumstance. She was trying to come up with something to add when two young men in loose jeans and hooded sweatshirts rushed toward them.

"Keufs," one of them muttered as he walked past.

Leila gave a derisive snort.

"What's that about?" Rune asked.

"It's a warning."

She followed Leila's gaze to a black van with tinted windows pulling in between Buildings A and B.

"Keufs is slang for flics. Cops," Leila explained. "It's kind of like pig Latin. The syllables and sounds are inverted."

Cops. The word nearly sent Rune to the ground again. Her heart leapt. Her breath felt like it was trapped inside her chest.

"They think we're idiots," Leila said, oblivious to Rune's distress. "Can you believe the van?"

"What are they doing here?" Rune asked. Her voice was taut and unnaturally high.

"Drugs, weapons, girls. Who knows?" Leila shrugged. "There was a shoot-out at La Paternelle last week. A couple of Félix Pyat dealers were involved. Maybe they're cracking down."

Rune wanted to believe that Leila was right—that the cops were there to quell the violence between two rival cités—but every cell in her body told her otherwise. Self-blame set in. This was her own damn fault. She'd lowered her guard. No, it was worse than that, she'd been downright careless, going to a packed bar, letting strangers into her life and home. Nosy Nathalie had clearly recognized her that night at Isa's. It wasn't a stretch to think she went to the police to collect the reward. Or maybe it was her one-night stand with Djamel. Who knew what secrets she divulged during their drunken roll in the hay?

"You look pale, Romy. Are you okay?"

Rune looked into her friend's concerned eyes. "I'm not feeling very well," she said. It was true. Fear was boring holes into the lining of her stomach. She couldn't risk going back to her apartment, but she couldn't leave without her go-bag. Everything that mattered was in there—her money, her papers, her old phone with all her contacts and photos.

"Let's get you home," Leila said, wrapping a protective arm around Rune's shoulders.

Rune leaned against Leila all the way back to Building A6. She cast a quick look over her shoulder before stepping inside. There was no movement in the black van, but out of an abundance of caution, she waited until the door closed behind them before speaking again. "Do you think I could lie down at your place for a few minutes? I hate to ask, but I don't think I can walk up all those stairs."

"Of course! I should have offered!"

Rune smiled weakly and allowed herself to be led down the hall to Apartment 106. She stood back while Leila wrestled with her key. It seemed Rune wasn't the only one with a sticky lock.

"Have a seat," Leila said once they were inside. "I'll get you some water."

Rune lowered herself onto the couch and surveyed the room. Leila's apartment was as rundown and depressing as hers, but there were colorful fashion magazines on the coffee table, right next to three oversized science tomes.

"Who do the books belong to?" she asked after Leila returned.

"My sister, Myriam. She's studying to be a nurse." Leila placed the glass on the table and sat down.

"She lives with you?"

"Mm-hmm."

The discovery reminded Rune that she really didn't know Leila, which meant that she really couldn't trust her. She was trying to figure out how to retrieve her go-bag when Leila did something few people managed to do. She surprised her.

"My family has a lot of problems," Leila said. "My father lost his job a few years ago. He started drinking. The situation wasn't good, so Myriam moved in with me."

"That must have been an adjustment."

"It was." She made a face, then brightened. "But it's gotten better. I only have one rule. She has to stay in school. I don't want her to get stuck here." The implied *like me* hung in the air.

Despite the circumstances, Leila's words moved Rune. They reminded her of how Kit had stepped up for Madee after their parents died. Theirs was a selfless love. The fact that it was between siblings and not a parent and child somehow made it even more precious. "Myriam is lucky to have you," Rune said softly.

Leila let out a small laugh. "Tell her that for me, will you?"

"I mean it."

Leila leaned in and placed her palm on Rune's forehead. "You feel hot."

"I'm alright. I just need my migraine meds."

"Medication? I can run to the pharmacy."

"It's okay. I have some upstairs."

Leila took the bait. "Why didn't you say so? I could have been there and back already!"

"That's really not necessary."

"N'importe quoi!" *Nonsense!*

Rune gave a well-timed wince. As she did, she realized that the stereotype of the mean French person was just that—a stereotype. French people might seem cold initially, but once they embraced you, they did so with their whole hearts.

"Give me your key," Leila said, proving the point. She held out her hand. "Come on. I won't take no for an answer."

"Well, if you really don't mind."

"I don't. Where are the pills?"

"In a bag on the floor in my bedroom, in one of the pockets. It might be easier if you bring me the whole thing."

"Say no more."

Rune didn't dare move until Leila was out the door. She waited for the latch to catch, then raced to the window. The van was still in the parking lot, but there were no cops in sight. She could still get away. She ran into the kitchen and tore through the drawers until she found a small knife. She jammed it into her jacket pocket, then hurried to the bathroom to raid Leila's makeup drawer. The bedroom came next. She hesitated before swiping a black-and-white headscarf from the dresser.

Loud whistles sounded outside. Rune dashed back to the living room in time to see eight police officers pour out of the van. Shouts of "keufs" and "flics" rang out across the complex as residents warned each other of the impending raid. Those who happened to be outside scattered. Rune turned to the front door and willed Leila to walk through it.

Come on!

The sound of boots clomping sent Rune into a panic. She thought about jumping out of the window, but she wouldn't get far without her bag. The doorknob turned.

"What are you doing with that?"

Rune looked down at the scarf in her hand.

"Well?" Leila didn't look angry, just disappointed. And hurt. She held up two passports—Rune's and Romy's—and tossed them on the coffee table. The duffel clunked to the floor.

Rune thought about spinning another lie, but instinct told her not to. It was time to come clean. She owed Leila that much. "What the waitress said about me—it's true. I stole the Bonaparte jewels. The police are here for me."

"I gathered."

"I got mixed up in something." Rune struggled with her next words. "I-I'm not a bad person."

"I would never think that."

Rune sat, mute, unsure what to do with Leila's compassion. She wouldn't have been so understanding had the roles been reversed.

"I don't care that you steal," Leila said. "And I won't say anything to the cops, but you can't stay here."

Relief and gratitude washed over Rune. Leila's contempt for the police ran so deep she was willing to forgo the reward and let her get away. There was so much Rune wanted to say. She wanted to apologize for stealing something that obviously mattered to Leila. She wanted to tell her that their friendship was real, even if nothing else about her was. But most of all, she wanted to thank her—for her openness, her kindness, her generosity. There was so much to say, but none of it would come out.

Shouts sounded in the hallway. Police sirens wailed nearby.

Leila pointed to the scarf. "Put it on. Quickly."

Rune draped it over her head and tied a knot beneath her chin.

"Not like that."

Her hands came down.

Leila adjusted the fabric so it covered Rune's hairline, then threw one end over the opposite shoulder. She stood back and nodded. "Better."

It was a small thing, but it meant the world to Rune. She gave her friend a grateful smile.

"What did I say about doing that, Romy from 703?"

Tears pooled in Rune's eyes. Leila blinked back her own. They sat with the moment, giving it space, knowing it would probably be their last.

"Go," Leila finally said.

Rune grabbed her bag and hurried toward the door. Her chin trembled when her hand found the knob. She held it together until the door closed behind her. Only then did she allow the tears to come.

18

PARC BELLEVUE (FÉLIX PYAT), MARSEILLE

Everything was different when Rune stepped out of Building A6. News of the police presence had spread through the cité like wildfire. No one knew why the cops were there, but that hadn't stop rankled residents from mobilizing outside the building to rally for one of their own. Some live streamed the gathering on social media. Others chanted "La police tue!"—*The police kill!*—over the discordant sounds of thunder sticks and cowbells.

Rune wove through a crowd that extended all the way to the adjacent building. She was somewhere in the middle of the pack when someone shouted, "Les voilà!" *There they are!* She turned in time to see a pair of officers emerge from her building. Having found her apartment empty, the two were now on crowd control duty. Their M4 carbines and black balaclavas made the hair on her body stand at attention. If this was who the authorities sent to arrest a solitary jewel thief, she hated to see who they sent after other types of criminals.

"Mort aux flics!" *Death to the cops!* someone yelled. Another person joined in, then another and another until the chanting reached fever pitch. A beer bottle zipped through the air, barely missing one of the officers before smashing into tiny pieces. Stirred up, the crowd began shouting profanities, none of which required a knowledge of French to understand: "Racistes! Assassins!" The vitriol was nothing new. If history repeated itself, the violence brewing between the police and the residents of Félix Pyat was a foregone conclusion.

A series of explosive *booms* sounded nearby. Rune spun around and saw a group of teenagers shooting fireworks at each other like they were playing a game of paintball. Out of the corner of her eye, she saw a masked man with a long metal rod race toward the police van. The cops saw him too. They ordered the man to stop, but their words went unheeded. The man raised his rod. The windshield shattered. A Molotov cocktail landed on the driver's seat, engulfing the van in orange and blue flames.

Rune was not violent by nature, but she was by no means a pacifist. More than anything, she knew how to seize an opportunity. "Forward!" she yelled at the top of her lungs. She moved back when everyone else pushed ahead. In no time, she found herself on the edge of the pack and a good hundred feet from Building A6. She was just starting to believe that everything would be okay when a dark BMW sped past. The passenger side window rolled down. Something glistened in the light.

"Flingue!" *Gun!*

Some people hit the ground. Others scattered to safety. Rune alone stood immobile, rooted in place in shock and fear. A spray of bullets erupted. Screams followed. Tires squealed as the BMW peeled away.

For a moment, Rune was the only person at Félix Pyat who knew the truth, the only person who knew that what happened wasn't a drive-by but something called a *fantasia,* when gang members drove into rival territory and shot in the air in a show of dominance and strength. It was a common occurrence in the cités but no less frightening for it.

The cops jumped to their feet as soon as they realized the danger had passed. One started shouting into his radio, the other pulled out his sidearm and aimed at the BMW. Rune was terrified he'd shoot even with innocents in the way. His weapon came down. Reason prevailed. He turned to check on his partner.

It was the act of turning that put Rune in the officer's sightline. This shouldn't have come as a surprise. She was the only person still on her feet. She might as well have had a spotlight on her. Their eyes locked.

Rune broke the connection by adjusting Leila's hijab. If the officer had any suspicions about her, they dissolved when she drew attention to her headscarf. He was looking for a half-American, half-Thai jewel thief, not a devout Muslim from the projects. He turned away. She did the same.

Only after Rune reached the outskirts of the cité did she begin to process what had happened. Her cover was blown. The life she'd created for herself at Félix Pyat was over. She'd have to start from scratch in a new place, with new people, under a new identity. How she was supposed to do that without a penny to her name was a big question mark.

A procession of police cars zipped past, sirens blaring. Rune expected them to make a U-turn and arrest her on the spot, but the sirens grew distant and faint. A furtive glance back confirmed they were gone. Her hands shaking, she swapped Leila's headscarf for a baseball cap and put on a pair of sunglasses. Minutes later, she lowered her head and slipped into the metro.

The southbound M2 was neither too full nor too empty when it pulled into the station not long after. Rune chose a forward-facing seat at the back of the car and kept her eyes down. She stayed that way until she reached Saint Charles in the city center. The station was home not just to Marseille's two metro lines but also to the long-distance railway. Rune knew it would be teeming with law enforcement from at least three agencies—the gendarmerie, the national police, and railway safety—but she didn't care. She needed to get out of the city, and this was the quickest option.

She was the first person off the metro when the doors opened. She joined the hordes heading to the escalator and stepped on. "Excuse me," she said to a couple occupying its entire width. The woman cracked her gum as she squeezed past. The man rolled his eyes. There were two types of people in the world: those who used escalators to get to where they were going more quickly and those who thought it was a ride. Rune disproportionately found herself behind the latter.

The long-distance train hall was packed. Rune located the departures board and gave it a quick scan. A train was leaving for Amsterdam in ten minutes. Perfect. But what would she do when she got there? She needed a plan. She needed help. She thought about calling Milo, but she'd promised she wouldn't and she didn't want to go back on her word. What she needed was someone she could leverage or someone who needed her as much as she needed them.

Romy.

The idea popped into her head and immediately took root. Romy, who was stuck in an abusive marriage. Romy, who was so scared of her husband she hid divorce papers under her child's mattress. Romy, who had access to unlimited wealth. The more Rune thought about the idea, the more convinced she was of its merits. But would Romy agree? And without a phone number, how was she supposed to contact her?

A woman with a small black suitcase walked past. She lit up when she saw a man with a baby in one arm and flowers in the other. The two embraced. For Rune, it was more than just a heartwarming sight.

She pulled out her phone and searched for an online florist with same-day delivery. She selected two identical bouquets of vibrant tropicals. One went to the Steiners' Deauville house, the other to the Berlin address on Romy's passport. With luck, Romy would be at one of the two. The tricky part was the card. Rune thought about it for a moment, then typed: *I know what he does to you. I can help. Meet me in Amsterdam, Dam Square, 11.19, 10:00* A.M. She used Romy's credit card to check out. Then she put her phone away and joined the line at a ticket machine. She didn't know if Romy would show, but with their meeting scheduled for the next day, she was about to find out.

PART 3

19

LEIDSEPLEIN, AMSTERDAM

L eidseplein in central Amsterdam was the perfect place to remain
anonymous. Every night, locals and tourists went to the square in
droves, crowding its restaurants and bars to the wee hours. Even on
this bracing evening, the outdoor terraces were packed with brave souls
in cozy knits yucking it up over shots of jenever and pints of beer. The
city was experiencing its worst cold snap in decades, but if the crowds at
the Leidseplein were any indication, the people of Amsterdam weren't
letting that get in the way of a good time.

Rune started shivering the instant she stepped off the tram. The
clothes she'd fled Marseille in were completely unsuited for the arctic
dome hovering over the Netherlands. She clenched and unclenched her
fists to coax blood back into her fingers before ducking into a clothing
store just off the plaza.

"We're closing in ten minutes," said a golden-haired saleswoman
with the physique of a runway model.

"I'll be quick," Rune replied through chattering teeth.

True to her word, she emerged from the store exactly six minutes
later wearing a black parka with an adjustable hood, a floppy wool hat,

and comfortable boots the clerk promised were the warmest money could buy. Next on the agenda was a pharmacy. Rune grabbed what she needed, then headed to a busy sports bar with three unisex bathrooms in the basement. She slipped into an empty stall. The air smelled like artificial freshener and stale beer. The tiles felt tacky under the soles of her new boots. The night was young, but the sink was already filthy.

Rune released her hair from the hat and shook it out. She pulled a pair of scissors from her shopping bag and snipped away until she was left with an uneven pixie and bangs slashed a bit too high above her eyes. Her sense of urgency grew as she opened a box of hair dye. She mixed the contents until they turned an alarming shade of blue and massaged the cream into her hair. She swapped her dark contacts for a lighter pair while she waited for the dye to set. By the time her transformation was complete, she barely recognized the gray-eyed blonde staring back at her from the mirror. Any misgivings she might have had about shedding her Romy persona dissipated when she heard the doorknob jiggle.

"Just a second," she called out. She used the kohl pencil she stole from Leila to line her eyes. A swipe of her friend's pink lipstick went on next. The results were iffy, but another jiggle convinced her it was time to go. She tossed her belongings into her new leather backpack and took a last look around the stall. Positive she had everything that mattered, she threw the door open and stepped out.

"Oh!"

The middle-aged man she slammed into had the physique of a former athlete, with an impressively broad chest that was just starting to soften. His nose and lips were fleshy. There were dark smudges under his eyes.

"Careful there," he said, grabbing her arm to keep her steady. He sized her up. His expression morphed into a leer. "Aren't you a pretty thing."

She turned away from him. His breath was foul, like garbage liquefying under the sun.

"What's the matter, blondie? Cat got your tongue?"

She cursed herself silently. She'd chosen to go blonde to blend in with the locals, but the color had drawbacks, one of which was blocking her path. She wrenched her arm out of his grasp and walked away.

"It's polite to say thank you when someone pays you a compliment," the man bellowed.

Rune kept walking. She was halfway up the stairs when she heard him yell, "Stuck-up bitch!"

The recriminations began as soon as Rune stepped outside. Why hadn't she told the man off? Why hadn't she come up with a clever retort? Why hadn't she said something—anything—to stand up for herself? But she knew why. Life on the run had fundamentally changed how she moved through the world. She'd squashed her old self, done everything in her power to make herself small. The realization filled her with deep sadness. Not only had she lost her freedom working for Lemaire, but somewhere along the way, she'd lost herself too.

20

CENTRAL AMSTERDAM

R une waited in line at the reception counter of the Kaartenhuis—the House of Cards—a boutique hotel just off Leidseplein in Amsterdam's historic center. The Dutch couple being helped had been arguing with the young clerk about noisy neighbors for what felt like an eternity, holding up a queue that was now six people long. A supervisor eventually arrived to placate the unhappy guests, freeing up the harried clerk. Rune didn't wait for him to make eye contact before approaching. If he was put off by that, he didn't let it show.

"Good evening. Welcome to the Kaartenhuis," he said, his voice as artificially bright as his smile.

"I'd like a room, please," Rune said, wasting no time on niceties. She sensed the collective gratitude of the people behind her.

"Do you have a reservation?"

"I don't."

"How long will you be staying with us?"

"Just one night."

The clerk typed a few words on his keyboard. He drummed his fingers on the counter while he waited for the results, then read from his screen. "I have a single room on the courtyard or a single facing the canal."

"Nothing larger?"

"Unfortunately not. It's the winter festival. We're fully booked."

"I'll take the canal."

"Certainly. I'll need your passport."

Rune had no intention of checking in under her real name, but she couldn't use Romy's either. Not after what happened in Marseille. If the French knew about her cover, there was a good chance the Dutch did too. She feigned a look of worry. "I don't have any ID."

"I'm very sorry," the clerk said. "But I can't give you a room without a passport. It's EU law."

Rune allowed her bottom lip to quiver. Not too much, just enough for him to notice. "My passport was stolen. I'm waiting for a replacement. It won't be ready until tomorrow morning."

The clerk started to shake his head.

"Please," Rune said, raising her voice just enough to draw the manager's attention. "It's cold outside, and I don't have anywhere else to stay."

He held up his hands like a traffic cop and glanced at his supervisor. The last thing he needed was another customer service fiasco. "It's okay. I can check you in now and you can bring the passport tomorrow, when you check out."

"Really? That's so nice of you!"

The clerk seemed chuffed by the compliment. "I'll just need your name and contact information."

Rune gave him a phony name and a California address.

"Your total is two-hundred-and-twenty Euros."

She counted out the bills and slid them across the counter.

"Room 501," the clerk said as he handed her a keycard. "Breakfast starts at seven. Check-out is before noon. Enjoy your stay."

Rune thanked him and took the elevator to the fifth floor. She found her room at the end of a hallway decorated with mass-produced prints of tulips and windmills. Like the artwork, the room was surprisingly generic for an establishment that called itself a boutique hotel. Exhausted from her long, stressful day, she stripped off her new parka and promptly collapsed on the bed.

A sliver of light filtering from between the curtains woke Rune early the next morning, interrupting the dream playing on repeat inside her head. It was a dream she knew well, one she'd had since she was a child. It started with her hiding in an industrial-sized workshop. Alone. Terrified. What she was doing there and who she was hiding from remained a mystery, even after all these years.

She was barefoot in her dream. Wood shavings dug into her soles as she scurried from one hiding spot to the next to evade an unseen pursuer. Her dream was soundless, like an old silent film or a new one playing on mute. The details varied—the color of her clothes, the tools on the walls, the arrangement of the machinery—but it always ended the same way: with her making a desperate run for the door. Then it restarted without her ever knowing if she'd escaped.

Rune never talked to anyone about her dream—not to her parents, not even to Kit—but when she thought about it, she always called it a dream, not a nightmare, as if using that word would somehow make it more terrifying. The dream was a defining aspect of her childhood, the thing that made her fight sleep from the time she entered first grade until the summer she started high school. After that, it was reality that kept her up at night.

Rune kicked the covers off her body and rubbed the sleep out of her eyes. Reliving her childhood dream was more unsettling than it was frightening. She didn't feel refreshed, but at least she wasn't afraid. She took that as a good sign as she got ready for her meeting with Romy. It wasn't for another few hours, but she wanted to get to Dam Square early. For all she knew, Alaric had intercepted the flowers and was waiting to pummel her.

There was only one guest in the restaurant when Rune came down for breakfast not long after. She watched a sullen businessman from the doorway for several seconds before concluding that it was safe to enter. Not once did he look up as she filled two plates and teetered toward a table with a clear view of the exit. She sat down and started shoveling food into her mouth. Her stomach gurgled in protest. She didn't let that slow her. She was so preoccupied with her breakfast that she didn't notice the waiter until he was practically on top of her. So much for staying vigilant.

"Would you like coffee or tea?" he asked.

"Coffee. Black," she said through a mouthful of pastry. She licked her lips. They were coated in icing sugar.

He returned a few minutes later with a cup that was larger than an espresso but smaller than the typical American coffee. She took a sip after it passed the sniff test, then checked her phone for alerts. There were dozens from various European news outlets. All described how the Bonaparte thief hid in plain sight. All mentioned Romy by name. Quotes from neighbors and coworkers ranged from "she seemed so normal" to "no one had any idea."

A camera hung in the corner of the room. Rune smoothed her hair, still damp from her morning shower. It was a good thing she'd changed her appearance. Everywhere she went, Big Brother was watching. There was every reason to believe the police had tracked her from the cité to the train station and then to Amsterdam. If they could do it, so could Lemaire. The thought was enough to kill her appetite.

The front desk clerk waved her down when she walked through the lobby. He gently reminded her that he needed to see her passport when she checked out. She lied and said she was heading to the consulate. "I'll be right back," she promised, knowing she'd never see him again. She truly hoped he didn't get fired.

A porter in a navy overcoat nodded at Rune when she exited the hotel. A burst of cold air clawed at her face. It wasn't unpleasant. On the contrary, it sharpened her senses. She raised her hood and adjusted her backpack before setting off on foot to Dam Square. Her app said it was twenty minutes away, but it didn't know she walked like a New Yorker. She dodged early birds with tripods and selfie sticks as she crossed four canals. Then she took a left on Kalverstraat, one of the busiest shopping streets in Amsterdam. From there, it was a straight shot to her destination.

Dam Square was bigger and grander than Rune expected. It was shaped like a rectangle, if said rectangle had been drawn by a toddler. Dominating the west side was the Royal Palace, a neoclassical building whose rigorous symmetry only emphasized the irregularity of its surroundings. Next to it, on the square's northwestern corner, was the Nieuwe Kerk, a fifteenth-century Gothic church turned exhibition hall. Historic buildings of various shapes, sizes, and vintages lined the rest of the square.

Rune scanned the area. She hadn't given Romy a specific meeting place, and the options were numerous. The area directly in front of the Royal Palace was a strong contender, but then, so was the entrance to the Nieuwe Kerk. She looked to the opposite end of the plaza and squinted. In the distance, framed by five-star hotels and luxury clothing stores, was a white conical pillar set on a series of concentric rings arranged to form a staircase. Two sculpted lions perched on circular pedestals flanked the pillar. Rune nodded once. It was perfect. She waited for a tram to pass, then strode into the square.

The pillar was the National Monument, a memorial to the victims of World War II, according to a tour guide speaking loudly enough to wake the dead. Rune tried to tune him out, but he took the idea of the outside voice to a whole new level. He went on and on about the personification of Victory on the front of the pillar and the figures representing the Dutch resistance below. He pointed to the semicircular wall behind the pillar and explained that it contained soil from war cemeteries from across the country. As for the lions, they were symbols of the Netherlands.

The crowd around the monument was thick, even at this early hour. *Good*, Rune thought. Crowds made for easy getaways. She walked around the pillar and saw several streets leading away from the square. The tram stop directly across from the monument might also come in handy. Worst-case scenario, she could disappear inside one of the hotels, a skill she'd honed during her many escapades in Bangkok.

Church bells rang. Rune looked at her watch. Her meeting wasn't for another thirty minutes. She planted herself at an outdoor café with a clear view of the monument and immediately started shivering. The space heaters were set to high, but they couldn't compete with the cold snap.

Ten o'clock came and went. Worry crept in. Maybe Romy was waiting on the other end of the square. Maybe she decided not to come. Maybe she hadn't gotten the message at all. Rune thought about bailing. This whole thing had always been a long shot.

And then she saw her. She blinked and looked again to make sure. Yes, it was Romy alright. She was even more beautiful in person than she was in her passport photo. She wore a cable knit scarf and a long coat that was cinched at the waist. Her dark hair was swept back and loosely tied at the base of her neck. Her makeup was at once put together and effortless. Rune swallowed nervously. Her pitch had to be perfect. Everything was riding on it.

She approached from the rear. Tension rose with every step. By the time she reached the halfway point, her heart was beating so fast it felt like someone was punching her in the chest. What if this was a mistake? What if Romy had figured out who she was and called the police? Everyone around her felt like a threat—the woman with the camera, the man on his phone, the nanny pushing a pram. Still, she kept walking. She walked until she reached the circular platform. She walked until Romy was just steps away. The urge to turn around and run swept over her. Instead, she steeled herself and counted down in time with her stride.

Five . . . four . . . three . . . two . . . one . . .
"Romy. Hi."

21

DAM SQUARE, AMSTERDAM

"Who the hell are you?!"

Romy's accent was as clipped as Rune remembered, her eyes as troubled as in her photos. It felt strange meeting the woman whose identity she'd stolen. "Come with me," she said, stifling the feeling. "We don't have a lot of time."

"I'm not going anywhere until you tell me what this is about."

A group of tweens chose that precise moment to charge toward the monument. Rune and Romy were surrounded in seconds. One girl lit a cigarette and stank up the area. Another started live-streaming without a second thought to anyone's privacy. Rune angled her head away from the pack. Romy nodded once.

"Who are you?" Romy repeated when they reached the back of the monument.

"I'm the person who can help you get out of your marriage."

Romy looked over her shoulder, like she was worried she'd been followed.

"I know what your husband does to you. I know you want to leave him. That's why you came here today."

"You don't know what you're talking about."

"I saw the divorce papers. I think you're scared of him. It's why you hid them, right?"

Anger flashed across Romy's face. "Deauville? That was you?"

"It was."

"You—you broke into our house. You took irreplaceable things!"

"Keep your voice down," Rune said. She glanced around to make sure no one had heard, then she gave Romy some unsolicited advice. "You can't keep the papers under the bed. It's a terrible hiding place. Put them in a safe deposit box or give them to a friend."

No response.

"I heard you fighting. I know he hurt you. How long before he does it again?"

Still nothing.

"What about your kids?"

"My kids?" Romy echoed. "You don't think I know what this is doing to them? You don't think I'm terrified he'll turn on them?"

"Then let me help you."

"You don't understand."

"Explain it to me."

Romy's features darkened. She studied Rune. Assessing. Calculating. Then she opened her coat and raised the hem of her sweater.

"Jesus," Rune said.

Romy's abdomen was a tableau of violence, an amorphous patchwork of greens and purples and reds. Rune looked away. The sweater came down.

"He always hits me where it doesn't show," Romy said.

Rune weighed her next words carefully. She'd experienced many kinds of violence, from the Muay Thai ring to back-alley fights, but this was something different. This involved the heart. What did she know about the heart? "Have you ever reported him?"

"Do you know who my husband is?"

Rune didn't. Not really, anyway. Her focus had been on Alaric's parents.

"He's not the kind of person you leave."

"I get it," Rune said. "He's rich and powerful. That doesn't mean he's above the law."

Romy scoffed.

"I'm serious."

Her scoff turned into a resigned sigh. She cast her eyes to something or someone in the distance. "Alaric is an old Germanic name," she said quietly. She turned back to Rune. "Do you know what it means?"

Rune shook her head.

"Ruler of all. Can you believe that?"

She could. Margot and Rolf seemed like exactly the type to give their son a grandiose name and raise him to believe it.

"Everyone loves Alaric—his friends, my friends—everyone. They think he's smart and funny and charming. But they don't know anything."

Rune shivered. From the cold. From talking about the Steiners.

"We met at university. I wasn't interested in him at first. He was too stiff and square. But he was persistent. He sent me roses every day for two weeks until I finally agreed to go out with him. He took me to the opera, the ballet, fancy restaurants. On weekends, when everyone else was studying, he'd whisk me away to Venice or Vienna or some other impossibly romantic place. It was a dream."

What Romy described sounded more like a nightmare to Rune. Over-the-top romance was never about the pursued, always about the pursuer.

"I knew something was off almost from the start. He'd get jealous if I mentioned my ex-boyfriends. Whenever I caught him in a lie, he'd turn it around and accuse me of not trusting him. He never apologized.

Nothing was ever his fault. In hindsight, the signs were everywhere, I just didn't want to see them." Romy expelled a breath, like she couldn't quite believe her own blindness. "It got worse after we had our first son. Alaric wanted constant attention, and when I couldn't give it to him, he raged. He punched holes in the walls of our bedroom. Drove like a maniac with us in the car. And once, when our nanny was away and our son started fussing during dinner, he turned the table over and screamed like a lunatic. Can you imagine? A grown man having a tantrum?"

Rune didn't know what to say. She'd encountered plenty of wackos, but she'd never had to live with one.

"Alaric went to work for his father's company after he finished his studies. He started traveling a lot, especially after the birth of our second son. He said it was for our family, but I think he just wanted to get away from us." Romy's voice turned bitter. "He treats us like dirt except when he needs us—at parties and work functions—then we dress up and smile so everyone can see what a perfect couple we are and what well-behaved children we have."

Doubt crept into Rune's mind. Maybe attaching herself to someone with these kinds of problems was a bad idea.

"I told my husband I was leaving him a few months ago. Do you know what he said to me?"

Rune indicated she didn't.

"He threatened to have me institutionalized. He could do it too. He's connected. There isn't a doctor or judge his family can't bribe. If I try to fight, they'll bury me in legal fees. My mother-in-law told me as much."

The guilt Rune felt about sending Margot flying down the Louvre's staircase evaporated. She was awful. The whole family was.

"Do you see now? There's no getting away from Alaric. I just have to protect my children and hope things get better."

"Really?" The word came out more harshly than Rune intended. She softened her tone. "Crossing your fingers isn't a plan."

Romy shrugged, despondent.

"Let me help you."

"You can't help me."

"I can." She believed it. She'd gotten out of worse situations. "What if I could make you disappear?"

"You couldn't even make yourself disappear."

Good point. Rune puzzled for a moment, then she realized she had it backwards. Alaric was the one who had to disappear. Not disappear as in die, he just had to be taken out of the equation. "I can get Alaric out of your hair," she said. She liked the idea even more now that she'd said it out loud.

"How?"

"I'll find away. Trust me."

"I don't trust you. I don't know you."

"My name is Rune Sarasin."

"You're nothing but a thief."

"I had to do that." Rune turned apologetic. "If I could give you your things back, I would."

"You think I care about the jewels?"

Rune tried a different approach. "Your in-laws are Big Pharma," she said, remembering Milo's disdain for the Steiners. "I'm sure they do all kinds of shady things. I can do some digging."

"And then what?"

"And then they get caught. And then they go to prison. Or at least they're not untouchable anymore."

Romy looked hopeful, but hope soon morphed into suspicion. "Why would you do this? Why would you want to help me?"

"Because I need you as much as you need me," she said bluntly. "The man who's pulling the strings—a man named Lemaire—I can connect him to a bunch of thefts. He's coming for me. He'll have me killed."

Romy's eyes softened. A bond started to form. She understood what it was to fear a powerful man.

"I can do this," Rune said. "But I need money to make it happen."

"Alaric handles our finances. He'd notice if money went missing."

Rune was stunned. Romy appeared to have it all—family, beauty, wealth—but she couldn't withdraw money from her own account without her husband knowing about it. Rune felt sorry for her. Then she felt sorry for herself. Without Romy's help, she was back to square one. She'd have to go back into hiding. She'd have to find another shitty job in another shitty place and spend the rest of her life looking over her shoulder.

Unless.

"Your ring," she said.

Romy glanced at her wedding band, an eternity ring of shimmery diamonds.

"Give it to me and I'll help you."

"How do I know you won't just take it and disappear?" Romy's tone was pleading. She wanted to believe. She was desperate for a lifeline.

"You don't," Rune said with a slow shake of the head. "The same way I don't know you won't call the cops on me. We just have to trust each other."

Romy toyed with her ring.

"I'll help you. I promise."

The word of a thief wasn't worth much, but doing something was better than doing nothing. Rune waited for Romy to realize that. The wait stretched on. Her stress rose.

"Alright," Romy finally said.

Rune's body loosened. She didn't actually know if she could help Romy or if Romy could help her. But it didn't matter. She had hope. She had a partner. After all this time, it was a relief not to be alone anymore.

Romy evidently felt the same way. She grabbed Rune's hand and turned toward the National Monument. The white pillar thrust skyward, majestic, triumphant. "See the sculptures over there?" she said.

Rune did.

"They're doves. They symbolize the liberation of the Netherlands from German control after the Second World War."

Rune smiled softly. Romy wasn't just making conversation. She was telling her something important. She was saying they were on the same page. She squeezed her hand.

Romy squeezed back.

"If we work together, we can both have that," Rune said. "We can both be free."

22

CENTRAL AMSTERDAM

Rune's father was big on Thai proverbs. Every night, he came home from work, loosened his tie, and recited a saying that captured a key aspect of his day. One of the most memorable was *Ni seua pa jorake. Escape a tiger, meet a crocodile.* Rune was seven when she heard the proverb for the first time. Her father had just resigned from a job he hated, only to hate the next one even more. She was only a kid, but she remembered thinking that the proverb didn't fit the context. Bad jobs were annoying. Tigers and crocodiles? Those could kill you. So could gemstone traffickers and pharma execs with everything to lose.

Rune and Romy had parted ways without a firm plan but with something that was arguably more valuable—a solemn pact to help one another. Each had something the other needed. Romy hadn't wasted time proving her worth.

Take the ring. It's yours.

I'll pay you back, I promise.

I don't care about that. Just deal with Alaric.

I will, but it might take time.

Not too long, I hope.

Rune's features clouded when she thought about those words. How much more would Romy have to endure? What if Alaric went after the children? She tightened her hold on her backpack. As she did, she couldn't help but wonder if Romy was the most brilliant woman she'd ever met, or a damned fool. What kind of person handed a stranger their jewelry?

Rune looked over her shoulder. Romy was in front of Madame Tussauds waving at a muscular woman shepherding two mischievous looking boys. The older boy ran into Romy's arms. The younger one was too busy eating a stroopwafel to notice. As she watched them disappear into the museum, she realized that her new ally was neither brilliant nor foolish. She was just a mother desperate to protect her children.

"Watch it!"

Rune jumped out of the way of the speeding cyclist.

"You're in the bike lane," a guy in a Michelin Man puffer pointed out.

Rune indicated she understood, then pulled out her phone to look for a place to unload Romy's ring. The options ranged from vintage jewelry stores to a not-for-profit municipal pawn shop. She picked the closest store, jammed her hands inside her pockets, and set off on foot. She managed to get there without getting lost, a small miracle given the labyrinth that was Amsterdam.

The shop was warm and full of treasures, a mix of pre-owned jewelry and antique housewares. Rings, watches, necklaces, and more filled the display cases. Silver and gold chains hung from velvet stands behind the counter. Rune ogled an Art Deco choker with a rock-crystal pendant and a Victorian broach covered in pink rubies while she waited for the clerk to finish with another customer. It took longer than expected.

"Are you looking to buy or sell?" the clerk finally asked her. His Donegal sweater was too big for his frame. His white hair was wispy and limp.

"Sell." Rune fished Romy's ring out of her coat pocket and placed it in front of him.

The clerk picked it up and peered at it through a jeweler's loupe. "This is nice," he said as he inspected it from all sides. "Very nice."

"It belonged to my mother. She passed away." The information was supposed to ward off questions, but the clerk took it as an invitation to share.

"I lost my mother when I was about your age," he said.

"I'm sorry to hear that."

"We were very close. I never got over it."

"Oh." The conversation was getting uncomfortable.

"Your mother's ring is exquisite. Are you sure you want to part with it? It may not seem important now, but you might want something of hers down the road."

Rune blinked at him.

He must have sensed he'd overstepped because he went into business mode. "I can offer you five thousand Euros," he said, keeping a firm hold on the ring.

Rune cleared her throat. The man thought she was a fool. It was time to educate him. "These are high-grade diamonds," she said matter-of-factly. "The color, cut, and clarity are near perfect. And we're looking at a total of four, maybe four-and-a-half carats. Thirty thousand Euros would be a bargain for a piece like this."

The man opened and closed his mouth without saying anything.

"Do we have a deal?" Rune asked.

"No deal."

She waited for his counteroffer.

"The resale value for diamond jewelry is between twenty and sixty percent of the original sale price," the clerk explained.

Rune knew that. Thirty thousand was an absurd ask, but as with any negotiation, it was smart to start high. "Five thousand is too low."

She plucked the ring from his fingers. "Thanks for your time. I'll try the Municipal Pawn Shop."

"I'll give you ten thousand," the clerk said quickly.

Rune thought about it.

"It's a fair offer. Take it or leave it."

"I'll take it."

He disappeared to the back of the store. The door burst open. A mother and daughter swept inside, cheeks red, cold on their breath. They went straight to the counter. The mother said hello while the daughter scrolled mindlessly on her phone. Rune snuck a peek. The Bonaparte story flashed on her screen.

No, no, no!

The clerk returned with an envelope in one hand and cash in the other. Rune felt sick watching him count the bills. The daughter was still scrolling.

"It's all here," he finally said.

She stuffed the envelope into her backpack and grunted her thanks. She had what she came for. It was time to get out of Amsterdam.

The street was eerily quiet when Rune stepped outside. She passed an empty stationary store, two bakeries with three customers between them, and a closed tobacco shop. A tram pulled into a stop down the block. The direction of the tracks suggested it was the line to Amsterdam's main rail hub. Rune started forward, then stopped. Train stations were full of people, and where there were people, there were risks. Prudence won out. She pulled out her phone and searched for a car rental office away from the historic center.

There was an Avis near Vondelpark, an urban oasis in the borough of Amsterdam-Zuid, one of the city's poshest neighborhoods. It was a bit of a hike from where she was, but it had the advantage of being on a major street that connected directly to several highways. She tapped "Directions" and typed the address of Steiner Pharma's Berlin office in the search box. It was an eight-hour drive. If she left now, she could be there by dinnertime.

The wind picked up. It wasn't a regular wind but the kind that felt like needles poking into your skin. Rune raised her hood and forged ahead. Her fingers went numb. Her nose felt like it was going to fall off. She couldn't arrive at the rental place soon enough. *Almost halfway,* she thought as she hustled through Koningsplein ten minutes later.

She was midway across the plaza when an unexpected sequence of events upended her plans. It started with a man on an electric scooter snatching the purse of the woman directly in front of her. It was the kind of thing that happened all the time in European cities, but on this occasion, the woman's companion reacted freakishly fast. His arm shot out. He yanked the thief off his scooter. Then the two got into it. Everything happened so quickly that Rune couldn't get out of the way of their flailing limbs. She found herself on the ground without knowing exactly how she got there. If that wasn't bad enough, the do-gooder's foot caught her right in the mouth.

A knight in shining armor ran to her rescue. He was tall and handsome, just like in fairy tales. He pressed his handkerchief against her lip and said something in Dutch.

"I'm okay, thanks," Rune said, waving him off. A split lip wasn't a problem. The crowd ballooning around her was.

"You're not okay. You're bleeding."

She looked at his handkerchief. It was stained with her blood. She took it from him with a grateful nod and brought it to her mouth. He helped her to her feet.

That might have been the end of it if a pair of policemen in fluorescent yellow vests hadn't chosen that precise moment to pull up on bicycles. She turned her back to them a bit too quickly. The man helping her noticed. Suspicion flickered in his eyes.

Does he know? she wondered.

She didn't wait to find out. She lowered her head, this time to hide her features, and followed the signs to the Bloemenmarkt, a floating flower market guaranteed to be packed at this midmorning hour. She cast a look back to see if the pedal police had followed, but they had their hands full wrangling the purse snatcher. Relieved, she joined a dozen or so Portuguese tourists making their way through the stalls. Fragrant spruce trees stood by the entrances, trussed and ready for Christmas shoppers. Inside were bouquets of dried lavender and more seeds than Rune knew existed. Older members of the group *oohed* and *aahed* at the eucalyptus wreaths on the walls. Younger members only had eyes for the cannabis starter kits.

The Bloemenmarkt was one of Amsterdam's most popular tourist sites, right behind the Red-Light District and Anne Frank's house. The barges supporting the stalls belonged to a bygone era when the city was a premier center of maritime trade. The Portuguese tourists were clearly charmed. Rune, not so much. She wanted to leave the group and sprint all the way to the Avis office, but the police were close by and nothing attracted attention like a person running.

The group moved to another stall. Rune followed and pretended to admire the souvenirs on offer—wood tulips, clog-shaped magnets, postcards of windmills and bicycles. A woman who assumed she belonged pointed to a pair of earrings shaped like canal houses and said something in rapid Portuguese. Rune gave her a thumbs-up and exited the stall before she could give herself away.

Her timing couldn't have been worse. The knight in shining armor from Koningsplein was just a few stalls behind. He noticed her immediately and tapped a gangly police officer on the shoulder. The officer's eyes narrowed. Rune walked away, not quickly, but not slowly either. She dared glance back a few seconds later. Prince Charming was gone, but the officer hadn't budged. In fact, he was more focused on her than before. She'd barely turned around when she heard him shout, "Police! Stop!"

Rune didn't think, she just ran. She elbowed her way through the crowd, her backpack bouncing in time with her stride. A burly merchant unleashed a torrent of vulgarities when she slammed into his display and knocked over a row of Christmas trees. She tried to get away, but he caught her by the arm and refused to let go. She gave him a fierce jab to the nose. Nothing happened, so she aimed for his eyes. He released her instantly. She spun around and ran as fast as her legs would let her. Her lungs burned. Her pulse raced. She hurtled toward the intersection directly ahead, then skidded to a stop.

It's the winter festival. We're fully booked.

The hotel clerk's words flashed through Rune's mind as she watched the mayhem unfolding in front of her. People from across the city had converged on the area to watch the annual Sinterklaas parade, an event marking the end of Saint Nicholas's seafaring journey from Spain and the start of the holiday season in the Netherlands. The procession began earlier that morning on the city's waterways. Dozens of boats snaked through the canals to the National Maritime Museum, where Amsterdam's mayor and her entourage waited to greet Nicholas. Wearing a distinctive red cape and miter, the bearded saint traded his boat for a white horse before continuing his journey across the city in the company of his helpers, the Black Petes.

A hard candy hit Rune on the cheek. It triggered a memory of her only other encounter with the Black Petes. The memory was so vivid it could have been yesterday. It happened during a visit to Amsterdam when she was eight years old, a business trip her father tried to pass off as a family vacation. A Black Pete in glistening blackface and quasi-Renaissance attire had leaned down to greet her. She was so terror-stricken that her parents were forced to cut the excursion short. She remembered crying all the way back to the hotel, her arms wrapped around her father's neck like a tourniquet.

When they got to their room, her father explained that she had nothing to fear. He told her that she was a good girl and that the Black Petes only punished ill-behaved children. What her father didn't understand was that she wasn't afraid of being judged by Nicholas's helpers, it was their face paint that frightened her. Even as a child, she understood that masks let people say and do things they otherwise wouldn't.

Rune blanched at the sight of children accepting candy from the Black Petes while the adults around them cheered and sang Christmas carols. Musicians, dancers, and acrobats added to the chaos. She looked back. The policeman from the flower market was nowhere in sight, but he could reappear at any moment.

Go!

She dashed into the street and catapulted onto a float shaped like a miniature house. Colorful gift boxes with perky bows were piled high on the Astroturf lawn, behind a white picket fence that appeared to be made of cardboard. Rune crouched behind them, earning bewildered looks from the two Black Petes on the float. She brought her index finger to her lips. To her astonishment, the two men simply resumed tossing candy at the crowd.

One minute passed, then another before Rune dared to raise her head. The policeman from the flower market was about thirty feet away peering into other floats. He was distracted. This was her chance. She lowered herself to the ground and zigzagged through the crowd until she reached a pack of costumed revelers armed with party poppers and noisemakers. One of them plunked a felt miter on her head. Another handed her a plastic crozier. They began chanting and cheering. Rune's voice merged with theirs as she joined their ranks and melted into the throng.

23

CENTRAL AMSTERDAM

N o sooner had Rune veered off the parade route than she got hope-lessly lost. She walked for fifteen minutes certain she was heading toward the Avis office only to find herself farther away from it than when she started. She paused by a quiet canal to get her bearings. It was lined with narrow houses, some brick, others stone, all capped with graceful cornices and whimsical gables. Denuded elm trees swayed in the wind. A strong gust sent a dead branch tumbling into the canal. It plopped into the water, creating ripples that gleamed under the warmthless sun. If the cold spell held for another few days, the canals would freeze over and transform the city into the world's largest ice-skating rink.

Rune spied an unlocked bicycle with a corroded metal frame and a torn leather seat propped against a lamppost. Biking was faster than walking, assuming she went in the right direction. She took a step toward it. The back tire looked a little soft, but everything else seemed to be in working order. Her eyes swung left to the young traveler strug-gling under the weight of his overstuffed backpack. They flicked to the right to the gaunt-faced woman crying quietly into her cellphone. Both were too wrapped up in their own problems to notice her.

"Just take it."

Rune spun around and found herself face-to-face with a young Dutch man with features so finely chiseled they bordered on feminine. He had the physique of a swimmer, with long limbs and broad shoulders that strained against his peacoat. Dark blond curls peeked out from beneath his tweed flat cap. His luminous eyes, a kaleidoscope of greens and blues, seemed to be laughing at her.

"What's the matter?" he asked. He took a step forward. "Cat got your tongue?"

Rune threw her leg over the bike. It teetered precariously to one side. The man grabbed the handlebars to keep her from falling over.

"What do you want?" she demanded.

"I don't want anything. I was just telling you it's okay to take the bike. It's been there for days."

"I wasn't *taking* the bike, I was just—"

"Stealing it?"

"Borrowing it." Her chin rose defensively. She was getting peeved. Who did this guy think he was?

"I see. Well, feel free to *borrow* it for as long as you like. I won't tell."

"I will." Rune realized she sounded like a snotty teenager the moment the words came out of her mouth. She tried to get on her way, but his hold on the handlebars was firm.

"You're not going to get very far with that back tire. I have a patching kit and pump at my house. It's not far. Do you want to come?"

She eyed him cautiously.

"Don't worry. I'm not a maniac or anything."

Said every maniac ever. "I'm not in the habit of going home with strangers."

"I'm Jakob. Now I'm not a stranger."

Rune weighed her options. She could try to make it to the Avis office and risk getting caught, or she could lay low at Jakob's place until the heat died down. The wind blew angrily. A siren howled in the distance. It was a no-brainer. "I'm Eve," she said, picking the first name that popped into her head.

"Eve," he repeated. He gave her a crooked smile. "Like the first woman."

"Jakob," she shot back. "Like the man who stole his brother's birthright."

His smile broadened.

⊙━━━⊙

"I thought you said you lived nearby," Rune said as she pushed her stolen bicycle across a busy intersection in the Oosterpark section of Amsterdam, an unexpectedly spacious neighborhood crisscrossed with wide avenues and historic buildings.

Jakob looked at her sideways. "Americans think everything is far when they're on foot."

"Who said I was American?"

"You're saying you're not?"

She declined to answer.

"Well, wherever you're from, you'll be happy to know we're nearly there." They turned onto a quiet street and stopped in front of a well-kept townhouse with an empty storefront on the ground floor and dormer windows at the top. Jakob grabbed the bike and carried it easily up the stone staircase to his third-floor apartment. He unlocked the door, stepped inside, and set the bike down in the middle of the room. He raised his eyebrows at Rune. "Are you coming in or not?"

She stepped inside and closed the door.

"Do you want something to drink?"

She nodded.

"You don't say much, do you?"

She shrugged.

He peeled off his coat and disappeared into the kitchen. She took a silent inventory of her surroundings. The room was spacious, the decor Spartan. The only furnishings were a leather sectional, a glass coffee table, and floor-to-ceiling shelves that spanned an entire wall. She appreciated Jakob's commitment to living in a clutter-free space. She walked over to the shelves hoping to learn something about the man who was now playing a role in her escape. Her eyes lingering on thirty-seven well-worn copies of Shakespeare's plays. She picked up *King Lear* and leafed through it. The pages were covered in handwritten notes and highlights. There were similar markings in the other plays, including *Cymbeline*. Who on earth read *Cymbeline*? "You've read all of Shakespeare?" she called out.

Jakob reappeared in the living room holding two bottles of beer in one hand and a tire repair kit in the other. "You haven't?"

"No."

"Don't feel bad, no one's perfect."

It took her a moment to realize he was kidding.

"Don't be impressed with all this," he said, glancing at the shelves. "I'm no poet."

Rune accepted the bottle Jakob gave her, but she didn't drink. She needed to stay clear-headed. She had to get to Berlin. She had to deal with Alaric. If she found something on him, then maybe Romy would do more than support her financially. Maybe she'd whisper Lemaire's name into Alaric's ear. The thought brought Rune immense pleasure. She didn't know what Alaric would do to the man who stole his family's jewels, but whatever it was, it wouldn't be good.

"Hold this," Jakob said.

Rune took the half-empty bottle and watched him get to work on the bike. She tried not to stare as he released the rear wheel, popped the tire off, and removed the inner tube.

God, he's attractive!

"Here's your problem," he said, pointing to a half-inch gash in the rubber. He buffed the area with a metal rasp, applied a thin layer of glue, and pressed a patch securely into place. Once that was done, he reassembled the tire, put the wheel back on the frame, and inflated it. He tested the pressure with the palm of his hand, gave it a few more pumps, and replaced the valve cap. "Perfect," he said.

Oh, yes you are.

"It should hold for a while. But you'll want to get the wheel replaced sooner rather than later."

"I will. Thanks."

"My pleasure."

Rune toyed with her cuff. She didn't want to go yet. She wanted to stay out of sight a little while longer.

"Sit," Jakob said, gesturing to the couch. "You haven't touched your beer."

She acquiesced. The leather was buttery soft. Jakob didn't have a lot of furniture, but what he had was top-notch. She sank deep into the cushion, suddenly wiped out. When she looked up, she realized Jakob was laughing at her. "What?" she asked.

"In the Netherlands, it's customary to take your outerwear off indoors."

Her face reddened. She took off her hat and parka and wondered why she'd suddenly turned into a bumbling idiot.

Jakob sat down. The couch sank under his weight, closing the space between them. He grabbed a metal box from the coffee table and pulled out a plastic bag filled with multicolored pills, each stamped with a cartoonish image. He selected a purple one with a unicorn and gave it to her.

"What is it?"

"A legendary beast with a spiral horn."

"I meant the pill."

"Something to take the edge off. No offense, but you look like you need it."

She couldn't argue there.

"It's Molly," he explained when the pill stayed in her hand.

"I've never done that."

"We learn by doing." He gave her a wink, then placed a yellow pill on his tongue and washed it down with the rest of his beer.

Taking that purple pill was a stupid idea and Rune knew it. But the last few months had left her with an overwhelming urge to forget. She popped it in her mouth and chased it with a big gulp of beer before she could talk herself out of it. Her eyes found Jakob's. "Now what?"

"Now this." Jakob walked over to the windows and pulled the curtains shut, plunging the room into semidarkness. He cued up a playlist and placed his phone on its dock right next to his collection of Shakespeare's play.

Rune didn't recognize the music, but the strong pulse and heavy bass had a hypnotic effect on her senses. She accepted Jakob's hand and allowed herself to be enveloped by him as they swayed in time with the music. He drew back to look at her when the song ended. Her pupils were dilated, her breath was quick and shallow. He placed a hand on her chest to feel her heartbeat. She didn't pull away.

"Someone's starting to roll," he whispered into her ear.

Perhaps it was the effects of the drug, or maybe the extraordinary circumstances in which she found herself, but Rune wanted very badly to lose herself with Jakob. He was handsome and funny and nice. His home was warm and safe. He leaned in to kiss her. She hesitated but only for a moment.

Rune felt surprisingly good when she awoke several hours later. Her stomach wasn't upset like it was when she drank too much. She wasn't dying of thirst. She didn't even have a headache. She gently lifted Jakob's arm off her body and inched toward the edge of the bed.

"Stay," he murmured, pulling her back.

"Why?" It was an honest question. She was under the impression that what happened between them was just sex.

"Because I like you and I think you like me."

He was right about that. There was a lightness about him that she found appealing. The fact that they were compatible in bed didn't hurt. Still, she untangled herself and started getting dressed. Jakob was fun, but she had to go before the car rental office closed.

"I want to get to know you, Eve."

"You already know me," Rune said pointedly. She wiggled into her jeans and swept the room for her bra.

"I'm going to Hamburg today. Come with me."

"I don't think so." Going anywhere near the train station was out of the question. Better to get on her newly patched bike and ride to Avis.

"It's a long drive. I'd love the company. I'd love *your* company."

Drive?

Rune considered the invitation as she pulled her sweater over her head. She needed to get out of Amsterdam, and traveling by car with Jakob was a lot safer than going it alone. Hamburg was also a stone's throw from Berlin. Getting to Steiner Pharmaceuticals would be easy from there. That sealed the deal. She crawled back onto the bed and nestled in the crook of Jakob's arm. She inhaled deeply. He smelled good, like the outdoors and a hint of aftershave.

"Is that a yes?" Jakob said.

"Yes," Rune replied.

He drew her closer, pleased.

She hooked her fingers with his. "What's in Hamburg?"

"Business."

"I've never been."

"It's nice."

"Better than Berlin?"

"Apples and pears."

"Oranges."

"Sorry?"

"The saying is *comparing apples and oranges*."

"In Dutch, we say pears."

"That's funny." Rune giggled.

"Why? Pears are less like apples than oranges are."

"Maybe the shape but not the texture."

"False."

"Not false! Oranges are pulpy and juicy."

"Are we really going to let fruit get between us?"

Rune smiled into his chest. "I'll let it go," she said. "But first you have to tell me, is Berlin the apple or the pear?"

"The pear, obviously."

"Thanks. I can *totally* picture it now."

Jakob pulled back so he could see her face. "Are you saying you've never been to Berlin?"

"Never."

"Eve, you *have to* go."

"I want to. It just hasn't happened."

"Let's do it. Today. Right now." His swirly eyes widened with excitement.

"Really? That's crazy."

"I do business there all the time. I was planning to go at the end of the month, but I'm happy to move the trip up. I'll do my thing in Hamburg, then we can spend a few days together in Berlin."

"That would be amazing. You're sure you can spare the time?"

"Of course. It's one of my favorite cities. I've been going since I was a kid."

"Tell me about that," she said, settling under his arm again.

"I was thirteen the first time I went. It was a class trip and the first time I traveled anywhere without my parents. I was so excited I didn't sleep the night before."

Rune grew pensive. She was about that age when she went on her first trip without her parents, the trip that changed everything, the trip that set her on her current path. She, too, had been eager to embark on her first solo adventure. But her dreams of kayaking and horseback riding at summer camp quickly turned into a nightmare. Weeks of bullying ended with her tormentor in the hospital and Rune taking the blame. She tried telling people the truth—that she wasn't responsible, that what happened was an accident—but no one believed her. Not the police, not the shrinks, not even her parents. She spent two years in the system. Restrained. Medicated. Full of pain and anger. When all was said and done, her life had veered so far off course she was never able to right it.

"The last day of the trip was pretty chaotic."

Jakob's voice pulled her back from the precipice. She forced herself to focus on him. She didn't want to think about the past. She'd put it to rest long ago. "What happened on the last day?"

"We spent the morning at the Berlin Wall Memorial, then we went back to the hotel to check out. We were getting on the bus to go home when I realized I'd left my retainer in the bathroom. I ran to get it, but I didn't have the key. I had to wait for the people at reception to sort me out. When I got back to the lobby, everyone was gone. Vanished. I thought they'd notice and come back for me, but my teacher didn't realize I was missing until the bus was an hour outside the city."

"Yikes. You must have been really scared."

"I was but not about being left behind. That part was fun. The hotel fed me and let me explore the grounds. It was my parents' reaction I was afraid of. I thought they'd blame me for missing the bus. Instead, my mom cried and my father apologized for not keeping me safe. It was the first time I saw them as real people and not just as my parents."

"You're lucky," Rune said. "It sounds like they really loved you." It was hard to keep the sadness out of her voice. Her parents had failed her so badly. They hadn't defended her. Worse, they hadn't believed her. That part still smarted, even after all these years.

"Hey, now," Jakob said when he realized something was off. "What is it?"

Rune tamped down the memories. Talking about her childhood wasn't on the table. That part of her life was closed to everyone, even herself. Still, she was tired of pretending to be okay when she was barely holding it together. She took a wobbly breath. "Jakob, I'm in trouble and I don't know how to get out of it."

"It can't be as bad as that."

"It is."

"There is a crack in everything, Eve. That's how the light gets in."

Rune pulled away so she could see his face. She tilted her head. "I thought you said you weren't a poet."

"I can't take credit for that," he replied with a crooked smile. He drew her back to him and kissed her hair. When he spoke again, it was in a serious tone. "Listen, Eve, whatever's going on with you, it will work out. Things always do."

That wasn't Rune's experience, but she was willing to entertain the idea that it could be. She closed her eyes and held him tightly. "Thanks," she said softly.

"For what?"

"For reminding me how lovely it is to forget."

24

BERLIN

Berlin was as fascinating as Jakob promised. Decades had passed since reunification, but Cold War divisions hadn't been fully effaced from the sprawling German capital. Keen observers compared the immaculate parks and historic architecture of the western neighborhoods to the gritty streets and monotonous apartment blocks of the eastern zones. They pitted the highly developed underground transit system of the west against the quaint trams that traversed the east. The most striking difference, however, was virtually imperceptible from ground level. Photos taken from orbit revealed two distinct sides to the city, one that radiated green and the other yellow. The explanation was simple: West and East Berlin historically used different streetlights. The installation of eco-friendly fluorescent lights, which produced a greenish tinge, coincided with the emergence of the environmental movement in West Germany in the 1970s. By contrast, East Berlin used sodium vapor lamps that produced a yellowish hue. Although Germany's eastern states now had the largest renewable energy sector in the country, Cold War lights were still the norm in the formerly communist sections of the capital.

Striking as they were, the differences between the eastern and western sections of the city were not at the front of Rune's mind as she paced up and down the U-Bahn platform at Unter den Linden waiting for sensation to return to her limbs. Her pleated slacks and white dress shirt looked smart, but they were completely wrong for the polar temperatures, even with a wool topcoat. She normally prioritized practicality over fashion, but this outing called for something different. She was so put together that even Jakob had noticed.

Where are you off to looking all gorgeous?

Shopping. Want to come?

I can't. I have a meeting.

That's too bad!

Hurry back.

Rune had spent the last three days playing tourist with Jakob, nervous, but not overly so. The police were on the lookout for a single American woman, not a couple vacationing in Berlin. They went to the Brandenburg Gate and the Reichstag Building, to the Jewish Museum and the Berlin Wall Memorial. They went further afield too, to a former Stasi prison and dank bunkers from the Second World War. Their days and nights had been full, but that didn't mean Rune had forgotten about Romy. Steiner Pharmaceuticals was at the top of the day's agenda. She wasn't sure what she'd do when she got there, but her best ideas usually came to her on the fly.

The U5 pulled into the station. Rune stepped onto the canary-yellow train, joining the sea of bodies already inside. She heard a chime followed by an announcement. The brusque voice startled her. She glanced over her shoulder.

That's when she saw them. Two men. Dark-haired. One tall and lanky, the other shorter, stockier. Lemaire's men. They'd found her. They'd come to get rid of her. She stole another look to be sure, but the men's faces were obscured by other passengers. A tremor of fear ran up her spine.

The subway doors opened. She pushed her way out. She looked back, but the platform was packed and the men were nowhere in sight.

The train inched forward. Someone pressed against her from behind. She spun around and raised her fists, ready for a fight.

"Sorry!" the teenager cried.

Rune's eyes swung from the distressed girl to the train. The two men were still inside. Random men. Not Lemaire's goons at all. She lowered her head, embarrassed, then transferred to the S-Bahn heading north.

The ride was long. The crowd thinned the further the train got from the city center. By the time Rune got off, there were only three people left in her car.

The borough was called Reinickendorf. The area was home to housing projects, a decommissioned airport, and a surprising amount of green space given the density of the rest of the city. Affordable rents and room to grow had drawn dozens of companies to Reinickendorf, including Steiner Pharmaceuticals, which moved to an office park on the south end of the borough at the turn of the twenty-first century.

Rune regretted not having a plan as soon as she stepped out of the station. The area had almost no foot traffic, despite being next to the S-Bahn. Maybe the cold was keeping everyone inside, or maybe Germans just didn't walk in semi-industrial office parks. In either case, Rune felt exposed. She thought about turning around and getting back on the train, but she hadn't come all this way for nothing. She hung a right, then walked past a bar, an auto repair shop, and a legal office. As she waited at the intersection, she couldn't help thinking that the services were being offered in the correct order.

The light turned green. Rune crossed the street and took a shortcut through a parking lot. Soon, Steiner Pharmaceuticals came into view. Her senses sharpened. Her heart gave a few hard pumps. She looked the building up and down, sizing it up like an opponent in the boxing ring. The nine-story building was made almost entirely of dark glass.

It was a bad choice as far as she was concerned. Soaring drug costs and high-profile recalls made Big Pharma one of the least trusted industries in the world. The dark glass was like a visual admission that the company had something to hide.

A fence that was more for show than protection encircled the grounds. Rune could have scaled it easily, but she didn't have to. The gate was wide open, the security booth unmanned. She waltzed through without being stopped.

The lobby was all white, from the polished marble tiles to the glossy modern furniture, the kind that showed every fingerprint. Rune silently berated the designer for making life hell for the cleaning staff. She paused by the door to look at the directory, then strode to the reception area like she was meant to be there.

A blonde woman with a runner's physique and combative eyes greeted her with a nod. Her name was Katrin, according to the shiny white name plaque on the counter.

"I'm Effie Davis from Johnson & Johnson. I have an appointment with Mr. Steiner," Rune said.

"Which one?" Katrin pronounced *W*s as *V*s, in typical German fashion.

"Alaric."

Katrin turned to her computer and typed a few words. Her lips turned paper thin. A deep crevice formed across her forehead. "I don't see anything on the schedule. Are you certain your appointment is today?"

"Of course I'm certain. Check again." Rune's tone was snappy. She wore an expression to match. She almost broke character when she saw the alarm on Katrin's face. As Steiner Pharma's primary gatekeeper, the woman was probably used to treating people shabbily, not the other way around. Rune transferred her weight from one side to the other to signal her impatience. She stopped short of tapping her foot.

"I'm sorry," Katrin said. Her eyes moved rapidly across the screen. "I don't see anything here."

"Just add me to the schedule."

"Herr Steiner is with someone at the moment."

"I'll wait."

"That's not possible. He's expected at the Capital Club at noon. I suggest you call his assistant to reschedule."

Katrin's resistance wasn't surprising. Everything about her screamed rule follower, from her subdued makeup to her pearl earrings. And with corporate espionage and cyber threats on the rise, a security breach could have serious consequences. But pushback wasn't a deterrent for Rune, it was just a signal to press harder.

"This is unacceptable," she said, raising her voice a notch. "I flew in specifically for this meeting. I'm due back in New York tomorrow."

Katrin's poise wavered. "I-I understand, but there's nothing I can do. If you contact Herr Steiner's office and explain the situation, I'm certain they'll be able to assist you." She fumbled for a business card and slid it across the counter.

"I have his number. What I need is—" Rune let out a huff. "You know what, never mind. You're obviously useless."

Katrin blinked as if she'd been slapped.

"Can you at least point me to your restrooms? Or does that also fall outside your job description?" Rune read the hesitation on Katrin's face. She was torn between crossing the angry American and keeping the riffraff out of the lobby.

"They're across the atrium and to the left," Katrin said. She gestured behind her with a thin hand.

Rune gave her a disapproving shake of the head, then walked away. Her posture was rigid, but she couldn't keep the smile off her face. Sometimes to get what you wanted, all you had to do was ask for something bigger first.

The atrium was all white, just like the lobby. The ceiling was a grid of glass, the floor covered with marble. A huge mirror angled to reflect sunlight levitated above the space, hanging from cables that were barely visible from below. The design was clever, but it was largely wasted on a city plagued by perma-clouds and general gloominess. Rune waited until Katrin was out of earshot to pull out her phone. "Pick up already," she whispered after the fourth ring. She was about to give up when the ringing stopped.

"Now's not a good time," Romy said over the sound of children laughing. Her voice grew muffled. She said something in French.

"I need a favor."

"I'm with my kids."

"I'm in Berlin. I need you to get the receptionist at Steiner headquarters away from her desk."

"How am I supposed to do that?"

"You'll figure it out. Do it now." Rune hung up before Romy could argue. As she did, she couldn't help thinking that this was a good test. If Romy was willing to do this, maybe she'd be willing to do other things, like give her husband Lemaire's name or lure Lemaire into a trap. Maybe she could even get Lemaire to admit to the Bonaparte thefts. If the police got their hands on him, they might stop looking for her.

The phone at the reception desk rang. There was a long pause, then the sound of footsteps. Rune looked over her shoulder and saw Katrin get on the elevator. She waited for the doors to close, then hurried to the emergency stairwell.

Alaric had a noon appointment at the Capital Club, a members-only organization for Berlin's movers and shakers. It would take at least forty-five minutes to get there in midday traffic, which meant that Alaric's current meeting was about to end. Rune pulled the door open and started her ascent. Alaric's office was on the twelfth floor, according to the directory down at reception. It was a long climb, but she was up to the challenge. She silently thanked the building manager at Félix Pyat for all those weeks of free cardio.

The stairwell ejected Rune into an empty hallway. She skulked around looking for Alaric's office until she happened upon a janitor's closet. She slipped inside. A strange woman wandering the halls attracted attention. Custodial staff was invisible. She knew that from experience. She traded her fancy coat for a dark blue smock that grazed the middle of her thighs and congratulated herself for her quick thinking. Then she grabbed a cleaning cart and went back to looking for Alaric.

She'd barely made it around the first corner when a deep voice stopped her dead in her tracks. She understood only two words of what the man said: "toilet" and "stopped." That was enough.

"Ja," she replied with a nod.

He said something else in German and made a shooing motion with his hands. She took a few steps toward the bathroom but veered away as soon as he was out of sight. She'd cleaned enough toilets to last a lifetime. She wasn't doing it again, not even for pretend.

Alaric's nameplate hung on the door of the coveted corner office. Rune wondered if he'd earned the spot or if it had been handed to him simply because he was the CEO's son. Two people were visible through the partially drawn blinds. Rune pulled the mop from her cart and started cleaning the floor a few feet away. She cleaned the same spot for nearly ten minutes, until Alaric's door opened and an elderly man with a stern expression came out. Alaric emerged moments later. He was taller than Rune expected—six foot five, if she had to guess. His hair was so blond it stretched credulity. He wasn't especially muscular, but with his combative posture and fierce eyes, he didn't need to be.

Alaric headed to the elevators without glancing her way. Men like him never noticed the help, not unless there was something wrong. Rune caught his office door with her foot right before it closed. She stepped inside and lowered the blinds. Then she started snooping.

The desk was the obvious place to start. It was sleek and minimalist, like everything else in the building. She cast the computer a longing look and wished that Milo was still in her corner before turning to the built-in filing cabinet. It was locked. Not a problem. She grabbed a pin from her hair and inserted it into the keyhole. A gentle twist was all it took for the drawer to pop open.

The files were organized alphabetically. Most of them pertained to pharmaceutical research and development. There was an HIV drug for adults on the cusp of approval, a plaque psoriasis medication in clinical trials, and a cognitive decline drug in early stages of development. Rune flipped through the files, then decided there were too many to read. She brought them to the copy machine and placed them into the feeder.

Beep!

"No, no, no!"

The beeping was loud, piercing. The panel flashed like a strobe light. Rune hit random buttons to get it to stop. When that didn't work, she opened the side cover and peered inside. "Shoot!" she said when she saw a crinkled sheet jammed in the fuser. She grabbed it with both hands and pulled. It tore in half. She swore quietly and pried it out one millimeter at a time. Only when every last shred was removed did the beeping finally stop.

Rune was about to restart the print job when she saw movement in the hallway. Whoever it was stopped outside Alaric's door. She froze. Had someone heard the beeping? She glanced at the janitor's cart in the corner of the room. It was a decent cover but not with Alaric's files in plain view.

Muffled voices sounded. Rune's eyes swung from side to side. Wide. Frantic. This was the corporate office of a pharmaceutical giant. If security found her, they wouldn't just kick her out, they'd hand her over to the police.

The knob turned. Rune launched herself behind the copier. Two people walked in. The lock clicked.

"Mmm."

Rune froze.

"Mmm."

Two moans were all it took for Rune to realize she was the third wheel in an office booty call. Relief came first, then embarrassment. Her cheeks prickled with heat when she heard the couple's passionate kisses. The heat turned to fire when the dirty talking started—no translation necessary. She brought her eyes to the ceiling and let out a slow, silent breath. Hearing things you couldn't unhear was an occupational hazard in her profession. But no matter how often it happened, it never ceased to mortify.

25

HOTEL DE ROME, BERLIN

"You're here!" Jakob exclaimed when Rune joined him at their hotel bar many hours later.

"I'm here." She settled next to him on the banquette and leaned in for a kiss. He tasted fresh and sweet, like Wrigley's Doublemint gum.

"I missed you today," he said, nuzzling her neck.

"Me too." The words came out automatically, but she meant them. "Sorry I'm late."

"There are worse places to wait."

She had to agree. The Hotel de Rome had the stiffness and formality of a nineteenth-century bank, but the bar overlooking Bebelplatz was surprisingly cozy, with matte black walls and red lampshades that cast a warm glow on everything in the room. She placed her hand on Jakob's lap and squeezed. Making people wait was bad manners, but so much of the day had been out of her control. The randy couple had taken their time in Alaric's office. They were so into each other that they hadn't notice the janitor's cart in the corner of the room or the file folders stacked on top of the copier. Rune had gone back to feeding the machine as soon as they'd left, only this time, she'd selected the scan option and downloaded the files to an empty USB drive she found on the desk. It took hours to scan all the files. Then she had to wait for Romy to lure Katrin away from the reception desk so she could make her escape. The never-ending ride back to the city had made the day even longer.

"Let's get something to drink," Jakob said. He twisted in his seat in search of the waitress.

"You didn't order?" Rune asked.

"She came by, but I told her I was waiting for my girlfriend."

"So, we're girlfriend and boyfriend now?" The idea made Rune happy. Kit tried to intrude on the moment, but she shoved him aside where he belonged.

"What would you call us?"

Her shoulders rose and fell. The relationship was so new she didn't know how to talk about it yet. All she knew was that Jakob was easy and fun and she liked who she was when she was with him. Not mopey or scared or angry, but closer to her old self.

"What can I get you?" the waitress asked, intruding on the moment. She looked like a young Peggy Lipton with straight blond hair that was parted in the middle and a spray of freckles across her nose. She only had eyes for Jakob.

"I'll have a glass of Sancerre," Rune said, asserting her presence. She didn't blame the waitress for flirting, but that didn't mean she had to sit there and take it like a chump.

"Grolsch," Jakob said.

The drinks arrived a few minutes later. The waitress gazed at Jakob from under her lashes as she deposited them on the table, but he was too busy smoothing a strand of Rune's hair to notice. His index finger found her earrings. "Are these emeralds?" he asked.

"Jade."

He looked like he wanted her to say more.

"They were a gift from my father."

"Tell me about him."

"No."

"Why not?"

"I don't want to." The disappointment on his face didn't sway her. She wasn't prepared to talk about her family. It was too messy. Too complicated.

"You were gone a long time."

"I was shopping." She'd meant to say it lightly, but there was an edge to her voice.

"Relax, Eve. I was just asking about your day. It's what people do."

Rune wondered if she'd ever stop feeling like a jerk for giving Jakob a fake name. The lies that followed made her feel even worse. "I went to the Mall of Berlin. Then I walked around for a bit and went to a museum."

"Oh, which one?"

"The Pergamonmuseum."

Jakob gave her an odd look.

"The one with the blue gate with all the animals."

"The Ishtar Gate."

"That's the one." That marked the limit of Rune's knowledge, all of it derived from a brochure in their room. She changed the subject. "How was *your* day?"

"It was okay."

"That's it? I thought we were doing the talking thing."

"My day was very boring."

"Try me."

"I met with some business associates to discuss expanding our footprint in Germany. We spent the afternoon crunching numbers."

"You're right. That's very boring."

Jakob laughed.

Rune joined in. As she did, she couldn't help thinking that she liked this man. *Really* liked him. The feeling was so intense she felt compelled to tell him something about herself that was true. "Berlin's great. There's an energy here that reminds me of Bangkok. That's where I lived before coming to Europe."

"Do you miss it?"

"Every day."

"Will you go back?"

"Probably. My father's from there."

"What's it like?"

"Hot, crowded, and dirty."

"Stop with the hard sell."

"It's also beautiful. More beautiful than any place I've ever been. It's not just the temples and palaces. Everything feels more . . . just *more*. Smells are sweeter. Colors are brighter."

"Sounds amazing."

"And the food. It's sooo good! There's a neighborhood called Saphan Lueng. A woman there makes the most incredible Thai congee. She's been making it the same way for fifty years. Same recipe. Same stall. She even uses the same pot. It's warm and savory and comforting all at once. I look for it everywhere I go, but no one seems to make it outside Thailand." Rune stopped babbling when she noticed Jakob smiling. "What?"

"Nothing. I've just never heard anyone speak so passionately about porridge before."

She leaned in. Her lips brushed against his. "It's not the only thing I'm passionate about."

"Oh, no?"

She pulled back slightly. "I told you something about me, now it's your turn."

"What do you want to know?"

"Whatever you want. I hardly know anything about you." It was true. He was quick-witted and kind, an easy companion, and a generous lover. But he hadn't offered many details about his life or his work.

"I'm an open book," he said, spreading his hands for emphasis. He'd barely gotten the words out when his phone started vibrating on the table. He gave her a look as if to say *saved by the bell*, then stepped out of the bar to take the call.

26

THE PALIMPSEST, BERLIN

"What are we doing here?" Rune shouted as they wove through the masses at The Palimpsest, a live music venue in the boho neighborhood of Kreuzberg. A girl band with zero effs to give played electropop at deafening levels. LED strips and glow sticks were the only sources of light. Rune didn't love being in crowded places, but the club was so dark—and the patrons so blitzed—that she couldn't have felt safer.

Jakob leaned down and cupped her ear. "I'm here to see a friend!"

She followed his gaze to the bar. It stood in the middle of what looked like an empty swimming pool complete with blue-green tiles and metal ladders. Rune noticed other signs of the club's past life: a two-tiered diving platform repurposed to serve as a speaker stand, aquatic motifs on the floors and walls, and seats that looked suspiciously like loungers.

Jakob led her to the bar, where a crowd four deep waited patiently for drinks. He made eye contact with one of the bartenders, a ravishing woman in a strapless white dress that left little to the imagination. Her hair was slicked back to make it look wet, a fitting choice given the venue. Expertly applied makeup gave her a sun-kissed glow. She raised her palm to indicate she'd be free in five minutes, then mixed two neon yellow drinks in record time. She added lemon wedges as garnish before reaching across a group of paying customers to hand Jakob the drinks. There was a collective groan. He mouthed his thanks. She blew him a kiss.

Rune took a sip of the yellow concoction. It tasted tart and fresh. She drank the rest in a single go, then followed Jakob to the dance floor. They joined the sweaty bodies swaying to the synthesized tunes coming from the stage. The alcohol warmed her body. Sheer abandon played on her face as she lost herself in the music, grateful for the sweet distraction Jakob was once again providing.

The feeling didn't last long. Jakob pulled away after just one song and pointed to the bar to show her where he was going. She nodded and went looking for the bathrooms. Her body was damp with perspiration when she joined the line behind a girl whose hair was so tangled no amount of brushing could ever fix it. The girl was no older than sixteen. Seventeen, at most. Either way, she wasn't old enough to be there. She leaned in and said something Rune didn't understand. Her voice blurred into gray static, lost amid the avalanche of sounds that engulfed them.

It was somewhat quieter inside the bathroom. Rune welcomed the break as she grabbed a handful of paper towels and ran them under the tap. She squeezed out the excess water and wiped her face and neck. She was touching up her lipstick when the girl suffering from acute bedhead emerged from one of the stalls and took her place at the sink next to Rune. If she was perturbed by the rat's nest on her head, she didn't let on.

"How much for pingers?" the girl asked.

"You're asking the wrong person," Rune replied.

"I'm not a cop."

"Clearly not. But I still don't have what you're looking for."

"Whatever."

Rune brushed off the encounter and went searching for Jakob. She hoped he was done with whatever it was he came to do. She wanted to get back to the hotel and get a start on Alaric's files.

She found him outside in an otherwise empty courtyard. He and the bartender were huddled next to metal chairs that had been stacked and trussed for the winter. They were so deep in conversation that they seemed immune to the cold. Rune paused in the doorway. Something about the scenario seemed off, but it wasn't something she could verbalize. The wind picked up, prompting Rune to wrap her arms around her torso. The movement drew the bartender's attention. She whispered something to Jakob. He looked up and waved Rune over.

"There you are!" he exclaimed, as if she was the one who went MIA.

"Here I am."

"Eve, this is Greta. Greta, meet Eve."

Greta shook Rune's hand, holding on a second longer than was comfortable. Her grasp was firm, her skin surprisingly warm given that it was freezing outside. "So, you're Jakob's girl," she said. She sized Rune up through false lashes.

Being someone's girl wasn't how Rune would describe herself, but she chose not to be contrary.

Greta ran her silver tongue ring back and forth between her front teeth. She leaned in, bringing her lips inches from Rune's ear. "Have you ever been to the Berlin Philharmonic?" she whispered.

Rune stepped back, perplexed by the randomness of the question and uncomfortable with the invasion of her personal space. She didn't say anything though. Jakob clearly liked Greta, so she'd make an effort to like her too.

"They're playing Thea Musgrave's *Voices from the Ancient World*," Greta said. "It's a six-piece composition inspired by figures from Greek mythology. The fourth piece is a flute trio called Circe. Do you know who she is?" She waited for Rune to answer. Back and forth the tongue ring went.

"Circe? She's the Greek goddess of magic." Rune couldn't hide her confusion. The conversation was getting weirder by the second.

"She was an enchantress, a sorceress who transformed men into animals. Musgrave's interpretation is outstanding. I've gone three times." Greta must have read the surprise in Rune's eyes because she seemed offended suddenly. "What? I don't look like the type who listens to classical music?"

Rune knew not to judge others based on appearances—too many people had done it to her—but the line between classical aficionado and Greta's in-your-face sex appeal wasn't a straight one. "It's not how you look," she said. "Well, maybe a little. But mostly it's that you do this." She waved her hand toward the bar.

Greta sucked her cheeks, irritated. "You think it's my life's aspiration to sling drinks? I study music at the Universität der Künste."

Rune tried to look interested, but she was getting tired of the massive chip on Greta's shoulder.

"Einstein once said that if he hadn't been a physicist, he would have been a musician. He thought in music, dreamed in music, and saw his whole life in terms of music. I feel that way too. I love classical music, but I can't bear the thought of never listening to anything else. It's one of the reasons I like working here." She smoothed her hair. Her eyes bore into Rune's. "Have you been to Paris recently?"

The question came out of nowhere. Rune wondered if Greta meant anything by it.

Jakob came to the rescue. "You have something for me?" he said to Greta.

Greta kept her eyes on Rune for a moment, then she tilted her head toward the door. "Behind the bar. Follow me."

She led them back into the club and through the drunken partyers. Her colleague glowered when they reached the bar. Rune didn't take it personally. She'd be upset too if she'd been left alone with the thirsty hordes. Greta crouched down. Rune watched her open a safe, pull out a Sailor Moon crossbody, and hand it to Jakob. He laughed and casually slung it over his shoulder.

"Thanks, Greta. You always come through."

"You bet."

"I'll be in touch." He kissed her affectionately on the cheek and took a step back to allow Rune to say goodbye.

She was doing just that when she felt a hard tug on her arm.

"Let's go," Jakob said with an uncharacteristic snap in his voice.

She wanted to ask him what was wrong, but he was focused on the area near the stage. She followed is gaze. Her eyes landed on two middle-aged men weaving through the crowd. They were older and more conservatively dressed than everyone else at the club. One looked like an angry marionette, with deep lines extending from the corners of his mouth to the middle of his chin. The other looked like his nose had been broken and reset by an inept surgeon. Even from a distance, Rune could see the bulge of their weapons at their waists. The men were cops, no doubt about it. She panicked. So did Jakob and Greta.

"Come on!" Greta said.

She led them into the bowels of the club, moving impressively fast for someone in a skintight dress.

"Out the back!" she yelled.

Rune didn't know why Jakob and Greta were running. She didn't care. All she could think about was not getting caught. She glanced back. The two men had them in their sights. Jakob pulled her hand to make her move faster, but it had the opposite effect. She lost her footing. Only a giant in a gold lamé shirt kept her from going down. He caught her by the waist and didn't let go until she was back on her feet. She gave him a grateful look and whispered desperately into his ear. Jakob pulled her away before the man could respond.

The pursuit continued. Greta led them to the rear of the club. Rune stole another look over her shoulder just as they were about to make a turn. She stopped abruptly when she saw the giant in gold lamé recruit three equally large friends and form a wall in front of the cops. Words were exchanged. Someone threw a punch. Then came the flurry of thrashing limbs.

"What did you say to him?" Jakob demanded.

"I told him my ex was after me. I said I was afraid he was going to kill me."

Jakob's expression was equal parts disbelief and respect.

Greta was less impressed. "Move!" she yelled.

Jakob grabbed Rune's hand again and hurried to keep up with Greta. They burst through a door marked "Employees Only" and ran down a musty hallway that doubled as a storage space. They rounded a corner. Then a second. The music faded into the background. Heavy breathing took its place.

"What was that about?" Rune demanded once she was sure they'd lost the cops.

"Maybe you can tell us that," Greta shot back.

"Excuse me?"

"I know who you are."

Rune felt Jakob's eyes on her. "I don't know what you're talking about."

"Right," Greta snorted. "The police just happened to come to the club tonight."

"That has nothing to do with me."

"You lying piece of—"

"Enough!" Jakob barked.

Greta snorted.

Rune blinked hard.

"The cops are still out there," Jakob said. He turned to Greta. "You need to get us out of here. *Now.*"

Greta scowled, but she didn't argue. She led them through a door, then through several others until they reached one that opened onto the alley behind the club. Rune shivered violently as they raced past an overstuffed dumpster to Jakob's BMW. They piled inside. Jakob threw the car into gear. Rune started to speak, only to clam up under Greta's withering glare.

27

HOTEL DE ROME, BERLIN

"**W**ill someone explain to me what the hell just happened?" Jakob said as soon as they reached the safety of their hotel room.

"Ask your girlfriend," Greta said.

Jakob turned to Rune, but she was too busy emptying the minibar of its tiny vodka bottles to notice.

"You think the cops came to the club by accident?" Greta said.

"Eve?"

"Wake up, Jakob!"

His forehead creased.

"You really don't know?" Greta waited a beat before laying into him. "For Christ's sake, don't you read the news? Your girlfriend's a thief. She stole a bunch of sapphires from some queen."

Deny, deny, deny.

"Give me a break," Rune scoffed.

And she wasn't a queen.

Greta tapped angrily at her phone and thrust it at Jakob.

"Don't," Rune said. She knew it was a story about the Bonaparte thefts. She knew that if he saw it, she'd lose him. She'd lose her cover. It would all be over.

He grabbed the phone. His features went from puzzled to shocked to furious in the space of seconds.

"I can explain," Rune said. "I—"

"What did you do?"

She opened her mouth to defend herself, but he cut her off again.

"What the hell did you do?"

"I-I didn't have a choice."

"That's your explanation?"

"I didn't want to do it, I swear."

"I don't believe a word that comes out of your mouth."

"I'm sorry I lied to you."

"I'm sorry I ever met you!"

Rune's temper flared. She'd had enough of men who deluded themselves into thinking their choices were somehow less questionable than hers. Something had gone very wrong at the club. The more she thought about it, the more certain she was that it had nothing to do with her. She was wanted internationally. The Germans would have sent a legion after her, not two undercover cops. "Are you sure you want to get all high-and-mighty on me right now?"

"Excuse me?"

She snatched the Sailor Moon bag off the bed and held it out like it was self-explanatory.

"Put it down."

There wasn't a snowball's chance she was doing that. She wrenched the zipper open and flipped the bag over. Loose bills floated to the floor. "Care to explain?"

"Like you don't know," Jakob snorted.

"Tell me."

"Talk about willful ignorance."

"Tell me!"

"You saw the Molly at my place. You took some, remember?"

Rune did remember. She felt foolish. She'd been so focused on keeping her secrets from Jakob that she hadn't even considered what he might be hiding from her. He was a dealer. Greta was his partner, one of many, she guessed. Of all the guys she could have hooked up with. She expelled a furious breath.

"You're angry with *me*?" Jakob said, stunned.

"You should have told me."

He let out a sharp laugh. "You're upset that I kept something from you when you told me a lie of epic proportions? I don't know who you are. I don't even know your real name!"

The words sucked the anger right out of Rune. Hurt crept in. Then remorse. "You know who I am," she said softly.

"I knew you were lying to me. I *knew* it! The museum you talked about is closed for renovation. It has been for years. I don't know why I didn't say anything."

Rune knew why. People only saw what they wanted to see, especially those with something to lose. Everyone had something to lose. She'd learned that long ago. "You didn't say anything because you like me and you didn't want anything to get in the way of that."

"You're a liar. And I'm a goddamn fool."

"I didn't lie about the important things. I didn't lie about how I feel."

"Enough."

"Jakob, I—"

"I said enough!"

Rune needed to explain. She needed Jakob to see that she hadn't meant to hurt him and that she wasn't a bad person. Her next words came out fast, before he could cut her off again. "Listen to me, Jakob. The Louvre, Deauville, I didn't want to do any of it. I have a debt that

I can't repay, that he'll never let me repay. I lied to you and I'm sorry. But the police are after me, and the man behind all of this wants me dead." She reached for his hand. "Please."

He yanked it away.

Rune knew right then that whatever they had was over. The disappointment that followed hit hard. Their relationship, though new, meant more to her than she'd realized. Through all the lies, she'd somehow caught a glimpse of him and liked what she'd seen. She swallowed the lump in her throat. "I guess I'll be going, then."

He turned his back to her.

She waited a beat, then grabbed her bag. She paused by the door, hoping he'd stop her. He didn't. She stepped out of the room. The moment she did, her freshly mended heart broke all over again.

28

HOTEL DE ROME, BERLIN

Berlin was no longer fascinating now that Rune was on her own. The plaza in front of the hotel was eerily vacant, the buildings along its perimeter oppressive in their sameness. Columns. Pilasters. Way too much symmetry. Rune looked to one side, then the other. She felt lost and vulnerable, adrift in unfamiliar surroundings. A light gleamed in the middle of the square. She went to it, not because she was curious but because her tears were drawing attention from the bellhops.

The light came from a rectangular well deep below the pavement. Rune peered through the protective glass. All she saw were empty bookcases. A few feet away was a bronze plaque inlaid into the cobblestone. She walked over and used her phone to illuminate it. The inscription was in German, but the date told her everything she needed to know: 10 May 1933. Berlin was a city of memorials—walls, statues, concrete slabs in the shape of tombs. They were nice gestures, but they couldn't change the past or shape the future. What was the saying again? *There's nothing in the world as invisible as a monument.*

Screeching tires drew Rune's attention away from the plaque. The sound came from the front of the Hotel de Rome. She squinted through the darkness as two men emerged from a black sedan. What started as mild curiosity turned into something far more alarming when she recognized the plain-clothed officers from the Palimpsest. Both bore scars from their run-in with the man in gold lamé. One had a bandage on his cheek, the other a black eye. They looked like they were on a mission. Rune fished her phone out of her pocket. Her hands shook as she typed.

POLICE!!!

Jakob had dumped her, but she couldn't stand the thought of him behind bars. A few seconds went by. The cops disappeared inside the hotel. An arctic wind snapped at the flags above the door. Rune willed Jakob to respond, then she lost patience and dialed the front desk.

"Hotel de Rome. How may I help you?"

"Room 415!"

"Please hold."

One ring. Then a second. Rune's knuckles turned white around her phone. She had to warn Jakob, not just because she cared about him but because there was no telling what he'd say to the cops if he got caught. Greta was an even bigger problem. The woman would throw her under the bus in a heartbeat if it meant making a deal.

"Hello?"

"The police are here! Get out now!"

"Eve?"

"They're in the building! Go!" She didn't wait for an answer. She raced across the square to a side street sandwiched between the hotel and a massive domed church. The cobblestones turned to pavers. Her feet slapped against them, disturbing a colony of rats feasting on food scraps. The scene was apocalyptic, but Rune was too distraught to notice. She reached the end of the street. Her head whipped to one side, then the other. The street was empty. The hotel's parking garage was to the right.

Come on!

She heard Jakob's BMW before she saw it. The nosed peeked out from the ramp. It turned toward her, blinding her with its headlights. She stepped into the street and raised her hand to tell Jakob to stop, to wait, to give her and them another chance. He sped away like she wasn't even there.

"Seriously?!" she screamed. She'd just saved him and this was how he was repaying her? By abandoning her to the cops? By leaving her alone in a foreign city? Fury set in, displacing the fresh sting of the breakup. The feeling roiled inside her, colliding with the anger she harbored for Kit and Milo and every other man who claimed to love her only to bail when things got hard. Had Rune been more self-aware, she might have noticed the patterns in her relationships and done the work she needed to do to address them. It was more complicated than daddy issues, but any therapist worth their salt would have started there.

"Halt! Polizei!" *Stop! Police!*

Rune startled back. Her anger vaporized at the sight of the two officers striding toward her. Would they recognize her from the club? Had they seen her face in the news?

Just breathe.

"Sorry, officers. I don't speak German. Ich spreche kein Deutsch." It took no effort to massacre the words. Keeping the tremor out of her voice, on the other hand, was a testament to her willpower.

"How long have you been out here?" the cop with the shiner asked.

"Not long. Is something wrong?" Rune's knees felt like mush. Any second now, the cops would figure out who she was. When they did, it would all be over. They would haul her in for questioning, then everything would come out and she'd spend the rest of her life inhaling secondhand smoke in a French prison.

"We're looked for two suspected drug dealers," said the cop with the bandage on his cheek. "We think they came this way."

"Drug dealers?!" Rune leaned into her panic. When you couldn't fight something, the only solution was to embrace it. "Oh my God! I could have been killed!"

The officers exchanged looks that said they were used to dealing with hysterical women. "Whoa!" the one with the black eye said. He pushed the air down with his palms, the universal gesture for "calm down." The one with the bandage was more concerned about his case than her mental health. "You're sure no one came out here just now?" he asked.

"I'm sure." Rune saw his eyes twitch. She read it as mistrust. His next words confirmed her suspicion.

"What are you doing out here so late?"

"Have I done something wrong?" She allowed her chin to tremble, but she held back the waterworks in case she needed them later.

"Just answer the question, please."

"I'm staying at the Hotel de Rome. My room is next to the elevator. They said it was soundproof but—" She let her words taper off. It was the right play. Bandage Man gave her a sympathetic look, like he knew a thing or two about insomnia.

"It's not safe for a woman to be out alone at this hour," he said, suddenly a friend instead of a foe. "We'll take you back to the hotel."

"Oh, that's okay. I'm sure you have more important things to do."

"It's no trouble. Keeping people safe is our duty."

"Well, if you're sure." Rune flashed him a grateful smile.

The officers accompanied her to the front of the hotel. Black Eye even opened the door to be extra sure she made it inside.

"Thank you so much, officers. I don't know what I would have done without you." Her words seemed to please them. She gave a little wave, then stepped inside like she still had a room there.

The front desk staff didn't look up when she walked into the lobby, neither did the drunk couple eating each other's faces. A neon birdcage hung from the center of the ceiling. Spherical pendants cast a warm glow on the space.

Rune took a deep breath. Something inside her shifted. Maybe it was the close call with the cops, or her anger at risking everything for a man only to be discarded once again. Whatever the reason, the melancholy that had been shadowing her slipped away. Her chin rose. Her posture straightened. She didn't need anyone to save her—not Jakob, not Milo, and certainly not Kit. She had herself to rely on. After all this time, she finally remembered that was enough.

PART 4

29

PARIS

Depending on the time of day, Le Relais at 4 Rue de l'Amiral de Coligny in Paris' 1st arrondissement was a swanky coffee house, an award-winning restaurant, and a buzzy after-hours bar where the young and beautiful came to see and be seen. Its location across the street from the Louvre's eastern flank should, by all accounts, have made it a tourist trap, but the food was consistently excellent and the local-to-foreigner ratio within acceptable limits, even to the most discerning Parisian.

Marcel Blaise, Le Relais' proprietor and self-professed gatekeeper, paced anxiously by the door wondering if the customers would come that day. He checked the tasteful Montblanc on his wrist. It was approaching 12:30 P.M. The lunch rush should have started by now, but he and his staff were the only ones in the place. He adjusted the sleeves of his smart black jacket and studied his appearance in the mirror by the host's station. His wavy hair was perfectly pomaded into place. His narrow face was smooth and clean-shaven. Only his dark eyes revealed his misery.

Le Relais had been dead quiet since the latest round of labor strikes. On the picket lines were not just the usual civil servants and railway staff but, tragically, members of the International Federation of Actors and the French Federation of Model Agencies. Gone were the emaciated actresses and vaping supermodels who ordered dishes they pretended to eat. The tourists had also jumped ship, scared off by heightened terror alerts and a new wave of health restrictions. Even the weather was conspiring against him. If business didn't pick up soon, he'd be forced to slash hours or even furlough some of his staff.

Marcel scanned the room through worried eyes. To the left, the dashing bartender sliced lemon wedges for drinks he'd never make. To the right, two baby-faced waiters tried—and failed—to look busy polishing silverware. Marcel turned his attention to the door and willed it to open. When it finally did a half hour later, he sincerely felt it was in answer to his prayers. The woman who entered was precisely his type: understated but well-dressed, stylish without being showy. He inhaled sharply when her dark eyes met his. He nearly swooned when she tossed her silky brown tresses over her shoulder. "Will anyone be joining you today?" he asked.

She shook her head. Her lips curled apologetically.

Good God! Marcel thought as he felt a familiar stirring. Even her smile was perfect. "This way, please."

He led her to a table at the front of the restaurant, hoping her presence by the window would drum up business. He could barely keep his disappointment in check when she requested a seat at the back of the room. Still, he helped her out of her plush wool coat and pulled out her chair like the practiced host that he was. She declined his offer to hang her coat and store her leather backpack. "Someone will be right with you," he promised after she settled in.

Marcel sent one of the waiters over to her table with a snap of his fingers. His heart dropped when he saw her wave the menu away. Despair set in when he overheard the waiter relay her order at the bar: sparkling water with a twist of lime. The bartender had just finished slicing four lemons and the woman wanted lime? It was all Marcel could do not to howl with frustration. He pinched the bridge of his nose with his thumb and index finger. Then he reminded himself that labor strikes didn't last forever and that fortunes could change at the drop of a hat.

Rune didn't normally turn down food and alcohol, but on this occasion, it seemed like the prudent choice. The next few minutes demanded her full attention. She blocked out the big feelings coming from the restaurant's host and directed her gaze to the window. Her table offered a clear view of the Gothic church of Saint-Germain-l'Auxerrois, a jewel of a building in a city that was full of them. But Rune wasn't interested in the church's massive windows and dizzying belfry. She only had eyes for the porch.

The church's bells rang at 1:00 p.m. sharp. The sound merged with honking cars and blaring sirens. Rune drew a breath. Everything hinged on what happened next.

Lemaire walked into her sightline exactly on schedule. He wore a black trilby that was stylish but wrong for the weather. The collar of his overcoat was raised protectively over his neck. He flicked a piece of lint off his sleeve with a gloved hand.

I need your help. Please.

That was how Rune had ended her message to him the day before. She'd asked for a meeting. She knew he'd show up. As the only person who could link him to the Bonaparte thefts, silencing her would be his top priority.

Movement in her peripheral vision caught her attention. It was Lemaire's two henchmen. The ones from the Crillon. The ones she thought she saw in Berlin. Lemaire had almost certainly instructed them to get rid of her. If they thought it would be easy, they would be sorely disappointed.

The waiter arrived with her sparkling water. The bottle hissed when he unscrewed the cap. Water splashed on her sleeve when he poured it into her glass. She didn't care. She kept her eyes on her mark.

Lemaire raised the cuff of his overcoat to look at the time. He was punctual, meticulously so. Her tardiness was probably driving him nuts. She took a sip of fizzy water and watched from the comfort of the restaurant as the wind whipped the trilby off his head. He was on his way to retrieve it when a chili-red Mini flattened it with its back tire. The sight pleased Rune more than it should have. She took her time drinking her water. Only after her glass was empty did she send Lemaire a text.

Can't make it. Cops everywhere.

She watched Lemaire retrieve his phone from his pocket. A scowl appeared on his face. He pulled off a glove and typed.

Where are you?

Rune snorted loudly enough to catch the attention of the staff. Lemaire was taking her for a fool. She thought for a moment, then wrote, *It's too dangerous. More soon.*

He must have understood that her words were final because he waved to his men and set off in the direction of the Seine River. Rune dropped a few Euros on the table, threw on her coat and backpack, and exited the restaurant before the host could even register what was happening.

She tracked Lemaire and his men to the Pont des Arts, a pedestrian bridge connecting the Left and Right Banks. A young couple with a brass padlock cast confused looks at the bridge's glass fence, apparently unaware of the war the city was waging against love locks. A beret-wearing accordionist softened the blow with a skilled rendition of *La Vie En Rose*. Rune paused to listen for a second. For someone who was decidedly bad at relationships, she was a sucker for romance.

The stately facade of the Institut de France, the country's premier learned society, loomed directly ahead. Rune watched Lemaire dismiss his men with a curt wave and words she was too far away to hear. He took a right past a stone personification of the Republic, then a left onto the Rue Bonaparte.

Rune eyed the street sign warily. *What are the chances?* she thought.

Handsome apartment buildings dotted the street. Pedestrians were few and far between. Concerned Lemaire would spot her, Rune stopped in front of a contemporary art gallery and pretended to admire a painting of a black dot. She saw Lemaire take a left beside an old church out of the corner of her eye. She hurried to catch up.

The street was quiet when she arrived. She was kicking herself for letting Lemaire get away when she caught sight of a door closing a few feet away. She approached it without hesitation.

16 Rue de l'Abbaye was a well-kept building made of limestone blocks that glowed even in gloomy light. A bookstore-cum-art gallery occupied the ground level. Above were four floors, presumably apartments. Rune pressed her nose against the glass panel. It was too dark to see inside. She tried the handle. It didn't budge. She was mulling over her options when the door swung open and just missed whacking her in the forehead. She yelped and jumped out of the way.

The woman who emerged had snow-white hair and a matching fur coat. An alligator-skin satchel dangled from her wrist. A sneer hung from her heavily powdered face. One look and she immediately pegged Rune as a foreigner.

"I suppose you're here to see the medieval refectory?" she said in a high-and-mighty tone that matched her appearance.

Rune's mind snapped back to high school history class. If memory served, a refectory was a monastic dining room. "Yes, the refectory," she replied with the solemnity the word seemed to require.

The woman gave her a careful once-over, like she was trying to gauge her trustworthiness. The bar must have been fairly low because she agreed to let Rune in. "I'll make an exception this time," she said.

"But you and your classmates can't keep coming here unannounced. This is private property."

Rune bobbed her head in agreement. She couldn't remember the last time someone had mistaken her for a student. She took it as a compliment until she noticed the milky film covering the woman's irises and realized she had the vision of a mole.

"Tell Professor Duclos to expect a call from the homeowners' association," the woman warned. "If she wants to use this building for teaching purposes, she *must* go through the proper channels."

"I'll let her know."

"Very well." The woman turned toward the keypad, then stopped. "Don't go anywhere but the lobby," she said, wagging her finger in Rune's face. "And for God's sake, don't touch anything."

"I wouldn't dream of it."

She entered the code.

The door buzzed.

Rune stepped inside. "Whoa."

She had every reason to be impressed. As the woman promised, the lobby encased the ruins of a medieval refectory. According to the plaque by the entrance, it belonged to Saint-Germain-des-Prés, one of the oldest monasteries in Paris. The eleventh-century church stood across the street, but the rest of the complex had long fallen into ruin. Bits and pieces were now scattered in museums around the world. Part of a chapel even stood abandoned to vagrants and pigeons in a small park next to the church. Unlike the rest of the ruins, though, what remained of the refectory was hidden from view, accessible only to the building's privileged residents.

Rune let out a low whistle of appreciation as she gazed at the ruins of a window that was more than thirty feet tall. Its stained-glass panels were long gone, but the intricate stonework that once held them in place was in exceptionally good condition. A metal staircase torqued upward next to the ruins, providing residents the opportunity to examine them up close each time they entered and exited the building, should they forgo the elevator. It was an ingenious design that interwove the old and new in a functionally and aesthetically concordant way.

The lights turned off automatically, leaving Rune in near darkness. They came on again when she moved toward the mailboxes. They were numbered one through eight, but they didn't list the occupants' names. She'd have to find another way to determine where Lemaire went. Knocking on doors wasn't an option, but neither was loitering in the lobby. Rune briefly considered waiting outside before homing in on the spiral staircase. The second-floor landing offered unobstructed views of the elevator. Plus, if a resident happened to see her, she could pretend to be one of Professor Duclos's pupils studying the ruins. Satisfied with her decision, she climbed the metal steps and took a seat.

There was nothing to do but think on that staircase. Rune thought about Lemaire and her plan to entrap him. She thought about the police and what they did and didn't know about her. But mostly, she thought about Romy and her children. About the damage that had been done to them, that was still being done. It had to stop. *She* had to stop it. Guilt gnawed at her, stubborn, unyielding. She hadn't even opened Alaric's files, much less sifted through them. *Soon,* she promised herself.

The one-hour mark came and went. Rune rubbed her neck and tilted her head from side to side to release some of her tension. She wanted to get up and start poking around, but her fear of drawing attention kept her exactly where she was. Getting caught by Lemaire wasn't an option. Not when the stakes were this high.

Two hours passed without movement. Rune's body was stiff now. The urge to use a bathroom set in. She trained her eyes on the elevator and silently begged it to move. It didn't comply, but something equally helpful occurred. An adolescent girl with facial piercings and platinum hair materialized at the front door. She wore a long black coat and the surly expression of a human in the throes of puberty. Rune knew right away that she could coax information out of her. If there was anyone she understood, it was the disaffected teenaged girl.

"Excuse me!" she called out from the staircase.

Nothing.

She hurried down the stairs. "Excuse me," she repeated, tapping the girl on the shoulder.

Off came the headphones. An aggressive guitar riff filtered through the earpads.

"Do you speak English?"

The girl nodded and cracked her gum.

"I teach at the American University. I'm writing an article about historic preservation and reuse. Would you mind answering a few questions?"

The girl looked surprised, like she wasn't used to being taken seriously by an adult. She shrugged her assent.

"How long has your family lived in this building?"

"A long time. Since before I was born."

Rune blinked at the incongruence of the girl's polished English and unvarnished shell. She recovered quickly. "Were your parents here when the staircase was built?"

The girl shook her head, causing her thick bangs to sway across her forehead. "The stairs are *really* old. Like, from the 1950s."

"Do you know if any of the other residents lived in the building at the time?"

The girl's eyes flew skyward as she tried to retrieve the information. "Maybe Madame Pelletier in 201. She's been here forever."

Rune wondered if Madame Pelletier was the elderly woman who let her into the building. "What about the other residents? Could they have been around?"

"Not the Blochs or the Desrosiers. Definitely not Monsieur Armand." The girl counted on her fingers as she rattled off more names. Lemaire wasn't among them.

"Are there any foreigners in the building?" Rune asked, approaching the issue from a different angle. "I'd love to get an outsider's perspective on the preservation of French culture."

The girl started to raise her shoulders, then stopped mid-gesture. "An American sometimes stays with Madame Vidal. I think they're together. Dating, I mean. Maybe you can ask him."

Rune was elated. Vidal was the name she'd seen in the travel log on Lemaire's yacht. She swallowed her excitement. "I'd love to connect with him," she said evenly. "What unit are they in?"

"401. But I don't know if he's there right now."

"That's okay. I'll leave a note in the mailbox. Thanks so much. You've been a huge help." Rune held out her hand.

The girl's handshake was firm, like the exchange had boosted her confidence. She wasn't the only one feeling proud of herself. Anything seemed possible to Rune now that she knew something about Lemaire's personal life. She waited for the girl to turn around, then practically danced out of the building.

The air felt colder leaving than it did coming in, but Rune was flying too high to notice. She retraced her steps down the Rue Bonaparte, passed the Institut de France, and over the Pont des Arts. Minutes later, she reached Le Relais, where the narrow-faced host with the slick hair greeted her like an old friend. He threw his hands up with delight when she told him she was there to eat. His delight turned to glee when she ordered the pan-seared sea scallops with brown butter sauce, the most expensive thing on the menu.

30

RIGHT BANK, PARIS

D ays were short in Paris at this time of year. A mere eight-and-a-half hours, hardly enough to ward off seasonal affective disorder, aka SAD, the most apt acronym in medical history. Although Rune could have done with more light, not even a 5:00 P.M. sunset could dampen her spirits.

She'd spent the afternoon eating and plotting her next moves. At the top of her to-do list was getting into Lemaire's luxury love nest to look for something useful. She had an idea about how to make that happen, but it required coordinating with Romy. She sent her a message asking her to contact Lemaire. The pretense? Buying gems. Lemaire never turned down an opportunity to make money. With that off her plate, she googled "Paris quiet place to work" and mapped out the closest option. The time had come to go through Alaric's files.

The wind was gusting. Rune lowered her head and hurried toward an arcade, hoping it would provide shelter. It didn't. She tucked her chin into her coat collar and picked up the pace. Only after she'd walked a full block did she realize she was on the Rue de Rivoli. Her good mood dampened. The street, one of the grandest in Paris, was named after

Napoleon's victory over Austrian armies at the Battle of Rivoli. The man was like her childhood dream—impossible to escape.

Beaux-arts lanterns swung from the arcade. The Louvre loomed across the street, immense and deserted. The museum was closed for the day, so were the shops pedaling trinkets to visitors keen on bringing bits of Paris home with them. Without the distraction of crowds, the beauty of the area was on full display.

The resplendent Hotel du Louvre appeared directly ahead. Rune was tempted to get a room, but without a passport, she was sure to be turned away. She took a right turn. It was early yet. Where she'd spend the night was a problem for later.

Google Maps directed her to the Palais-Royal, a former cardinal's palace with a public courtyard and park at its center. She walked through the vaulted entrance and found herself amid a forest of black-and-white columns, some taller than her, others only a few inches high. Had she done her research, she would have known that they were part of an art installation designed to hide the palace's ventilation shafts.

The courtyard led directly to a rectangular park with leafless trees aligned like soldiers in formation. At the center was a circular fountain whose jets were turned off for the season. Rune's soles crunched against the dusty gravel. A powdery residue clung to her boots when she exited the park a short time later. She didn't notice. Her focus was on the gated entrance of France's renowned national library.

A security guard with a walrus mustache greeted her in the vestibule and took a cursory look inside her backpack. Had he opened the interior pocket, he would have discovered the envelope of bills she'd stashed inside. He waved her through. She walked away relieved not to have to explain herself. She was still trying to get her bearings when a door opened directly to her left. A woman with horn-rimmed glasses and a cardigan covered in orange cat hair emerged. She held the door open. Rune stepped inside.

The room was a bibliophile's dream, an enormous oval lined with floor-to-ceiling bookcases. A shallow dome levitated above the space. Below were sixteen windows, each named after a city with a historically significant library—Alexandria, Athens, Rome, and many others Rune had never heard of. Long oak tables with green opaline lamps occupied one end of the room. On the other end were upholstered chairs arranged around metal tables. The design was at once grand and intimate.

Rune chose a seat at one of the library's computer stations, next to a man who looked to be nearing retirement. She smiled inwardly when he started typing using only his index fingers. She reached into her pocket for the thumb drive she'd swiped from Alaric's office. She stuck it into the USB port, clicked on the first file, and drew closer to the screen. There was no time to waste. Romy and her boys were counting on her.

Minutes stacked into hours. Three to be precise. Then the overhead lights started flickering to signal that the library was closing. Rune leaned back in her chair and rubbed her eyes. She'd gone through about half of Alaric's files, including drug trial reports, proposals to purchase new equipment, and earnings projections. So far, there was nothing amiss. She wanted to go through the rest of the files, but her time at the library had just about run out.

The staff chatted loudly as they went about their end-of-day tasks. One shared too much information about a medical problem. Another provided a blow-by-blow of an argument she had with her partner. It was their not-so-subtle way of telling patrons it was time to leave. The man next to her let out an unhappy grumble as he gathered his belongings. A set of keys fell out of his coat pocket. He bent over to retrieve them, but Rune beat him to it.

"Here you go," she said, dropping the keys in his wrinkled hands.

The man was not a people person. He thanked her awkwardly, then busied himself with his extensive collection of HB pencils.

Rune guessed from the pencils and frumpy sweater vest that he was an academic. She tried again, this time in a language he'd understand. "I wish the library wouldn't close so early. It's such a busy time of the semester."

"So many meetings," the man complained with a dismayed shake of the head.

It wasn't much, but it was all the encouragement Rune needed. She leaned closer, as if she was sharing top-secret information. "I heard extended hours are in the works."

"Really?" The man stopped organizing his pencils and looked her in the eye for the first time. "That would be marvelous!"

Charmed by his enthusiasm for extended library hours, Rune pressed on. "I teach at the American University. The library there closes at five. Can you believe that?"

"I'm at the Sorbonne. It's not much better."

The librarian with the health problems planted herself nearby and cleared her throat. Rune and the man exchanged looks.

"I hope you don't think I'm being too forward," Rune said as they made their way out of the oval room. "But would you like to have dinner with me?"

"Excuse me?" The man put a hand to his ear as though he'd misheard.

"My boyfriend broke up with me yesterday. I don't want to eat alone." She gave him a pained smile, then added, "I'm Rune, by the way."

"Hugo."

She held out her hand. Hugo accepted it. He seemed more comfortable now that they'd exchanged names. They passed the guard's station and stepped outside. The wind had died down, but somehow it felt colder. "What do you say, Hugo? Will you save me from the pitying looks of strangers?"

That drew a chuckle.

"Well?"

"Why not?" he said. "Come with me."

Rune followed him across the street to the Galerie Vivienne, a skylit passage washed in warm ambient light. The sinuous notes of Ravel's *Bolero* filled the air. Serpentine mosaics made of gold and black stone twined under their feet. They passed a toy store and an optician's office, then a hair salon and a bookshop, the oldest in Paris. They turned a corner, climbed a few steps, and continued to the Bistrot Vivienne, a quintessentially Parisian eatery that looked like it hadn't changed in two hundred years. The matronly hostess recognized Hugo. She gave Rune the side-eye, then led them upstairs to a room with red velvet chairs and matching carpeting. A career waiter with salt and pepper hair approached. He took their order in an unmistakably Provençal accent.

"I'll have a pastis," Rune said, suddenly nostalgic for Marseille.

"Ricard or Duval?"

"Ricard."

He turned to Hugo. "And for you, sir?"

"I'll have my usual."

"Very well." The waiter disappeared down the stairs, leaving them alone for the first time.

"So, your boyfriend dumped you," Hugo said.

"Wow. Sugarcoat, much?"

"Sugarcoating is for children. You're not a child."

"Is that what you tell your students when you give them bad grades?"

"I don't *give* them bad grades. They *earn* them."

"Right."

Silence descended. Rune didn't feel compelled to fill it. The waiter returned with their drinks.

"I met my wife on our first day of university," Hugo said. He gave his wineglass a few swirls before setting it down without drinking. "She was two rows ahead of me in a course on Early Modern Literature. One look and *paff*!" He slapped his hands together. "We call it a thunderclap in French. Love at first sight."

Rune knew what that was. She took a sip of pastis to keep the memories at bay.

"We got married a few months after graduation. I continued my studies while she raised our two daughters. Next week would have been our forty-second anniversary. Isn't that something?" He gave his wine another swirl. Again, he didn't drink. "It was a dream. It really was. Oh, we had our share of disagreements, like everyone. But I never once doubted her love for me. She never doubted mine either. She told me as much." He fell silent, letting the low hum of nearby conversations fill the space. When he spoke again, his voice was soft, barely higher than a whisper. "It went by so fast."

Rune downed what remained of her drink. She didn't know what happened to Hugo's wife, but the tears in his eyes told her it wasn't good. She felt stupid. How could her days-long fling with Jakob compare to the life Hugo built with his wife? Even her relationship with Kit seemed small in the face of "till death do us part."

"They say Paris is for lovers, but I think that's bullshit." The softness was gone from Hugo's voice. He stopped playing with his wine long enough to taste it.

"The poets would probably disagree with you," Rune said. "The tourists too."

"Paris is for suckers who content themselves with dirty streets and clichés. There's nothing special about this place."

"That's a pretty cynical thing to say for someone who found love here."

"That was a long time ago. Things are different now."

"What about the art and the monuments and the lights? Those haven't changed." Rune wasn't sure why she was arguing with Hugo, but she wasn't prepared to admit that Paris was all smoke and mirrors.

Maybe she needed to believe that some places were in fact special and that those places could provide hope, even for people like her.

"You're young," Hugo said with a dismissive wave of his hand. "You'll understand when you get to be my age."

Rune hated being talked down to, but in this instance, she chose to let it go. A broken heart could make people say and do things they otherwise wouldn't. She would know. She signaled the waiter for another round. "Keep up," she said to Hugo.

He blinked, surprised.

"What?" she shrugged. "Grumpy old men are my vibe."

31

RIGHT BANK, PARIS

Rune went home with Hugo that night. She didn't complain when he dropped his head on her shoulder in the taxi, nor did she push him away when he pressed up against her in the elevator. And when he fumbled with his house keys, she took them from his hand and slipped them into the lock like she was the woman of the house and not a virtual stranger.

She pushed the door open. He pawed around for the light switch, nearly taking her down in the process. Somehow, she kept them both upright.

"Sorry," he slurred.

"It's okay," she said, as much for her sake as for his. "Let's get you to bed." She peered through the darkness to find the bedroom. It wasn't hard. The apartment, while not without charm, was as small as one would expect for a French civil servant.

Hugo was practically deadweight by the time Rune got him on the bed. He didn't react when she unlaced his boots and pulled them off his feet, nor did he stir when she grabbed a spare blanket from the armoire and draped it over his body. She swept his thin gray hair off his forehead, then she left him alone to sleep it off.

The only computer in the apartment was in the cramped living room, next to shelves that held twice as many books as they should have. The Jurassic-era desktop was enough to make Rune regret not choosing a younger, more tech-savvy mark. But those people tended to expect sex, and she had neither the time nor the desire for a hookup. She pressed the power button. The startup chord was so loud she felt compelled to check on Hugo. She relaxed when she heard him snoring. Then she removed her wig and ran her fingers through her choppy hair, still unnaturally blonde from her time in Amsterdam.

The computer took a long time to boot up. Rune lost patience and went to the kitchen to get some water. She filled a glass straight from the tap, then opened the fridge. The shelves were bare, just as she suspected. She grabbed a jar of tiny French pickles from the door and brought them to the living room. To her surprise, the computer was ready to go. She pawed around the messy desk until she found a crinkled sheet with all of Hugo's passwords. He used the same one for everything—Rose—presumably his wife. She plugged in her thumb drive and picked up where she left off at the library.

Steiner Pharmaceuticals' files were a fascinating read for anyone interested in drug research and development. Unfortunately, Rune had no such interest. Maybe it was the lateness of the hour, but the more she read, the less thorough she became. She caught her mind drifting during an especially technical file on new antivirals for chronic hepatitis C. Her vision grew appropriately blurry when she tackled a market research analysis about macular degeneration.

"Enough," she said when she saw the company's quarterly earnings report. She stood and did a few stretches. When that failed to revive her, she went back to the kitchen to search for coffee.

Hugo only had a stovetop espresso maker, the aluminum kind that consistently made undrinkable sludge. Short on options, she put a pot on and waited for it to brew. The telltale gurgling started, followed by a dry hiss signaling that the coffee was done. She poured it into a small white cup, gave it a sniff, and drank it like a shot. The caffeine kicked in almost straight away. She returned to Hugo's computer sharper and more motivated than before.

The quarterly earnings report contained run-of-the-mill information about Steiner Pharma's performance, the kind of information that could be important but that Rune didn't have the skills to interpret. She was about to close it, but the caffeine flooding her system prompted her to read to the end. It was the right decision.

+ €993 million, Neuilly.

The note was handwritten and squeezed in the top right corner of the page, like an unconscious doodle or scribble. Rune scrolled back to the beginning of the file and went through it slowly. It listed all of Steiner Pharma's branches, fourteen in total, including the Berlin headquarters. The handwritten note was the only mention of Neuilly. Rune did a quick search and learned that Neuilly was, in fact, Neuilly-sur-Seine, a wealthy enclave just west of Paris. The town was not just Paris' most expensive suburb but also one of the most affluent areas in France, home to exclusive residential neighborhoods, foreign embassies, and multinational corporations.

Rune found no link between Neuilly and Steiner Pharmaceuticals, but she knew it existed. The proof was in the scribble on the quarterly earnings report. Her leg bounced up and down as she considered what to do next. The jar of mini pickles beckoned. The lid popped when she turned it. She reached in with her fingers and pulled one out. It was crunchy and delicious. She pulled out a few more. It took her about half the jar to come to the decision to text Romy.

You up?

The screen brightened the dark living room. It dimmed after a few seconds. Rune let out a brief sigh and resigned herself to waiting until morning. She reached into the pickle jar again. Her screen lit up.

What is it?

Sorry to wake you!

You didn't.

Rune didn't have to ask what was keeping Romy up to the wee hours. She'd lose sleep too, if she shared a bed with Alaric. She cut to the chase.

Does Steiner Pharma have a branch in Neuilly?

No.

Rune sat back in her chair. Maybe she was wrong. Maybe the scribble was just a scribble, completely unrelated to the company's earnings. She was about to sign off when another message popped up.

But we keep a pied-à-terre in Neuilly. It's where we stay when we visit my family.

The words piqued Rune's interest. She didn't believe in coincidences.

We're there now. Got in an hour ago—to take care of the other thing you asked me to do.

Rune nearly knocked the jar of pickles off the desk. *You're meeting Lemaire?!*

Yes.

And you're only telling me NOW?

No time. Alaric is with me. I was going to call in the morning.

When are you meeting him?

We'd agreed on tomorrow afternoon, but he changed it. We'll probably do it in a few days.

Where?

The Crillon.

Rune couldn't believe Lemaire had taken the bait. She could set her plan in motion. She could search the Saint-Germain apartment.

Was there anything else?

Rune thought for a moment, then typed, *Send me your Neuilly address.*

Why?

So I can look through your husband's things. Rune worried Romy wouldn't agree, but the address arrived seconds later. She pulled it up on Google Maps. It was in a residential part of Neuilly, across from the Bois de Boulogne, a two-thousand-acre park and paradise for nature lovers.

Come by tomorrow at 9:00 A.M. The apartment will be empty.

Great!

You'll have an hour. I'll leave the key under the doormat. The code to get into the building is 2468.

"Who do we appreciate?" Rune chanted softly. She laughed at her own joke, then shook her head at the absurdity of using the same security code for multiple homes, especially after one of those homes was burglarized.

Rune said goodbye to Romy and glanced at the clock on Hugo's computer. Dawn was approaching. In just a few hours, she would leave the safety of this apartment and make her way to Neuilly. She stripped down to her underwear and curled up on the bed next to Hugo. He whimpered softly. She wrapped her arms around him until he quieted, then closed her eyes. Sleep wouldn't come. Something shady was going on at Steiner Pharmaceuticals. If she could figure out what it was, she would have what she needed to help Romy. Once that happened, she could focus all her attention on Lemaire.

32

NEUILLY-SUR-SEINE

It took Rune forty minutes and two transfers to get from Hugo's Right Bank apartment to Neuilly. The ritziness of the area was apparent the moment she stepped off the metro at Les Sablons. The station was on one of only two lines equipped with expensive screen doors separating the platform from the tracks. The white tiles on the walls and ceiling were free of graffiti and grime. Homeless people were nowhere in sight. Rune tucked an errant strand from her brown wig behind her ear and took the escalator to the exit.

The sky was clear and the air crisp when she emerged from the station. Her phone led her across the multilaned Avenue Charles de Gaulle, down the Boulevard des Sablons, and left on Boulevard Maurice-Barrès across from the Bois de Boulogne. She passed several attractive limestone buildings before reaching Romy and Alaric's address. It was more ornate than the others, with classical moldings and garlands articulating each story. Fanciest of all were the shirtless Atlas figures supporting the third-floor railing.

Rune opened the iron gate and followed the paved path to the entrance. She used the code Romy gave her to get into the lobby and then made her way to the elevator. Up to the fifth floor she went, toying with her wig to prevent the camera from capturing her face. The doors opened. The smell of expensive perfume mixed with carpet cleaner filled the air. Rune sneezed twice as she walked down the long hallway to the Steiner's apartment. She lifted the corner of the welcome mat and found the key Romy left for her. A neighbor chose that precise moment to emerge from the only other unit on the floor.

"Ménage," Rune called out. *Housekeeping.*

It was one of the few French words she remembered from her time in Marseille. It did the trick. The neighbor raised his nose and shuffled to the elevator with his well-groomed Pekingese in tow.

Romy and Alaric's pied-à-terre was bigger and more luxurious than most people's primary homes. A spacious foyer led to the main part of the apartment—an open kitchen, dining room, and living room that overlooked the Bois de Boulogne. There were two bedrooms on one end of the unit, one for the parents and one for the kids. On the opposite end was a guest suite and a well-appointed study. Rune went straight to the study. With only an hour, she had no time to lose.

The locked filing cabinets were no barrier for Rune. One by one, she opened them, scanning the folders for references to Neuilly and nearly a billion Euros. Nothing. She tackled the drawers next. Still no luck. She plunked herself in Alaric's chair and leaned back. She could continue to spin her wheels, or she could try Alaric's computer. She pulled out her phone.

I need Alaric's password.

A few minutes went by with no word from Romy. She hit dial.

"Your timing is terrible," Romy said after three rings.

"I can appreciate that, but I need to access Alaric's computer."

"I can't help you."

"Yes, you can."

"You think he gave me his password?"

"No. But I think you know it."

"I don't."

"Wives always know."

Romy exhaled loudly.

"If you were to guess. Maybe your birthday?"

The exhale turned into a snort. "Alaric has to be reminded every year. His assistant sends lovely flowers."

"If not you, then who? The kids? Someone else he cares about?"

"Alaric only cares about himself."

"Let's go with that."

"With what?"

"Him. His birthday, the street he grew up on, his first-grade teacher."

"His birthday is November 15, 1987. He grew up all over the place. And I don't know who his teachers were."

Rune tried a few variations of Alaric's birthday. None of them worked. "What else could it be? His childhood pet? His mother's maiden name?"

"Our dog is the only pet he's ever had. He hates it, and he hates Margot almost as much."

"Is there *anyone* he likes?"

"No."

Rune scanned the room for a clue. There were framed diplomas on the walls and books and knickknacks on the shelves. The only personal item on the desk was a photo of Alaric in his younger years hamming it up with two friends. She picked it up and looked for signs of his violent tendencies, but all she saw was a normal guy doing what normal people did when someone pointed a camera at them. "Who are Alaric's best friends?" she asked, setting the photo down. "The ones in the picture on his desk."

"Karl and Edgar. Karl with a *K*."

Rune tried each name separately. Neither worked. Then she tried Alaric's and the other two as a single word. The login screen vanished.

The progress bar started loading. She couldn't believe it. "I'm in!" she exclaimed.

If Romy responded, Rune didn't hear in her rush to search Alaric's files. The first thing she did was go to his documents folder. There were hundreds. She typed Neuilly in the search field to narrow the results. It yielded a handful of hits, mostly documents related to the apartment—the mortgage, home insurance policy, and utilities. She checked the time. "Focus," she said when she saw she only had ten minutes left. The time crunch lit a fire under her. She tore through the remaining documents. She was down to the last three when she finally stumbled on something useful, an invoice for carnauba wax, colloidal silicon dioxide, and dibasic calcium phosphate, ingredients that wouldn't be out of place in a lab. The delivery address was in Neuilly but not the apartment. It wasn't a smoking gun, but it wasn't nothing either.

Rune was taking a picture of the document when a metallic sound caught her attention. She stopped what she was doing and listened. She'd nearly convinced herself she'd imagined it when she heard a door open and close. Someone was home. Adrenaline surged. Then she reminded herself that the apartment was huge and full of hiding places. With remarkable composure, she turned off the computer and slipped out of the office.

Most people would have moved away from the sounds, but Rune was experienced enough to know that being near the exit increased her chances of getting away. She advanced to the foyer in silence. Movement in the kitchen told her the coast was clear. She was a breath away from the front door when she heard the lock turn. It opened faster than she could react.

"Oh!" the woman exclaimed.

Rune recognized her as the Steiners' nanny. Behind her were Romy and Alaric's two sons and their giant dog. "It's okay," Rune said, raising her hands to indicate they had nothing to fear.

Four pairs of eyes blinked at her.

"Everything's okay. I'm here to see Mr. Steiner."

A look of doubt crossed the nanny's face.

"I'll be going now." For a blissful moment, Rune thought she would get away with it. Then all hell broke loose.

"Herr Steiner!" The nanny's voice shattered the quiet of the apartment. The boys started crying. Brioche barked and yanked at his leash. Rapid footfalls approached from the kitchen.

Rune lunged to one side, but getting around the hysterical nanny was like trying to circumvent a mountain. The woman must have thought she was being attacked because she tried kicking Rune. Unfortunately for her, she had neither the skill nor the athleticism to pull it off. Rune caught her foot midair, leaving the nanny to balance perilously on one leg. She swept the woman's standing leg with her opposite foot. The nanny dropped to the floor.

"You're safe," Rune assured the wailing children. "I'm not going to hurt you."

The boys cry harder. Brioche snarled like he meant business. Rune fled to the elevator.

"Hey!"

Her head jerked back. Alaric was in the hallway looking taller and blonder than ever. He wore athletic gear. His chest was puffed, his face all angry and red. Rune ditched the elevator idea and ran for the stairs.

"Halt!" *Stop!*

Down the steps she went, her stomping feet echoing in stairwell. She'd barely made it past the first landing when she heard Alaric above her. She raced past another landing, then another and another until she reached the ground floor. Her shoulder hit the door. The sun exploded around her. The wintry air bit her cheeks. She sprinted down the paved path to the front gate.

Alaric burst from the building seconds later. Rune looked back and knew instantly she couldn't outrun him. The Bois de Boulogne lay directly in front of her. The Boulevard Maurice-Barrès stretched to either side. She chose the latter. If Alaric was going to catch her, better on a public street than in an empty park. She knew what he did to women when he thought no one was looking.

"Halt!"

Rune didn't have to look back to know that Alaric was gaining on her. His voice was loud. The sound of his shoes striking the pavement grew closer with every stride.

Vvvvrrrr!

The e-bike motor caught Rune's attention. The sound was ubiquitous in the age of Uber Eats and Deliveroo but for her, it was a lifeline.

"Move!" she yelled at the delivery guy getting off his bike three buildings down.

He looked up. His face registered his surprise.

"I said move!"

He took a step back, completely oblivious to what was about to happen.

Rune torpedoed past him with a breathless "Sorry!" Her leg flew over the bike, then off she went, the electric motor propelling her already quick feet.

The delivery guy swore. Alaric added his own expletives.

Rune pedaled madly, not looking back until their angry voices had faded to nothing.

33

NEUILLY-SUR-SEINE

"**W**hat the hell happened?" Romy demanded.

"I'm fine, thanks for asking," Rune replied as she ditched her stolen e-bike and wrenched her wig off her head. A garbageman looked at her sideways when she tossed it directly into his truck. She bulged her eyes as if daring him to say something, then headed to a busy street lined with expensive looking boutiques. She chose one at random. A saleswoman with a pageboy haircut greeted her in rapid French. Rune waved her hand to indicate she didn't need help.

"I wouldn't have let you into my apartment if I'd known you were going to attack my nanny and terrify my children," Romy hissed.

"Give me a break! I didn't—" Rune stopped mid-sentence and lowered her voice. "That's a complete mischaracterization of what happened."

"Tell that to my kids."

"Don't lay this all on me. You said I had an hour."

"You *did* have an hour. Alaric always comes home from his run at the same time. *Always.*"

"Whatever," Rune mumbled. She wasn't prepared to admit that she'd lost track of time. She scanned the racks until she found what she was looking for—a scarf in the perfect shade of don't-notice-me beige. She snatched it from the hanger and looked for the matching hat she was certain existed. "I may have found something, in case you were wondering."

"Really?" Romy suddenly sounded a lot less upset.

"Does Alaric have dealings on Avenue Charles de Gaulle?"

"Not that I know of."

"Hmm." Rune spied the beige hat on a shelf by the cash register. She went to retrieve it. The only size available was a large. She bobbed her head at the saleswoman to indicate she was ready to pay and pulled a hundred-Euro bill from her backpack. She reached for two more when the price came up on the register.

"What's next?" Romy asked.

"I'm going to check out the address." Rune put the hat on before the saleswoman could offer her a bag. Her eyebrows were the only thing stopping it from slipping over her eyes. She pocketed her change, then looped the scarf around her neck and headed to the exit.

"Don't you ever get tired of it?" Romy said.

"Tired of what?"

"Of going where you're not supposed to go."

"No. Not really."

"How will you get in?"

"I'm not sure." Rune heard muffled French on the other end of the line. Something approaching regret crept in. "Are those your kids?"

"Yes."

"I didn't mean to scare them."

"It's fine. They're fine."

"Go be with them. I'll call if I learn anything."

"Okay. Be careful, Rune."

"Always."

Rune entered the Charles de Gaulle address into her phone as soon as she hung up. There were no informative hits. She mapped out the route and was surprised to learn that the building was just a few minutes away. She stepped outside. Police sirens sounded nearby. A woman across the street looked around, concerned. But Rune didn't break stride. The cops were looking for a brunette in head-to-toe black, not a bottled blonde with beige accessories. And that was assuming the sirens were for her.

A right turn took Rune off the main shopping drag. Another led her directly to Avenue Charles de Gaulle. Only when she saw Les Sablons metro did she realize she'd been steps from the mystery address when she first arrived in Neuilly. She passed a private branch of the French multinational bank, BNP Paribas, the headquarters of Warner Brothers Discovery France, the Comcast building, and Chanel's Paris headquarters. The next building lacked any identifying features, but its massive footprint and hypermodern design told her it was home to an equally important company. She hung back knowing the opportunity to get inside would invariably present itself. She didn't have to wait long.

The woman who walked through the sliding glass doors looked like everyone else coming in and out of the building. She wore corporate attire under a dark coat. Her phone was pressed against her ear. The only thing distinguishing her was the royal-blue lanyard dangling from her free hand. Rune smiled at the sight. Where there was a lanyard, there was an ID card. She strode toward the woman. Their shoulders smacked. Rune let out a yelp, then collapsed onto the sidewalk.

"Help! My knee!" she cried, writhing in pain.

"I'm so sorry! I didn't see you!" The woman crouched down, her expression full of concern. "Are you alright?"

"It really hurts."

"Don't move. I'll call an ambulance."

"No!" The word came out a little too abruptly. Rune backpedaled. "I mean, please don't. I don't have travel insurance and I can't afford an ambulance or a hospital."

"But you're injured."

"I'll be fine. I just need to rest."

"Are you staying nearby? I can call you a taxi."

"That's okay. My boyfriend will come get me. He's at the Eiffel Tower."

"The Eiffel Tower is very far! You can't wait out here!"

"I'll be fine," Rune repeated.

"There's a café across the street," the woman said. She pointed to a Pret a Manger. "Do you think you can make it?"

Rune gazed across the eight lanes of traffic separating them from the café and gave the woman a determined nod. The woman wrapped her arm around Rune and helped her to her feet. She allowed Rune to lean on her as they made their way to the median and then to the other side of the road. She even opened the door for Rune and offered to buy her coffee to warm her up.

"Maybe a hot chocolate?" Rune proposed instead.

"Of course," the woman replied.

Rune wobbled getting into her chair.

The woman set her phone and ID card on the table to steady her. "I'll be right back," she promised after she was sure Rune wouldn't topple over.

Rune waited until the woman's back was turned to slip the ID card into her pocket. She pulled out her phone and pretended to make a call. The woman caught her eye from the counter. Rune waved and gave her a small smile. Her smile grew when the woman returned with a hot chocolate and a flaky pastry. "Ooooh!" she cooed when she opened the lid and saw the whipped cream. "You didn't have to!"

"It's the least I can do," the woman said. "Is your boyfriend coming? Do you want me to wait with you?"

"Oh, no. You've done more than enough."

The woman looked relieved. "I'll be going, then. Take care." She took a step away from the table.

"Wait!" Rune called out.

The woman turned around.

"Don't forget your phone."

The woman's eyes were full of gratitude when she reached for her phone. Rune blew on her hot chocolate and watched her walk out of the restaurant. Then she grabbed the pastry, took a big bite, and headed to the door.

34

NEUILLY-SUR-SEINE

T he lobby of 137 Avenue Charles de Gaulle was as cryptic as the
exterior. No sign announced the name of the company, no logos
hinted at its function. The waiting area was free of brochures and adver-
tisements. Rune took all this in as she walked through the sliding glass
doors and past the reception desk. No one stopped her. Why would
they with the ID card hanging around her neck?

Security consisted of one guard overseeing four optical turnstiles.
Rune chose the lane furthest from view and held her ID over the digital
reader. A soft beep sounded. The light on the barrier went from red to
green. The glass doors retracted.

A frazzled-looking man waited by the elevators, shoulders stiff, hand
wrapped tightly around the handle of his briefcase. Rune stopped at
a respectful distance and gave him a polite nod, but he didn't notice.
His eyes were fixed on the numbers above the doors. That suited her
just fine.

The elevator dinged. The man stepped on, swiped his card, and
pressed the button for the top floor—the sixth. Rune chose the fifth.
It was as good a place to start as any.

The doors opened onto an empty hallway. All the lights were off. Rune wandered past dozens of cubicles that had clearly never been used. She backtracked to the elevator and went down to the fourth floor. It was virtually identical. Never before had she spent this much time in a place and not known what went on there.

The veil of mystery lifted when she reached the third floor. Instead of cubicles, she encountered a spacious lab full of pharmaceutical equipment, including tablet presses, capsule filling machines, X-ray inspection systems, and many other things she didn't recognize. Refrigerators with glass doors lined one side of the room. Workstations occupied the other. Whirrs and beeps sounded at regular intervals, not so loudly as to be disruptive but loudly enough not to fade into the background. Rune stashed her belongings in an empty locker and grabbed a lab coat from a peg. A surgical mask and goggles went on next. The haircap came last. She looked ridiculous, but so did everyone else.

The people in the lab were from all over the world. Rune heard at least four languages as she lingered by the lockers—some French, a bit of Italian and Japanese, and a lot of English. A heavyset scientist with a pronounced limp grabbed the iPad from his workbench and exited the lab. Rune took his place.

Checking out the man's computer was the first order of business. The screen lit up when she touched the trackpad. He'd left two documents open. One contained chemical formulas, the other described drug manufacturing processes. Both were labeled "Keytruda." Rune memorized the word, then scanned the folders on the desktop: Lecanemab, Biktarvy, and Mounjaro. The first two meant nothing to her, but she'd seen enough American TV ads to know that Mounjaro, a drug developed to treat type 2 diabetes, was the next weight loss miracle cure. She also knew that the Indianapolis-based company that made Mounjaro, Eli Lilly, was not shy about plastering the world with its corporate logo. The Neuilly facility was not one of theirs.

The limping scientist returned to the lab with a group of well-dressed executives. Rune saw a flash of blond at the front of the pack. She felt a stab of fear when she realized it was Alaric. Margot and Rolf were by his side. Whatever was going on, it was a family affair.

Rune stepped away from the workstation before anyone noticed and planted herself next to a tablet-coating machine. An air-atomized spray system covered hundreds of pills in deep maroon as they rotated in a circular drum that looked a lot like a front load dryer. The spray guns stopped suddenly, but the pan kept moving, allowing the tablets to cool and dry. By the time the executives were within earshot, the machine was spitting the tablets into a large plastic bin.

"Production has fallen slightly behind schedule," the limping scientist said in an unplaceable English accent. "Still, I think you'll be pleased with our progress."

Alaric exchanged looks with his parents. His lips pulled downward with displeasure. "What's the reason for the delay?" he asked. His own accent was stilted, like he'd learned English from a textbook but never practiced making the sounds.

"The fault isn't ours," the scientist was quick to say. "One of our suppliers was late on a shipment. It had a domino effect."

Rune winced. The Steiners looked like the kind of people who wanted results, not excuses. The group walked past. She kept her eyes down and followed. It was risky, but she didn't want to miss a word.

"What's the new timeline?" Alaric asked.

"The first shipment will be ready to go a week from today, barring the unforeseen."

Rolf gave his son a slight shake of the head. A discomfiting silence fell over the group, amplifying the hum of the machinery. Rune skirted a vat of bubbling liquid and pretended to check the temperature gauge. She strained to hear the rest of the conversation.

"A week is too late," Alaric said. "You'll have to work faster."

"That's not possible," the scientist replied before quickly correcting himself. "What I mean is the team is already working overtime. We can't speed things up without sacrificing their safety."

Alaric stopped walking. Everyone behind him fell in line. His next words came out with chilling clarity. "We decide what is and isn't possible. Not you. Is that understood?"

"O-of course, Mr. Steiner. I didn't mean to imply—"

"You have three days."

Rune saw the scientist open his mouth to reply and knew instinctively that nothing good would come of it. Had the circumstances been different, she might have done something to stop him. Others in the lab apparently shared her opinion, if the nervous glances and general air of unease were any indication.

"Perhaps we can speed things along somewhat if we extend the workday by an hour or so," the scientist offered. "But the team has been working overtime for months and everyone is exhausted."

Rune knew the man's words would have consequences, but she couldn't have predicted what happened next. Alaric grabbed him by the forearm, knocking the iPad out of his hands. The man's eyes widened in surprise. His mouth formed a perfect *O*. The almost comical symmetry of his features vanished when Alaric dragged him to the bubbling vat. His eyes bugged out. His mouth flew all the way open. Petrified. Maw-like. Rune watched in stunned terror as he tried to resist, but his efforts were futile against Alaric's superior strength.

"No!" the man yelled.

Rune covered her ears, but nothing could block out the screams and stomach-turning sound of flesh hitting boiling liquid.

Alaric let go.

The man slumped to the ground.

Cries of shock and horror ripped through the lab.

"You," Alaric said.

Rune jolted to attention. Alaric had noticed her. Worse, he was addressing her. She searched his face for signs of recognition.

"What's your position here?"

She couldn't speak, partly out of fear, partly because she didn't have the faintest idea what her position might be. Her face mask moved in and out in time with her panicked breath.

"Well?"

"Junior scientist . . . I'm a junior scientist," she stammered.

"Congratulations. You've just been promoted."

"What?"

"You're now in charge of the Keytruda shipment. It needs to be ready in three days. No one goes home until the work is done. Understood?"

Rune stayed mute.

"I asked if you understood."

She forced her head up and down.

Alaric's eyes turned to slits. His forehead creased into a frown. Fear clawed at Rune, but she made herself hold his gaze. He took a step forward. She flinched, thinking he was about to attack her. Instead, he bent down to retrieve the injured man's iPad. He tapped the screen to make sure it still worked.

"Everything you need is here," he said, giving it to Rune.

Her hand shook as she accepted it.

"Don't let me down."

Even in these extreme circumstances, Rune understood she had a choice to make. She could fall apart, or she could be brave and play along. She glanced at the scientist cradling his ruined hand. It was an easy decision. "I won't let you down, Mr. Steiner," she said in a surprisingly steady voice. "You have my word."

She must have sounded convincing because Alaric and his entourage walked away, leaving her alone with the team. If any of them had questions about who she was and why she was in charge, they didn't dare voice them. She surveyed the lab from behind her safety goggles. She straightened her back. Then she clapped her hands and shouted, "You heard Mr. Steiner. Get to work on the Keytruda shipment. No one goes home until I say so!"

35

STEINER PHARMACEUTICALS, NEUILLY-SUR-SEINE

T he lab ran like a well-oiled machine. Everyone had their assigned tasks and knew how to perform them. And perform they did, not because Rune had ordered them to but because they were terrified that Alaric would do to them what he did to their former boss. Rune shared their fears, but she didn't let it get in her way. After sending the injured scientist to the hospital to attend to his "accidental" burn, she appropriated his workbench and set about learning everything there was to know about the Neuilly lab.

The facility didn't exist on paper. Rune wondered why until she realized that its sole purpose was to produce counterfeit drugs. The illicit activities went unnoticed amid the Steiners' legitimate operations, which included everything from sourcing raw materials to distribution. It occurred to Rune that the family was just a clean-cut version of the dealers she'd encountered in Marseille, the young men loafing on stained couches at Félix Pyat. They were the same. So was Jakob, for that matter. The difference was one of degree, not of kind.

Steiner Pharma's biggest money-maker was Pembrolizumab, sold under the brand name Keytruda, an injectable immunotherapy drug used to treat a wide range of cancers, including inoperable melanoma, Hodgkin lymphoma, and metastatic lung cancer. The drug made the company a quarter of a billion in profits in the last year alone. That was all well and good, except that the Steiners didn't hold the patent for Keytruda, the pharmaceutical giant Merck & Co. did. The other drugs produced at the Neuilly lab were also counterfeits: Eisai and Biogen developed Lecanemab, an injectable used to treat Alzheimer's disease; Gilead Sciences held the patent for Biktarvy, a once-a-day pill used to treat HIV; and Eli Lilly made the diabetes and weight loss medication, Mounjaro. Steiner Pharma's stable of counterfeits included dozens of other drugs, ranging from antibiotics to erectile dysfunction medications. Rune thought about the note in the company's quarterly earnings report: + €993 million Neuilly. Not a bad chunk of change for a company whose legitimate annual earnings topped at about 24 billion.

Nothing on the iPad or at the lab suggested that the Steiners tested their drugs. No one seemed to care if they worked, or if they were safe. With profits this high, it was hardly surprising. Rune learned that the global counterfeit drug industry was worth 200 billion US dollars per year and that an estimated one in ten medical products in low- and middle-income countries was either counterfeit or substandard. But the problem extended far beyond the developing world. Closed drug distribution systems in the US offered some protection, but rising costs were pushing more and more Americans to purchase their medications online. Counterfeits were an international problem. Governments were falling short.

Rune spent the afternoon deciphering the ins and outs of the Steiners' illegal business. Only once did someone interrupt—an earnest-looking lab technician alerting her that it was time to order more pipettes. Rune assured him she was on it.

The staff started side-eyeing her at 7:00 P.M., the typical end of the French workday. The looks grew more intense when 8:00 P.M. rolled around. About half an hour later, a lanky man wearing his mask under his chin approached like a dog scared of its owner.

"I have to get home to my mother," he said, pushing up his goggles. "She's disabled. The nurse left two hours ago."

"Go," Rune said magnanimously. Other workers poked their heads up from their stations hoping that they, too, would be shown mercy. Somewhere nearby, a stomach growled. The sound reminded Rune that she hadn't eaten anything since the pastry at Pret. She was suddenly ravenous. "Okay, everyone. Wrap it up," she called out.

The floodgates opened. Workers streamed out of the lab. A few expressed their thanks, but many clearly blamed her for ruining their dinner plans.

"Go home and get some rest," she said, ignoring their morose expressions. She didn't care that they were angry with her. She cared even less that sending them home would probably mean missing Alaric's deadline. He'd hold her responsible. No matter. She wouldn't be around when he unleashed his wrath.

The sounds of machinery tapered as more workers called it a day. The facility eventually went silent, save the steady hum of the refrigerators.

Rune waited until everyone had gone before removing her protective gear and exploring the lab. She found a vending machine in the employee breakroom, fed it a couple of coins, and selected something that looked like a cookie. She tore the package open with her teeth and took a bite. It tasted awful. She shoved the rest in her mouth anyway, then she tossed the wrapper in the garbage and continued her search.

The far end of the lab looked like a completely different facility. Gone was the state-of-the-art drug manufacturing equipment. Replacing it were conveyor belts, electric lifts, and cardboard boxes shrink-wrapped and stacked almost to the ceiling. Rune tried prying one of the boxes out from the bottom of the pile but stopped when the stack threatened to come down on her. She found a rolling ladder and pulled it over to the boxes. Going up was no trouble. Coming down was another story. She lost her grip on the box, then tripped over her own feet trying to hold on to it. She hit the floor with a dull *thunk*, bruising her thigh in the process.

It took several minutes for Rune to locate a utility knife. She brought it over to the box she almost died retrieving, sliced the plastic wrap and tape, and folded back the flaps. Out came the foam inserts, revealing vials of clear liquid that had somehow survived the fall. She picked one up. It was the fake Keytruda. It looked exactly like the real thing, down to the label:

Keytruda (pembrolizumab)
Injection
100 mg/4 mL (25 mg/mL)
For Intravenous Infusion Only. Rx Only.
Single-use vial. Discard unused portion.

The bottle may have looked legit, but Rune knew that whatever was inside wouldn't cure anyone's cancer. Even if the formulation was the same—and there was a big emphasis on the if—the storage conditions were not. She'd read that Keytruda had to be kept between thirty-six and forty-six degrees. The vials were supposed to be packaged in individual cartons to protect them from light. They weren't meant to be shaken. Rune couldn't be sure, but she guessed that dropping them from a six-foot ladder counted as shaking.

She returned the vial to the box and glanced at the address. The recipient was a company called Pharmacologically based in Mamaroneck, New York. She made a mental note to send an anonymous tip to *The New York Times*. Then she took a photo of the vials and sent it to Romy along with the message: *Did you know?*

It was an aggressive question, but Rune was starting to have doubts about Romy. How could she fail to notice that her husband had an office around the corner from their apartment? How could she not know that he was producing counterfeit drugs? Her screen flashed. *Speak of the devil,* she thought.

What am I looking at?

Fake cancer meds. courtesy of Steiner Pharma's Neuilly lab.

????

You didn't know?

No!

The lab is five minutes from your apartment.

I don't know anything about it.

Where did you think Alaric was going every day?

Paris. The company has an office near the Champ de Mars. It's the largest branch aside from Berlin.

Rune paused. Romy seemed sufficiently clueless. And outraged. But then, tone was hard to gauge via text.

How did you get into the lab?

You don't want to know.

Are you there now?

Yup.

What's the address?

Why?

I want to see it.

You won't be able to get in.

You did.

Rune couldn't argue there, but she didn't change her mind. She wasn't persuaded Romy had what it took to get past security. And even if she did, what then? It was hard enough to get herself out of sticky situations. She didn't need anyone slowing her down if things went sideways.

It's my family. Please. I have to see for myself.

Had it been anyone else, Rune would have put her foot down. But Romy had been there when everyone else turned their backs on her. She hadn't just handed over her ring, she had believed her. Maybe because she knew what it felt like not to be believed.

Well?

Rune hesitated. Involving Romy went against every instinct she had. Her screen went dark. She tapped it back to life. She could practically hear Romy say "you owe me" in her clipped French accent. And so, against her better judgment, she dropped a pin on her location.

36

STEINER PHARMACEUTICALS, NEUILLY-SUR-SEINE

Maybe it was Rune's nerves. Or the stale cake she'd recently inhaled. Whatever the case, acid swelled inside her as she waited for Romy to arrive. The wait felt eternal, not least because she knew exactly how long it took to get from Romy's apartment to Avenue Charles de Gaulle. She ran the numbers in her head: five minutes to get dressed, eight minutes to walk to the lab (ten if Romy dawdled), five minutes to talk her way past the guard, and a two-minute elevator ride to the third floor, for a grand total of twenty-two minutes. Rune looked at the time. More than an hour had passed since she'd sent Romy the address. She worried something terrible had happened. That Alaric had caught Romy or that Romy was reneging on their deal. Then what? Her plan to get Lemaire hinged on Romy's involvement.

The distant ding of the elevator sounded outside the lab. Rune took a step forward, then changed her mind. What if it wasn't Romy? What if it was someone who realized she wasn't who she claimed to be?

The lab door opened and closed. She flattened herself against a refrigerator. Footsteps rang out, sending fear rippling through her body. The footsteps came closer.

"Rune?"

Relief flooded her system. Then embarrassment. She stepped out from behind the fridge. "Jesus, Romy! You scared me!"

"I told you I was coming."

Rune silently chastised herself for being a ninny. Then she deflected. "What took you so long?"

"I had to wait until Alaric was asleep. And it took me a while to find this." She held up Alaric's ID card.

Rune was impressed until she noticed Romy's fur-trimmed coat and Yves Saint Laurent bag. Her eyebrows rose. "This is how you fly under the radar?" she asked.

"Everyone in Neuilly dresses like this."

Good point.

"Show me."

Rune understood that Romy was referring to the drugs. She angled her head toward the back of the lab. The walk there felt longer this time around. Or maybe she was just tired. She couldn't remember the last time she'd gotten a good night's sleep.

"This is it?" Romy said when she saw the stacked boxes.

"See for yourself. The vials are labeled Keytruda. It's a cancer drug made by Merck. Their bestseller, apparently."

Romy picked up a vial from the open box. Her eyes scrunched as she read the fine print. She set it down, apparently convinced that what Rune was saying was true.

"They were here earlier," Rune said. "Alaric, Rolf, and Margot. They're all in on this."

"I'm not surprised."

"They're working on a big shipment. Alaric attacked the scientist who couldn't meet their deadline." Rune stopped speaking as the memory of the scientist's screams came rushing back. She pushed it aside and gestured to the boxes. "These will hit the market in three days. We have to stop it." She expected Romy to agree, but all she got was silence. She pressed harder. "Keytruda isn't their only knock-off. I found paperwork for dozens of others. An HIV drug, an Alzheimer's medication, antibiotics . . ." Rune's words trailed off. She eyed the pile of boxes. How many doses did they contain? How many people would they kill?

Romy must have had similar thoughts because she shuddered suddenly. "This is monstrous," she said.

"You really had no idea?"

"No." She shook her head. "Alaric is violent and controlling. His parents are the same. But I never imagined they were capable of this."

Rune didn't say anything.

"I don't understand why they would do this. Steiner Pharmaceuticals is a Global 500 company. Their profits are huge."

"I'm guessing it's not just about money."

"It's not, is it?"

"Have you seen enough?"

No response.

"We should go."

"Not yet."

Rune didn't understand why Romy wanted to linger. There was nothing left to see, and staying only increased their chances of getting caught.

"Did you ever hear that fable about the king's son and the painted lion?" Romy said.

Rune shook her head, confused.

"There was a king whose son was a risk-taker. The boy spent his days playing dangerous games. The king tried to steer him to safer hobbies, but the boy refused."

Rune frowned, unsure of where Romy was going with this.

"One day, the king dreamed that a lion would kill his son. Thinking it was a premonition, he built a fortress to keep his son safe and painted the walls with life-size animals, including a lion. But his son didn't like being confined. He became angry, so angry that he grabbed a branch and beat the painted lion with it."

"Okaaay."

"The branch the boy grabbed was thorny. It left a deep cut on his finger. The wound became infected, then the boy developed a fever and died."

"That's messed up. Can we go now?"

Romy continued as if she hadn't heard Rune. "My children love Aesop's fables, especially the morals. Do you know what the moral of this story is?"

Rune didn't know, nor did she care.

"It's better to confront problems head-on than to try to escape them."

It took Rune a few seconds to understand what Romy was saying. By the time she did, it was too late. Her eyes flicked sideways at the sound of the door opening. Her pupils ballooned when she heard footsteps on the other end of the lab. She turned back toward Romy, eyes wide with disbelief. "What did you do?" she demanded.

"What I should have done the first time my husband laid a hand on me."

Panic shot up. Rune knew enough about Alaric to know this wasn't going to end well.

"Go," Romy said. "This isn't your fight."

Rune didn't need to be told twice. This wasn't what she'd agreed to. If Romy wanted to be a hero and confront Alaric, she could do it on her own.

"Romy!"

Alaric's voice thundered through the lab. Rune's head swung from one side to the other. She spied a forklift nearby and ran toward it with every intention of escaping at the first opportunity. It was a good plan, a great one even. Then Alaric arrived and everything went to hell.

<hr>

"Was machst du hier?"

"What am I doing here?" Romy scoffed. "That's what you have to say to me?"

Rune peeked out from behind the forklift. Alaric was within arm's reach of Romy. He towered over her.

"Whatever you think you know, you don't," he said.

"There's no sense denying it. The proof is right in front of us."

"This?" He gestured to the boxes. "We order many of our competitors' products. It's standard practice."

Rune saw the doubt creep into Romy's face. Alaric had responded without missing a beat. He was the posterchild of believability.

"We can talk about this tomorrow. It's time for you to go home to the children now." Alaric's words dripped with condescension. He placed his hand on the back of Romy's neck to get her to move. It was a possessive gesture. It left no question about who was in charge.

Romy jerked away. "Don't touch me!" she spat. "Don't ever touch me again!"

The blow that followed came hard and fast. Romy's head snapped sideways. Her hand rose to her cheek.

"Are you ready to go home now?" Alaric's voice was level. Reasonable. Like what happened was completely normal.

"I'll go home," Romy said.

He smirked triumphantly.

"But not with you."

His smirk disappeared. He raised his hand to strike her again.

"Do that and I'll go to the police. I'll tell them about this lab. I'll tell them about the counterfeit drugs you've been dumping on the market. It won't just ruin you, it will destroy your company."

Alaric's cool demeanor melted. He drew himself up to his full height.

Run! Rune wanted to scream.

Romy did the opposite. She stood her ground, chin raised, defiance pooling in her eyes. Her punishment was instant. Alaric pulled his fist back and slammed it straight into her stomach. She crumpled on impact, but her ordeal wasn't over. He grabbed a fistful of her hair and dragged her screaming across the floor like a dirty mop. Then he flung her to the other side of the room, sending her crashing into an industrial shelf full of plastic jugs.

"Imagine if this whole thing came down on you," he said.

Romy whimpered like a scared animal.

"Your bones would snap. Your skull might even cave in."

The whimpering turned into incoherent babbling.

"That might be the preferable outcome."

Romy's eyes swung toward the shelves. So did Rune's. The jugs were labeled H2SO4. Rune couldn't immediately identify the formula, but she recognized the individual parts: H2 was hydrogen, S was sulfur, and O4 was some sort of oxygen. She was still trying to piece it together when Alaric did it for her.

"Sulfuric acid is a corrosive. It can dissolve most metals. Just think what would happen if one of these containers were to spill on you. What that would do to your pretty face."

Romy raised her hand defensively. "Don't!"

Alaric let out a cruel laugh.

"Please! What about the children?"

"The children will spend the rest of their lives thinking their mother died in a tragic accident." His eyes narrowed. His expression turned frightful. "The doctors will hook you up to every machine, I'll make sure of that. By the time they're through with you, you'll be begging to die."

Romy was sobbing now. Rune couldn't tell if it was for her own fate or her children's. It didn't matter. She couldn't stand on the sidelines and watch this happen. She had to step in. Her eyes bounced around the lab and settled on three fire extinguishers. Two were labeled Dry Chemical, the third CO2. She skirted the forklift, then paused. She told herself it was to wait for the right moment, but what she really wanted was a chance to change her mind.

Go!

She moved swiftly, silently. She glanced over her shoulder expecting to see Alaric launching himself at her, but he was still laser-focused on Romy. Her hands closed around the smaller of the two chemical extinguishers. She took a breath. The element of surprise was the only thing she had going for her. She couldn't afford to squander it.

The bracket clicked when it released the extinguisher. Rune held it tightly and circled until she was directly behind Alaric. Her hands rose, ready to strike. It was then that she realized the flaw in her plan. Alaric was tall, so tall she couldn't possibly knock him out from this angle. Her mind raced for a solution.

Do something!

She was reaching for the extinguisher's handle when Alaric sensed her behind him. He spun around. His mouth dropped. A deranged look crossed his features.

"You!" he said.

She pointed the hose at his face and squeezed the handle. Nothing happened.

The safety pin!

She reached for it, but it was too late. Alaric tore the extinguisher out of her hands. She fully expected him to smash her head with it. Instead, he tossed it aside and wrapped his hands around her neck. A scream rose from deep inside her. She opened her mouth to release it, but all that came out was a strange gurgle. The pressure on her trachea increased, sending jolts of pain through her body. She went for his eyes. He dodged her. She tried again. Still no good. Desperate, she raised her right arm and rotated her shoulder to break his hold on her throat. She followed that with a knee to the groin. He folded like a ragdoll.

"Let's go!" Rune gasped.

Romy remained an inert heap on the floor.

"Now!" She grabbed Romy's wrists and pulled.

The jerking movement must have flipped a switch because Romy's eyes suddenly cleared.

"Come on!"

Romy sprang to her feet. They raced through the lab side by side, moving so quickly everything around them turned blurry. They were about halfway to the exit when Rune dared look back. "Faster!" she screamed when she saw Alaric closing in. She picked up speed. So did Romy. But rage propelled Alaric faster than either of them could move. Still, they kept pushing, grunting in effort as Alaric got closer with every stride.

Romy screamed. Rune spun around. Romy was on the floor again, curled in a ball to protect herself against the kicks raining down on her. Rune grabbed a metal stool from one of the workstations and swung it across Alaric's back. He turned around as if she'd merely tapped him on the shoulder. She swung again, this time aiming at his chest. He caught the stool before it could do any damage and used it to push her to the ground. She landed hard on her back, limbs splayed like a broken doll. She instinctively scooted away, but he grabbed her by the shoulders and lifted her straight off the floor.

The shaking that followed was so violent she thought her neck would snap. Then came the punches. The first struck her in the left eye. The next caught her square in the jaw. She didn't know where the rest landed. That didn't register amid the pain. She looked down at the maroon stain spreading across the front of her lab coat like a Rorschach test come to life. It took her a moment to realize that what she was looking at was her blood. A galaxy exploded behind her eyes.

This is it.

The thought filled her with profound regret. There were so many people she wished she could see again. So many things that remained unsaid. Maybe it was just as well. Her life was a maze of broken relationships—her parents, Kit, Milo. Leila and Jakob were just the most recent.

The punches stopped abruptly. Rune fell to the floor. She saw movement through the scarlet film over her eyes. Then she heard a long, agonized cry. She lifted her head to see who it was, but the movement cause so much pain she nearly threw up.

"Get up!"

Rune heard the voice, but she didn't respond. She was sinking further and further into the abyss. The cottony darkness enveloped her, warm, welcoming.

"I said get up!"

A hand grabbed her shoulder. Her eyelids fluttered. Romy's face came in and out of focus.

"We have to go!"

She blinked a few times to clear her vision. When she could finally see, she realized why Romy was hell-bent on leaving.

Alaric was sprawled on the floor, mouth agape, eyes fixed and vacant. Sticking out of his neck was a shard of glass from a broken beaker. There was blood. A lot of it.

Adrenaline kicked in. Rune's pain contracted. Her energy surged.

"Hurry up!" Romy said.

"What did you do?" Rune asked hoarsely. It hurt to talk. Her throat was raw from being choked.

"I had to. He would have killed you. And then he would have killed me."

Rune struggled to her feet. She knew it was useless, but she leaned over Alaric and placed two fingers on his neck. There was no pulse. She held her palm over his mouth and nose to try to feel his breath. Nothing there either. "Shit," she whispered.

"I know."

"Shit! Shit! Shit!"

"I know!"

Every part of Rune wanted to flee—to run far and fast and never look back—but she knew running wasn't an option. "We can't leave," she said. "People saw us. There are cameras in the lobby. In the elevator too."

"We can call the police and explain what happened," Romy said. "Alaric attacked us. It was self-defense."

"I can't talk to the police, remember?"

"Right." Romy paused to think, then said, "You should go. I'll tell them I did it. You were never here."

"They'll watch the security footage. They'll send a forensics team. My DNA is everywhere."

"What's your solution, then?"

Rune heard the tautness in Romy's voice. It was as if she finally understood how much trouble they were in. She ran through various solutions in her mind, each more preposterous than the last.

"You're right," Romy said. "We can't call the police. What if they don't believe me? I can't go to prison. What would happen to my boys?"

Rune knew Romy would kill again before letting Margot and Rolf raise her kids. She didn't blame her. The people who created one monster couldn't be trusted not to do it again.

"We'll get rid of the body," Romy said, bobbing her head like she was trying to convince herself. "No body, no crime. I'll report Alaric missing in the morning. No one will ever know."

Rune had already considered that idea. They could wheel Alaric out of the lab on a dolly. Cleaning up would be easy with all the chemicals lying around. But then what? What would they do with the body? How could they be sure no one would see them? She tried to think of a solution, but the pain from her thrashing was creeping in.

"Help me move him," Romy said. She grabbed Alaric by the ankles and gave a hard tug. The body slid forward a few inches, leaving a smear of blood on the floor.

"Stop."

"We just need to get him out of the building."

"I said stop!"

Romy dropped Alaric's feet.

"Find me a lighter."

A look of confusion crossed Romy's face. It morphed almost instantly into understanding. She didn't say anything. Words were unnecessary. Off she went to search the workbenches.

Rune hurried to the rear of the facility, to the shelving unit Alaric had threatened to bring down on Romy. She scanned the containers until she found one she recognized: acetone. She'd had her nails done enough times to know it was highly flammable. She grabbed a jug and retraced her steps as fast as her injuries would let her. She needed to do this before she thought about it too hard.

Romy was there when Rune got back, a look of determination on her face, a book of matches in her hand. Their eyes met. Romy gave Rune a nod. Rune twisted the lid off the jug and poured the acetone over Alaric. Romy struck a match. She tossed it onto the body. Flames burst up. Then the two ran like hell.

37

STEINER RESIDENCE, NEUILLY-SUR-SEINE

The explosion could be heard from Boulevard Charles de Gaulle all the way to the center of Paris. Those atop the Eiffel Tower were treated to an extraordinary show of orange and red plumes shooting into the inky sky. The tremor was felt for a five-mile radius. Windows in the immediate vicinity shattered from the shockwave, including those of Chanel's glossy headquarters. The BRGM, the government agency tasked with monitoring seismic activity in France, recorded strong ground motion not unlike a 5.1 earthquake.

Rune and Romy were home looking like filthy swamp things by the time any of this happened. They had eschewed the elevator at Steiner Pharma and sprinted for the emergency staircase, flying down three flights to the building's lobby. The sprinkler system had kicked in midway through their descent. Romy burst out of the stairwell first. Rune had been right on her tail. She'd screamed at the nightguard to get out of the building. Everyone else was long gone, though she didn't learn that until the following day.

The Steiners' apartment was stocked with the most expensive liquor money could buy. Rune grabbed a bottle without looking to see what it was. She filled a crystal tumbler to the brim and chugged it down. It hardly took the edge off. She poured herself another. The soft clinking of Brioche's collar sounded behind her. She grabbed a second glass knowing Romy was now in the room.

"How are the kids?" she asked. Her voice sounded strange, like it belonged to someone else. She couldn't stop her teeth from chattering.

"Asleep, thank goodness." Romy accepted the glass with a shaky hand and drank half its contents.

"What are you going to tell them?"

Romy shrugged.

"Really though."

"I'll say that their father was in a terrible accident. That he won't be coming home." Romy peered at Rune, then walked to the kitchen with Brioche on her heels. She returned moments later with an icepack and a tea towel. She handed them to Rune.

"Thanks," Rune said. The cold felt good against her throbbing jaw. She sank onto the couch.

Romy took a seat next to her. The dog rested its giant head on her lap and let out a satisfied sigh when her fingers found the sweet spot behind its ears. She peered at Rune again. "It looks bad. Does it hurt?"

"Like a son of a—"

Romy held up her free hand, then glanced back to make sure her kids hadn't wandered into the living room.

"You don't look so great yourself," Rune said. "Do you have any arnica cream? Your eye is ten shades of purple."

Romy didn't respond. Rune didn't press the issue. They didn't have to speak to know what the other was thinking. There was an understanding between them, the kind rooted in shared trauma.

Rune drained her glass and cast a longing look at the liquor cabinet. She wanted more than anything to drink herself into oblivion, but prepping Romy for what came next took precedence. She turned her back to the booze. Out of sight, out of mind. "We should prepare," she said. "The police will be here soon."

"I know."

"Your story needs to be solid."

"It will be."

Rune frowned when she heard the wobble in Romy's voice. "Tell me what happened tonight."

Romy's face crumpled.

"It's okay. Your husband just died. The police will expect you to be upset. It would be weird if you weren't."

"Alaric and I had dinner at home with the children. Then I tidied up and put the kids to bed."

"What happened after that?" Rune pressed. It was what the cops would do.

"Alaric made some calls. I watched a movie. *Anatomy of a Fall.*"

"They can check that. Don't offer details unless they ask."

"Alaric made some calls. I read for a few hours."

"What did you read?"

"Kundera. *The Book of Laughter and Forgetting.* Alaric was still up when I went to bed."

"Around what time was that?"

"It must have been ten. Ten-fifteen at the latest."

"Did he tell you he was going out?"

"No."

"You didn't hear him leave?"

"No."

"You're sure?"

"Of course I'm sure."

Rune detected a snap in Romy's voice. Sadness was okay. Fear and anxiety too. But anger wasn't going to fly. "You can't come across as combative. You're a grieving widow, remember?"

"Right."

"And I wasn't kidding about the arnica cream. You have a spectacular shiner. The cops are going to ask about it."

"Alaric and I were together for fifteen years. You don't think I know how to cover a black eye?"

Rune was sorry she'd said anything. She went to the liquor cabinet and poured herself another drink to wash down her foot.

"We solved my problem," Romy said when Rune returned. "We should deal with yours."

"You mean Lemaire?"

Romy nodded.

"You're still willing to help me?"

Romy looked confused. "Why wouldn't I be?"

"Because I made a complete mess of things!" Rune hated how pathetic she sounded. She hated that Kit's last words to her were still going around and around in her head.

Everything you touch turns to shit!

Realizing he was right hurt almost as much as Alaric's blows. She looked at Romy's ballooning left eye. A knot coiled inside her stomach. She *was* a screwup. The proof was right there in front of her. She exhaled loudly. "I was supposed to get Alaric out of your life, not kill him."

"You didn't kill him. I did."

"Only to save me. He'd still be alive if I hadn't broken into his lab." She let out another sharp breath. "You told me he was dangerous. You *told* me." She squeezed her temples with the tips of her fingers as if it would fix whatever was wrong with her brain.

"What happened to you?" Romy asked softly.

"What do you mean?"

"Why would you think I'd drop you just because a crazy plan went wrong?"

It didn't take an advanced degree in psychology to figure that one out. Everyone who ever mattered had dropped her. *Everyone.*

"I'm not sorry he's dead, you know," Romy said when it became clear Rune wasn't going to answer.

That came as no surprise. But hearing the words out loud made Rune profoundly uncomfortable. She was many things—a thief, a scammer, a liar—that didn't mean she was okay with murder.

"You must think I'm a terrible person," Romy said.

"I don't." The words came out automatically, but Rune realized right away that they were true. She hadn't walked in Romy's shoes. She didn't know what it was like to live with someone like Alaric. And if she was being honest, she wouldn't shed a tear if Lemaire met with a similar fate. She grabbed Romy's hands. "I don't," she repeated, squeezing them tightly.

Romy squeezed back. They stayed that way for a long time, face-to-face, hands entwined. It was Rune who finally let go. "Thanks for saving my life," she said softly.

Romy nodded and replied, "Thanks for saving mine."

38

LEFT BANK, PARIS

Napoleon reputedly said that secrets traveled fast in Paris. The indomitable emperor was referring to the speed at which political gossip spread through all levels of the French court, a phenomenon that might be described as the nineteenth-century version of a story going viral. Rune had left Romy's Neuilly apartment determined to quash police and public interest in the Bonaparte heists. Her goal was simple: to reorient the story so that she wasn't the bad guy. Or, at the very least, not the bad guy who mattered. The plan she and Romy hashed out would not only let her off the hook with the cops but also get Lemaire out of her life once and for all.

Are you almost there?!

Rune ignored Romy's text. It was the third she'd sent in ten minutes, each more urgent than the last. She gave an exasperated shake of her head, sending strands of her new brown wig swinging across her shoulders. Not for the first time, she wondered why it was that her partners-in-crime were always such worrywarts. She closed the door to the Saint-Germain apartment that belonged to Lemaire's mistress and headed to the elevator. Her finger had already hit the button when she decided it would be more prudent to walk. Apparently, Romy's caution was contagious.

Rune took the spiral stairs slowly, as much to avoid breaking her neck as to admire the ruins of the Saint-Germain refectory. The last time she was in the building, she'd been so focused on finding Lemaire that she hadn't fully appreciated them. The centuries-old window looked every bit its age. The fact that it had survived wars, revolutions, and the vagaries of time was nothing short of miraculous. She stretched her hand to touch the weathered stones. Pride swelled inside her chest. She, too, had weathered raging storms. She, too, was still standing.

The lobby was empty when Rune finally reached it. It didn't stay that way for long. The front door swung open. The air that rushed in so cold she felt it in her bones. She squinted at the backlit figure. Only after the door closed and blocked the sunlight did she recognize the elderly woman with the snow-white hair and matching fur coat. An alligator-skin satchel dangled from her wrist, just as it did during the first encounter. A frown distorted her heavily powdered face.

"You again!" the woman exclaimed.

"Yes, it's me," Rune replied as if it wasn't a dumb thing to say.

"I told you last time. You can't keep coming here without going through the proper channels."

"I did. Professor Duras spoke with a member of the homeowners' association."

"Professor Duras? What happened to Professor Duclos?"

"Did I say Duras? I meant Duclos."

The woman eyed her with mistrust. Rune didn't flinch. The sound of the front door unlatching broke the standoff. Rune knew it wasn't Lemaire. He was at the Crillon waiting for Romy. Still, she didn't want to linger.

"I don't want to see you here again until I hear directly from Professor Duclos," the woman said.

"This is the last time. I promise." Rune meant it. She had no intention of returning to the building. If the next few hours went as planned, Lemaire wouldn't be going back to the building either.

Romy had kept Lemaire waiting at the Crillon only to change the location of their meeting. The new meet-up was at the Jardin des Plantes, a botanical garden masquerading as a public park in the heart of the city's Latin Quarter. Two things spoke in favor of the location: First, it was relatively close to the Saint-Germain apartment; second, given the subzero temperatures, it would likely be deserted. Parisians were renowned *flâneurs* but they understandably drew the line at lounging in the cold.

Rune stepped out of the subway at Jussieu and lowered her head against the wind for the three minutes it took to get to the park. She walked through the metal gate and passed a brasserie that was empty of diners. A right turn took her toward the labyrinth, where Romy was scheduled to meet Lemaire. Even with the barren hedges, it was an ideal site for a clandestine meeting. It was also the perfect place from which to eavesdrop. She was nearing the entrance when her phone vibrated in her coat pocket.

SOS!

Unlike Romy's previous texts, this one warranted immediate attention.

"We have a problem," Romy said. She was breathing hard, like she was in the middle of a spinning class.

"I gathered."

"Lemaire called. He changed the location."

"Where?"

"The dinosaur gallery."

Rune wondered if Lemaire was suspicious of Romy, or if he just didn't want to meet outside.

"It's on the northeast corner of the park," Romy said. "We're meeting by the big crocodile."

"The Sarcosuchus?"

"You know that?"

"I know a lot of things."

"Hurry."

"I'm on my way."

Rune veered away from the labyrinth and speed walked to the opposite end of the park, passing empty planters and leafless trees arranged in perfectly straight lines. A brick building appeared in the distance. She broke into a jog. She couldn't be late. Everything was riding on this.

She was short of breath when she finally reached the entrance. A bored teenager reeking of BO sold her a ticket. She grabbed an English-language floorplan, located the dinosaur exhibit, and rushed upstairs.

Romy stood in the middle of the gallery dwarfed by the Sarcosuchus skeleton. Lemaire was nowhere in sight. It wasn't like him to be late. Rune caught Romy's eye, then climbed the stairs to a mezzanine that ran the length of the room.

Three sets of footsteps sounded not long after. Rune knew even before seeing anyone that they belonged to Lemaire and his men. She pulled a wireless microphone from her pocket, connected it to her phone, then tapped record. Lemaire's men patted down Romy.

"My apologies for that, Mrs. Steiner," Lemaire said after his men moved a respectful distance away. "One can never be too careful."

"I understand."

Rune was impressed by how calm Romy sounded.

"So, tell me, what kind of gems are you looking for?"

"Sapphires. The ones you stole from my family. I want them back."

Direct. Unemotional. Rune nodded her approval.

"I'm afraid you've been misinformed," Lemaire said.

"I know it was you. There's no point denying it."

"I'm in the business of importing and exporting gemstones, Mrs. Steiner. Not stealing them."

Rune tensed. She needed hard evidence for the police. She needed Lemaire to admit he was behind the Bonaparte heists. But Lemaire wasn't a stupid man. He wasn't going to confess just like that.

Romy stuck to the script. "My sources made a very convincing case," she said. "They tell me the handoffs happened at the Crillon. In the Marie Antoinette suite."

Rune could almost hear the wheels in Lemaire's head turning. Who were these sources Romy was talking about? How did they find out about the meetings? What else did they know about his operation? She was waiting for his response when a family of five barreled into the gallery. The two enervated parents tried in vain to corral their children, but the noisy trio flew out of their reach the moment they spied the dinosaurs.

"Don't touch that!" the mother hissed when the oldest child lunged toward the long-necked Sauropoda. His hands were all over the display. "Stop it right now!" Her words were just shy of a scream.

Lemaire adjusted the sleeves of his topcoat and tilted his head to the opposite end of the gallery. It was a good sign. He was taking Romy seriously. Rune followed from the mezzanine as the pair moved away from the feral family. They stopped beside a woolly mammoth, one of the largest skeletons in the room.

"What is it you want from me, Mrs. Steiner?" Lemaire asked.

"Only what's mine," Romy replied coolly.

He gave her a patronizing smile. "Like I said, you've been misinformed. But don't worry. I won't hold it against you. It's no secret you've had a hard time of it lately. First the thefts. Then your husband . . ." He let his words dangle.

"I could go to the police with what I know."

"Why aren't you there now?"

"Because I don't want to punish you. I just want the jewels. They were important to my husband."

Lemaire eyed her carefully. He was a businessman. He recognized an opportunity when he saw one. "I'm not the person you're looking for," he said. "But I might be able to help you."

"How can you help if you didn't steal my jewels?"

"I've been in the trade for many years. I keep my hands clean, but I may know people who know people. I'd be happy to put out feelers. For a price."

Rune wanted to repel from the mezzanine and beat the arrogance out of him. He was so confident. So convincing.

"I have to warn you. The information won't come cheap. And that will be on top of the cost of the jewels."

"Naturally," Romy said.

Lemaire approximated a smile. "I suppose money is no object for the newest board member of Steiner Pharmaceuticals."

Romy didn't say anything. Rune tightened her grip on the microphone and willed her to keep pressing. As it stood, Lemaire had admitted to little more than knowing a few shady characters. Those were a dime a dozen in the gemstone trade.

"I'll be in touch soon," he said.

Rune swore silently and watched him saunter away. She was disappointed, but if she was honest, she wasn't entirely surprised. Lemaire was more careful than most. He wouldn't have lasted this long if he weren't. She looked down at the gallery and caught Romy's eye.

Sorry, Romy mouthed.

It's okay, Rune mouthed back. And it was. Only a fool would go after Lemaire without a backup plan. She was no fool.

39

RIGHT BANK, PARIS

Lemaire reached out to Romy less than twenty-four hours later. Rune got word just as she was entering a bistro in the 11th arrondissement, a working-class neighborhood where people knew to mind their own business. The host suggested a table in the middle of the restaurant. She opted for the mahogany bar at the back of the room. The modal sound of manouche jazz filtered from ceiling speakers as she hopped on a stool with slightly wobbly legs. A glance in the mirror behind the bartender confirmed that no one was paying attention to her. She removed her hat and ran her fingers through her choppy hair, newly dyed to its natural color. She reached into her bag for her cherry-red lipstick and applied a generous coat. Only then did she direct her eyes to her phone to read Lemaire and Romy's most recent exchange.

I found what you're looking for, Lemaire had written.

That was fast.

I'm a man of my word.

Who has my sapphires?

That's not important.

It is to me.

Do you want them back or not?

Yes.

Twenty.

Rune's brows arched when she realized Lemaire meant 20 million Euros. It was a ludicrous ask. Romy apparently shared her opinion.

That's unreasonable.

It's the cost of doing business.

Let me get back to you.

Rune glanced at the timestamps. Romy's next message didn't come for another hour. Her patience was admirable.

I can get you half immediately. Anything more will require liquidating assets.

The seller is firm.

Fine. I'll need a few days.

Don't wait too long. There are other interested parties.

Understood. You'll hear from me soon.

The string of texts ended. The bartender approached. His eyes crinkled with pleasure at the sight of her. She asked for a glass of Sancerre before changing her mind and ordering a diabolo menthe. He dropped a cardboard coaster in front of her, then a highball glass full of ice cubes coated in dark syrup. She watched him pour lemon soda into it, turning the contents Leprechaun green. She gave the stir stick a quick turn and raised the glass to her lips. The minty drink tasted as awful as it did when she first tried it in Marseille with Leila. She didn't care. It was memories she was chasing, not flavor.

<hr />

"What happened to your hair?" Romy asked after sidling up to Rune.

"Eyes forward," Rune replied, smoothing her dark strands.

They were at the Palais de Chaillot, on the famous esplanade over-looking the Eiffel Tower. The sun was inching toward the horizon, painting the sky in pinks and purples. The meandering Seine shimmered under the waning light. The view was so spectacular that Rune momentarily forgot why she was there. She raised her phone and took a few pictures. If everything went as planned, she would soon be leaving Paris. She lowered her phone but kept her eyes on the tower. "How did your meeting go?"

"Lemaire is now 20 million Euros richer."

Rune whistled quietly. What it must be like to have that kind of wealth. "And the jewels?"

"I have them."

"You're sure they're the real thing?" She wasn't trying to be difficult. She'd simply had a bad experience with someone swapping a real gem with a fake one.

"They're real alright."

Rune felt something brush against her thigh. She knew without looking that Romy was trying to hand her the bag of jewels.

"What are you planning on doing with them?" Romy asked.

Rune pushed the bag away. Then she broke her own rule and looked Romy straight in the eye. "Not me," she said. "You."

<hr />

It was early evening when Rune emerged from the metro at Concorde. One day had passed since her meeting with Romy. One busy, nerve-racking day. She was about to find out if her hard work had paid off.

The Hôtel de Crillon stood across the plaza, elegant as ever. Rune hurried toward it. A biting wind stung at her cheeks. Her fingers and toes went numb instantly. For once, she didn't mind the cold.

A porter in a black fedora opened the door. Rune swept in like Marie Antoinette reincarnated. Crystal chandeliers twinkled from the vaulted ceiling. The stone floor glistened under the refractive light. She found a plush armchair with an unobstructed view of the lobby and settled in.

The commotion started not long after. First came the loud voices. Then the stomping feet. The night manager materialized out of thin air, but his objections were ineffective against the two police officers who insisted on accessing the second floor. The pair disappeared into the elevator. Rune watched its ascent play out on the gilded dial above the doors. Long minutes passed. Her body vibrated with anticipation. Just when she thought she couldn't stand it any longer, the dial began its slow descent.

Five . . . four . . . three . . . two . . .

Ding!

"This is outrageous! Do you have any idea who I am?"

Lemaire's voice sent shivers through Rune's body. He sounded angry. Defiant. She clamped the arms of the chair when he appeared in her sightline. His tailored suit jacket was rumpled. His hands were cuffed behind his back. Strangely, the former was more shocking to Rune than the latter.

"You'll be hearing from my lawyers!" Lemaire seethed. "I'll have your badges!"

"Do what you must, sir," one of the officers replied. "But you should know that the evidence against you is sufficient to obtain a conviction. More than sufficient."

Lemaire stopped struggling. "What evidence?"

"We have it from a reliable source that you conspired with Margot and Rolf Steiner to commit insurance fraud. They hired you to steal the Bonaparte sapphires. You outsourced the job to a small-time thief who's now disappeared. We searched the Steiners' home in Deauville. The necklace and earrings were in the safe."

"Wh-what?"

Rune smiled. Romy had done her part.

"Our colleagues in Hvar obtained a warrant to search your yacht. They found jewels that our source claims were given to you as payment for the Bonaparte heists. It was quite a stash—a vintage emerald choker, five Tiffany bracelets."

"I believe it was six bracelets," the second officer interjected.

"I stand corrected."

Rune crowed at her foresight to plant the jewels on Lemaire's yacht back in Mallorca.

"We also conducted a search on an apartment in Saint-Germain. We confiscated a Cartier watch registered to the Steiners. Madame Vidal, the owner of the apartment, claims you're the only one who had access."

"That's impossible," Lemaire stammered. "I'm being set up!"

"Save it for the judge."

Lemaire wrenched his arms out of the officer's grasp.

The officer smashed his face into a wall.

Rune exhaled sharply. A weight lifted. She rose from her seat and strode past the trio. Her eyes locked onto Lemaire's. She didn't speak. She didn't have to. She knew as well as he did that, after all this time, she was finally free of him.

She crossed the lobby and made her way back to the hotel entrance. She walked outside. Cars zoomed noisily around the oblong plaza. The gold-capped obelisk gleamed under the stars. She gazed at the Champs-Élysées dressed for the holidays in thousands of flickering lights. She took a step forward. The future was all questions and no answers, but Rune wasn't scared. Whatever it promised, she was hungry for it all.

THE END